Praise for the

The Tree Shepherd's Daughter

"The constant
will keep [r

"One of those
becomes comple
only in its own
anticipating books two and three in the promised trilogy."
—*KLIATT*

Into the Wildewood

"Compelling and beautifully written ... a great
follow-up to an already breathtaking first novel.
Fans of the series will be very satisfied."
—TeensReadToo.com

"*Into the Wildewood* brings a fresh perspective to the
genre with a crackerjack plot and razor sharp writing."
—*ForeWord Magazine*

The Secret of the Dread Forest

"The pleasant mix of fairy dust and romance—hallmarks of
the previous two books—is still present in *The Secret of the
Dread Forest*. The book zips along—fans of the series will not
be disappointed."
—*VOYA*

"New and old characters combine in a breakneck plot that
will have readers turning pages in class
and long after bedtime."
—*ForeWord Magazine*

The
Quicksilver
Faire

To Brian and Sandy, my liaisons at the High Court
of the Shining Ones, Minnesota Division.
And to my family, including the dogs and cats, who
put up with deadline-induced frenzy with good spirits.

THE FAIRE FOLK SAGA: TRILOGY 2

The Quicksilver Faire

GILLIAN SUMMERS

THE SCIONS OF SHADOW TRILOGY

Woodbury, Minnesota

First Edition
First Printing, 2011

Book design by Steffani Sawyer
Cover design by Kevin R. Brown
Cover illustration by Derek Lea

Flux, an imprint of Llewellyn Worldwide Ltd.

Library of Congress Cataloging-in-Publication Data
Summers, Gillian.
 The quicksilver faire / Gillian Summers.—1st ed.
   p. cm.—(The scions of shadow trilogy ; 2)
 "The faire folk saga: Trilogy 2."
 Summary: At the Fairy High Court, sixteen-year-old Keelie Heartwood learns that her mission in Canada is not to settle a conflict between the elves and the fae, both of whose blood she shares, but to resolve an imbalance in magic that threatens to destroy the world.
 ISBN 978-0-7387-1571-1
 [1. Magic—Fiction. 2. Elves—Fiction. 3. Fairies—Fiction. 4. Goblins—Fiction. 5. Canada—Fiction.] I. Title.
 PZ7.S953987Qui 2011
 [Fic]—dc22

                                                    2010054515

Flux
Llewellyn Worldwide Ltd.
2143 Wooddale Drive
Woodbury, MN 55125-2989
www.fluxnow.com

Printed in the United States of America

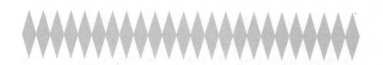

one

It was like having study hall on a roller coaster. Keelie Heartwood could hardly read the spidery lines of the Elven Compendium of Household Charms before her, thanks to the wild motion of the impossibly tiny airplane she was riding in.

Don't throw up, don't throw up, don't throw up. She swallowed hard. Her mantra wasn't working. The thick pages of the ancient book swayed back and forth as if she were reading on a swing, and the writhing letters jumped on the moving page. It seemed to be a recipe for a charm to turn flowers into weeds.

Pointless, except that the book was written by elves. Keelie was half elven, but she knew that a lot of what the elves did made little sense in the modern world. Case in point: Lord Elianard, her stuffy lore teacher, would be proud of her for reading Elvish writing but he would never stoop to tell her so. She wondered if she'd get extra points for reading on a plane that was staggering through the clouds like a kid in high heels on a sandy beach.

Her seat dropped a foot, roller-coaster style. She grabbed the book's thick covers to keep it from flying into the aisle as her stomach contents rose into her mouth. She swallowed hard and turned to look out the little window by her elbow, staring at a cloud landscape and the plane's silvery wing. She wished her boyfriend, Sean, was in the next seat, rather than the bulky carrier that contained Knot the cat. But Sean was sitting in the seat in front of her to allow Knot to stay near Keelie. She could just see the gilded top of one sun-bleached lock of Sean's hair.

It was the stupid cat's fault. She had to keep an eye on Knot, who had a fairy's wicked and inappropriate sense of humor and the power to wreak havoc, a dangerous combination on an airplane of any size. Her old frenemy Elia, Lord Elianard's daughter, was also on the plane, even farther to the front thanks to their last-minute tickets. Keelie did not miss having her nearby.

The plane dropped again, and then a persistent chime sounded. Her heart pounded as a light began blinking above her head. Seat belt. She took a deep breath. The one thing she could ignore, since she'd never unbuckled hers.

Her lips moved with the other words she'd chanted since they'd left Portland: *I am safe, I am safe*. But this mantra wasn't working either. She didn't believe it.

Keelie hated airplanes. They reminded her of her mother's death last spring, and this commuter jet must be a lot like the one in which Mom had spent the last moments of her life.

She closed the book and put it into her pack, even though it was her only source of distraction. She just couldn't concentrate. Instead of seeing the tiny picture of flower leaves in the Compendium, she'd envisioned Mom's plane breaking up in the sky, the passengers cartwheeling like Lego people into the fathomless Pacific. She shook her head, trying to clear it of bad thoughts, and wished once more that she'd checked inside her backpack before getting on the plane. Someone had dumped out her copy of *Hall Pass*, the novel she'd been dying to read and had finally snagged at the bookstore in town, and replaced it with the Compendium, a massive volume of spells and charms guaranteed to put anyone to sleep in five minutes.

"Someone" was probably Lord Elianard, since her grandmother was still in California, serving as the newly installed tree shepherd of the Redwood Forest.

It was because of her time in the Redwood Forest that Keelie was now headed to the Northwest Territories—to Big Nugget, a dot on the Canadian map, and to the Crystal Faire held there. Unlike the Ren Faires that her elven father, and now she, worked at every summer, which lasted anywhere from a week to the whole season, the Crystal Faire went on year-round, rain or snow. And from what Keelie had heard, they usually got a lot of snow in Big Nugget, along with seriously sub-zero temperatures. But that was months away; it was springtime now. And apparently it had been unnaturally warm, too. Bears had not hibernated over the winter and were wandering the Northwoods, grumpy. Scientists were blaming it on everything from global warming to sun spots.

But Big Nugget and the Crystal Faire were just a stop on her journey. Keelie was really headed to the elven village of Grey Mantle, on Mount Faron, and from there to the fairy High Court. She was on a diplomatic mission. Someone had been giving humans access to magic, and the elves and the fairies were accusing each other of this dangerous deed. Allowing humans to use magic put both the elves and the fae at risk, since preternatural creatures were supposed to keep themselves secret from humans—who, like clumsy children, broke things that fascinated them and which they did not understand.

An angry yowl sounded next to her, and she patted the metal-grate door of the plastic cat carrier strapped to the seat.

Within the darkness of the carrier, large green eyes glowed. Knot the evil kitty pressed his face to the bars and yowled his displeasure again. When she didn't make a move to open the door, he drew back and the carrier heaved and bounced on the chair as if a monster was in it. The elderly woman across the aisle paled in alarm.

Keelie pasted on the fake smile that she'd perfected from

dealing with the evil kitty and aimed it at the woman. "He's so playful."

"He seems upset. Is he old? I understand air travel upsets older cats."

Lady, you wouldn't believe. Aloud she only said, "Oh no, but then my dad says you're only as old as you feel."

The old lady nodded. "A wise man." She winked. "Of course, he's probably young too, compared to me."

Keelie upped the wattage on her smile. Her dad, Zekeliel Heartwood, was over three hundred years old, so this seventy-year-old would be like a baby to him. A wrinkly baby with an expensive hair weave and a fleece top that read, "Watch The Skies, They're Coming."

She checked her watch. They should be only minutes from their destination. The flyer for the Crystal Faire crackled in her jeans pocket, and she fished it out and unfolded it on her tray table. The map of the area was marked in thick black pen in her father's angular hand, his stretched-out letters marking where their escort would wait for them at the airport in Yellowknife.

The plane shook once more, then dropped a few feet like a clunky elevator slipping on its chain. Keelie imagined that this was what Mom felt in her last moments. She'd probably thought that the rough ride would soon be over and she'd be back home in Los Angeles with her feet up, sipping a hot cup of tea. Mom's trip had been over soon, all right, but not the way she'd expected.

Had she thought about Keelie in those last moments? The school counselor at Baywood Academy had told her that Mom didn't feel a thing, that she'd died instantly, but Keelie doubted it. She'd watched TV shows about planes going down. There were flames, and screaming, and stuff tossed around the cabins, crashing into people and seats. Mom would have been afraid, and maybe sad.

Her jeans pocket buzzed. She looked around; no one had noticed. She wiped her eyes and jimmied the smooth, oiled-wood cell phone out of her pocket.

This wasn't a real cell phone like her friends in California used. Nope, this was an elven-made phone, and it was charmed to connect all of the forests through the trees, making communications between the technology-phobic elves easier.

She answered cautiously, feeling sure that whatever magic powered the phone would not interfere with the plane's navigation instruments, but hunching over nonetheless. The flight attendant and other passengers wouldn't understand.

"Keelie, what's happening on that plane?" demanded her father's voice.

"Nothing, Dad. We'll be landing soon. Why'd you call? It's illegal, you know."

"You need to stop thinking sad thoughts," her father commanded. He hadn't been quite so bossy before, but he was Lord of the Dread Forest now and it seemed to have gone to his head.

"Dad, I'm on a plane," she whispered. "I'll call when we land and you can give me a pep talk then."

"Keelie, feel the forest—you're broadcasting your fears and grief. I can hear them all the way in Oregon."

Uh oh. Keelie opened her tree sense, the part of her mind that gave her a direct link to the forests. When they'd first gotten to know each other a year ago, Dad had been surprised that her connection to the forests was so strong—her mother was human, and Keelie had grown up far from the woods. But her connection to the trees had grown deeper with every moment Keelie spent with the elves. What she'd thought, as a child, was an extreme allergy to wood turned out to be an affinity that allowed her to identify the origins and species of everything wooden, from toothpicks to doors and furniture. If it was wood, it spoke to her.

She connected to the forest thousands of feet below her, and jumped as she felt the wail of the trees. She extended her touch, then shrank back in her airplane seat as the full force of the trees' anguish flooded her. It seemed familiar, which made it even more horrible as she realized why. It was her grief for Mom, amplified, expanded, and infecting thousands of acres of forest. Not exactly the best way to make a good impression on the Northwoods elves.

"What do I do?" Her voice was hoarse.

"Relax, and link your power to mine."

A thread of green light seemed to wrap itself around her power. The familiar feel of Dad's magic fortified hers, and she let her darker-hued power sink, melting into the sparkling green.

A moment later she felt calm, adrift in peace. Below her, the trees relaxed, quieted. *Sorry*, she whispered in tree speak.

"Beg pardon?" The old lady leaned across the aisle.

"Just chatting with my cat." Keelie turned off the cell

phone and put it away. The chime sounded, but there was no more turbulence.

"We are now approaching Yellowknife Airport," said the captain's calm voice. "Please fasten your seat belts as we start our descent." Twenty minutes later, they landed with a small, anticlimactic bump.

As soon as they were allowed to stand, Sean popped up over the headrest of the seat in front, his blond surfer hair flipped into his eyes. Except he wasn't a surfer. He was a jouster, riding horses for a living in a warrior sport that was old four hundred years ago. He was now the head of the Silver Bough Jousters, his father's troupe, which had headed to the High Mountain Faire in Colorado without him. Keelie knew he resented coming here, but then, so did she. At least they'd get to spend more time together.

"I'll wait for you outside. Everything okay?" His eyes flicked to Knot's cage. The two of them had a rocky history.

"Yeah, now that we're on solid ground," Keelie said. "Where's Elia?" Speaking of rocky.

Sean turned and looked around. He shrugged, lifting an eyebrow.

Keelie and Sean waited until everyone else deplaned, leaving just the crew and someone in the bathroom—likely Elia. Keelie lifted the carrier and looked in at her cat, who stared back impassively. But he couldn't fake his reaction to flying—his eyes were dilated to the size of dimes.

"Poor widdle kiddy scared? Aw."

Knot hissed a promise that she'd pay for making fun of him.

"Don't worry, we'll be off this plane in just a bit." She scrambled out of the row and grabbed her carry-on bag from the overhead bin, then headed down the narrow aisle, making sure to bang the cat carrier against the back of each empty seat. No point wasting the opportunity. The contrary cat's purr filled the cabin.

As they passed the bathroom, Keelie wrinkled her nose at the sound of its occupant being very sick inside. Definitely Elia.

"Gross," she muttered. At least it hadn't happened out where everyone could participate in the nausea.

Blue sky showed through the jet's narrow open door. The air was brisk, and instead of a Jetway to the inside of a concourse, a flight of painted wooden stairs on a wheeled platform led down to a pitted tarmac. Very classy. A colorful bus was being loaded with luggage, everyone from the plane crowding around it.

From the top of the stairs, Keelie saw walls of green forest. The hills and mountains surrounding the valley were densely wooded, a throbbing presence that made her itch as its magic skittered over her skin. Her work awaited her in these mountains—the mission she'd been sent on. According to her father and the Elven Council of the Dread Forest, the High Court fae were on the brink of war with the Northwoods elves over who had caused magic to leak to the humans, and the conflict could spread worldwide in very little time. Despite her inexperience, Keelie's part-fairy, part-elf blood made her father think that she was best suited for the job of arbitrator. Other elves disagreed, but

Dad was Lord of the Dread Forest. On top of that, Lord Norzan, the tree shepherd of the Northwoods, had specifically requested Keelie. He'd been impressed with what she'd done to save the Redwood Forest.

"You'd think they'd send someone more qualified than a sixteen-year-old mall rat," Keelie muttered aloud. She knew she'd proven herself to be more than a kid, but had no idea where the extent of her powers came from. Knot meowed from inside the crate and she looked at him. "Not from you, furface." The cat was freaky, but not telepathic. At least she didn't think he was. His kitty lips spread in a smile.

"Right. Time to get started. I can't wait to see who Elia's family has sent to greet us." Elia had come on the trip to meet her kin in Grey Mantle.

"Someone nice, I'm sure," Elia said from behind her. Her hair hung in two tight yellow braids and her eyes were as gorgeous as ever, but the elf girl's skin was greenish. She clutched the sides of the plane's doorway.

"You look like you have chlorophyll poisoning, but I know it's morning sickness." Keelie tried to sound sympathetic. "Need some crackers? Maybe there's a vending machine around here."

Elia put her hand over the little swell that bumped out her embroidered tunic. "I swear it was dancing a jig," she moaned.

"Maybe you should have listened to Uncle Dariel and stayed home," Keelie said. Dariel was the Unicorn Lord of the Dread Forest, and he'd stayed behind, cross. Even though

Keelie called Dariel "uncle," she just couldn't bring herself to start calling Elia "aunt."

"Dariel wanted me to come," Elia said sharply, her attitude resurfacing. "He wouldn't keep me from meeting my people."

"Yeah, he's nice that way." Keelie picked her way down the rickety steep stairs (pine, with lots of lead paint suffocating the wood).

Sean was standing in front of the long wooden building that occupied one side of the single runway. The bus had rumbled off, leaving them alone. It was like the set of a zombie movie. Keelie joined him, looking around. "I wonder if the elves keep their rescue helicopters here or up in Grey Mantle?" she said. The Northwoods elves were famous for their teams of Healers, who traveled far to aid other elves.

A figure, wearing the Healers of the Northwoods uniform, stepped around the end of the building. Keelie recognized the outfit from the Redwood Forest, when they'd evacuated Norzan. She'd been surprised to see the Healers lift off in a sleek helicopter, a reminder that elves had modern resources even if they sometimes seemed stuck in the Middle Ages.

No helicopter was in evidence anywhere around the airfield.

The Healer elf strode toward them, then bowed. "I'm Miszrial of the Stones, here to drive you to our village." She had thin lips, a beaky nose, and yellow hair scraped back from her face, making her look like a hawk in uniform.

Elia bowed back and Keelie dipped her head. She knew

Elia was excited about this visit, a triumphant homecoming for the princess whose pregnancy was cause for celebration across the land. Most elves were infertile, and Elia's offspring would be the first child born to elves since Elia's own birth sixty years before.

Despite her advanced age, Elia looked only a little older than Keelie's sixteen years and probably would stay that way for the next fifty years. Keelie had no idea how long her own life could be, since her mother was mostly human.

Miszrial didn't seem impressed with either of them. She led the way to a strange vehicle, a compact SUV with a roof made up of glassy black solar cells. "Please sit in the back." She bowed, then glared at Sean when he reached for a suitcase. He backed away, hands raised in mock surrender as she started shoving their luggage into the back of the SUV.

Keelie reached across the gated front of the cat carrier and a clawed paw lashed out and snagged her sleeve. She snatched back her arm.

"A fairy cat. It rides in the back."

Keelie grabbed the handle of the carrier. "Knot rides with me," she said firmly.

Sean picked up the cat carrier and shoved it onto the back seat, then stepped aside to allow Keelie to climb in and sit next to it. He followed, taking the spot next to her and closing the door.

Keelie pulled out her elf phone. "I'm going to call Dad and tell him we're here."

Miszrial rolled her eyes and opened the front door for

Elia, who held out an arm, silently asking for assistance. Miszrial helped her in.

Elia lifted her chin. "Call him if you wish, Keliel, but if I were you, I'd wait until we reach Grey Mantle. You'll be able to tell him about the unique Northwoods Ceremony of Welcome. I hope you don't feel slighted when they honor me."

Keelie gritted her teeth. "Don't start. We've managed to get along this far, and I'd hate to tell Uncle Dariel that I decked his pregnant wife."

The elf girl's chilly smile flicked up the corners of her mouth like tiny commas. "You wouldn't hurt me. You're too *kind*." She said "kind" the way others said "dog poop."

"You're probably right. I'd probably sic Knot on you."

Elia's eyes widened briefly before settling back to their bored stare. Keelie grinned. Score one for the half-elven mongrel. Sean poked her in the ribs, making her stifle a snort.

Miszrial drove toward the paved road, turned left, then pointed the SUV toward the forested mountains.

Unlike the Redwood Forest she'd just left, these woods didn't seem threatening to Keelie. She opened her tree sense a crack, then wider when she felt the welcoming green of the trees around her. All the anxiety she'd transferred onto them was forgotten. To think that just a year ago she'd thought trees were frightening, that she'd dismissed the magical buzzing that danced over her skin as an allergy.

Mom's fault, of course. Mom had tried to protect her from her otherness, from the half of her that was destined to be a tree shepherd like her father. And lately she'd discovered that Mom had other secrets, too. Mom's mother—Keelie's beloved Grandma Jo, whom she considered the ultimate cookie-baking granny—had fairy blood. This meant that Keelie's so-called "human half" was not fully human after all. Elia sometimes called Keelie a mutt. She was being deliberately mean, but she was right on target.

The green forest crowded closer to the road, and ahead, the black-asphalt ribbon wound around a hill covered with squat, slate-roofed buildings. They swung around the curve and there was the town of Big Nugget. Brightly colored pennants fluttered from peaked rooftops, and a ferris wheel towered over the shops, seats rocking in the morning breeze.

It was as if a big party was going on. They passed the first of the shops, with glittering mullioned windows and a wooden sign that read "Freat's Treats." A woman with wildly curling flame-colored hair was sweeping the sidewalk. She released the broom to drag her sign to the curb, and waved at them. Keelie gasped as the broom continued to sweep on its own.

"Did you see that?" Sean asked.

Two boys ran across the street, dressed in medieval-style, loosely woven trousers and belted tunics, caped hoods around their shoulders. They headed toward a bright blue maypole where other children danced, weaving silky, colorful ribbon streamers. The children's shoes hovered two feet above the ground. Their watching parents did not seem to notice anything amiss.

"Is this due to the magic leak?" Keelie asked.

"Yes, the humans have sensed the magic and are using

it for their pleasure. The Shining Ones at the High Court have put us all in peril. This must be stopped." Miszrial's hands tightened on the steering wheel. "Big Nugget used to be a quiet village, but when the wild magic was discovered two years ago, it drew this carnival." The elf's upper lip curled. "Their so-called Crystal Faire." She sniffed, as if the humans were silly.

They wound their way through the town, passing even more examples of magic. Kites with no strings hovered around a vendor, and a dazzling flock of fantastically colored birds swooped, chattering, over the SUV on their way to a silver-haired woman who controlled them with a gesture.

"My father has long cautioned elfkind on the dangers of letting humans see us," Elia murmured, sounding shocked. "Many think that the Renaissance Faires are a clever way of hiding in plain sight, but Father would be appalled at the flagrant use of magic here, and by human beings." Lord Elianard was not fond of humans.

Keelie touched her very human, rounded ear. Even with her unusual elven powers, she had never been able to fly, or summon fairy birds, or make brooms sweep by themselves (although that last one could come in handy). There was definitely something wrong going on at the Crystal Faire.

As soon as she was able to, Miszrial picked up speed, shot out of Big Nugget, and headed up the mountain.

Keelie caught her breath. She thought she saw faces peering at them from the underbrush that bordered close by the narrow road. "Stop the car!" she said loudly. Had it been her imagination?

Elia covered her mouth. "Yes, please. I don't feel so good after witnessing that nauseating display."

"We can't stop. Our destination is Grey Mantle," Miszrial stated. Elia craned her neck to look back imploringly at Keelie and Sean.

Keelie stared at the passing greenery, looking for more faces. Had they been animals? She started as they passed a gate made of twisted trees, the top of its arch decorated with the skull of a great deer. Even more startling was the sight of Peascod, the jester she'd last seen in the Redwood Forest. He waved at her, his eyes glittering behind his rigid, eternally smiling mask. They zoomed past, and then he was gone.

Keelie grabbed Sean's arm. "Did you see Peascod?" Fairies, elves, and now this. Had Peascod come here to take advantage of the leaking magic? Miszrial had called it wild magic. That was certainly fitting, if Peascod could use it.

Sean looked back, over her shoulder. "You're seeing things. It was probably a bear."

"No, it was Peascod," Keelie whispered. Her upcoming diplomatic duties were making her nervous, and she didn't need the added worry of the presence of the criminal jester. Dad needed to know.

"What?" Sean's eyes examined the blur of trees. "Maybe you imagined it. Maybe it was a strangely shaped twig."

"Bears and twigs don't wear masks."

He nodded slowly. "If it was really him, what does it mean?"

Keelie shuddered as she thought of what Peascod could do if he wielded magic. "He could take revenge on us. Bad things would happen that would seem like accidents."

Sean looked out the window at the seemingly endless forests, seeming as troubled as she was.

"What are you two whispering about? It's not polite." Elia glared at them from the front seat, still looking queasy. "I hope you're not hurt that the elves here may treat you with disdain. They dislike the fae even more than humans, and they *hate* humans." Elia looked at Miszrial. "Is there a place we can stop?"

"Don't listen to her, Keelie," Sean said.

"I'm used to it. Don't worry about me." Keelie felt Sean's warm hand envelop hers.

"That's why I'm here," he assured her. "I'll remind them that you are the daughter of the Lord of the Dread Forest." He smiled at her, making her stomach all fluttery. His smiles always did that to her.

"I'm not sure I can complete my diplomatic mission if I'm treated like a walking infection." Keelie leaned closer to Sean, enjoying his strong, warm presence.

"And while we're here, I will call you Keliel. My kin are so much more formal than the elves elsewhere," Elia continued.

Did she ever shut up?

"Of course they are." Keelie turned her face so that Elia wouldn't see the smirk on it. She needed to get serious to make her father proud. He'd sent her to impress the North-woods elf clan, to help them resolve their problems, and since their problem had to do with the fae's High Court, she was glad she had fae blood no matter how much of a mongrel it made her in the elves' eyes.

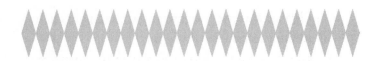

two

Keelie hoped the rest of the drive to Grey Mantle would be short and swift. She was squished in the back seat between the cat carrier and Sean, behind a queasy elf girl who was looking worse with every fast turn on the twisty road that wound through the mountains. Knot meowed louder with each stomach-churning curve.

Keelie felt a warm greeting from the local trees. She caught telepathic snatches of greetings as she passed them.

Greetings.

May your roots find comfort in our soil.

Let the sun bless you with many leaves.

The Great Sylvus bring you happy days.

Keelie sent a foresty embrace back to them.

After another hairpin turn, Elia slapped her hand over her mouth. "We need to stop." She burped.

Keelie scrunched closer to the door because the sound of the burp wasn't an I've-had-a-great-dinner-and-my-belly-is-full sound. It was an I'm-going-to-lose-the-contents-of-my-stomach sound.

"We need to stop." Keelie used Grandmother Keliatiel's commanding tone to get the elf guide's attention and cooperation.

Miszrial shook her head. "Can't. Need to get to the village."

Surprised, Keelie snapped her mouth closed. Normally when she used her commanding voice, she got results. Quickly.

Ahead, she saw a "You've missed the Crystal Faire, turn around!" sign. Below this was the small word "Restrooms."

Keelie leaned forward and pointed at the sign. "We need to go back."

"No. Can't. We need to get to Grey Mantle."

"If you don't stop, one pregnant elf and one cat might not make it there alive." Keelie studied Knot, who was staring balefully at Miszrial. His tail twitched, swishing sharply left, then right.

"Stop now," Sean barked.

Brakes slammed, pushing them all forward, then back again.

Miszrial glanced out the driver's side window and did a

double take. Keelie watched her face in the mirror and saw fear slip into the elf woman's eyes.

"Something's out there," Miszrial said.

Keelie peered out the window and thought she saw, once again, faces peeking through the underbrush. Maybe the *bhata* dwelled closer to the ground in this section of Canada; each region and area was different. She wondered if she could encourage a swarm to come and attack the SUV—then elf guide would be forced to listen.

If she were honest with herself, Keelie was nervous, too, especially about meeting with the fae. She shivered, thinking about being in a room full of fairies. She was used to the *feithid daoine*, who were bug fairies, and the *bhata*, who were mossy, sticklike creatures. What if she encountered a goblin? She'd pass. One encounter in the Redwood Forest was enough, thank you very much.

There was a definite change in the atmosphere around the SUV. It was as if a dark cloud had descended over them. She lifted her head and studied the sky. Puffy clouds floated in the air. Nothing ominous about them.

Keelie thought about the fairies. Perhaps she was sensing them. She'd been much more sensitive ever since restoring the Dread, the elven curse that kept humans away from her home forest. Or else she was just spooked from glimpsing Peascod.

Another loud burp issued from Elia, who then leaned over and threw up.

Keelie gagged, and pulled Knot's cat carrier closer to shield herself from the splatter.

"She can't do that," Miszrial shouted.

"Guess she did," Keelie replied, with at touch of I-told-you-so in her voice. "Now you *have* to go back to Big Nugget to clean out the SUV, because there's no way I'm going to ride in this smelly vomit car."

"You'll just have to wait until we reach Grey Mantle." Miszrial bit her lip and glanced nervously out the window as if searching for something. Keelie wondered if fairies might be in the woods. Though the elves and the fae had never gotten along.

"We have to get to the village for dinner," Miszrial added, clenching her jaw. "It's four o' clock. We can't turn around—we're going to have to drive straight through. It will only take an hour."

Elia gagged. Perfect timing.

"Fine. We will return to Big Nugget, but it will be a quick stop," Miszrial said. She pulled a U-turn and drove back toward town. When they reached Main Street, the Crystal Faire was still in full swing. Miszrial parked the SUV and they all clambered out.

Keelie was glad for the chance to get a closer look at the Crystal Faire. It was a strange combination of medieval faire meets Wild Wild West. Bright pennants snapped jauntily in the cool breeze, and the boxy buildings were painted in a variety of dizzying bright colors. It was as if somebody with ADD had opened a box of crayons and decorated the town.

Sean had read up on Big Nugget, and as they strolled, he told them about it. It had been a mining town back in the late 1800s. Legend had it that dwarves lived in the mines. There was even an entire city down there, according to some miners who had dug deep into the Earth seeking treasure, only to return to the surface with fairy-tale stories.

Another local myth said a dragon lived under one of the mountains. While the trees grew strong and tall toward the sky, the creature guarded its treasures from would-be robbers. Keelie started to laugh, then stopped. *There really could be a dragon.* She'd often wondered if Finch, the scary administrator at the Wildewood Faire, had some draconic relatives somewhere.

Knot was staring longingly at the Rollicking Mermaid Tavern. Keelie told him to go ahead. "One mead. That's it." Knot crooked his tail and strode away—which meant *yeah, yeah, yeah!*

"Maybe I should go along to keep an eye on him." Sean looked thirsty.

"Not a bad idea. Just one mead for you, too. We have elves to impress."

Sean gestured toward his blond surfer hair, whose careless curls covered his pointed ears.

Keelie laughed. "Yeah, but you're not from around here. We still have to make a good impression."

Miszrial had returned to the SUV and gone on a quest to find a car wash. Good luck, Keelie thought. She hoped Miszrial became lost and had to drive to Grey Mantle without them. Maybe she would tell Norzan she'd lost her passengers in Big Nugget and they'd send another car for them.

Not a bad idea. There had to be a hotel here. They could hide out until knights came to their rescue. Or would that be cavalry, in this place? They might have knightly cowboys. Keelie surveyed the myriad of brochures at the tourist center welcome desk while she waited for Elia to return from the ladies' restroom.

A middle-aged woman with curly blond hair smiled at them. She wore a purple tie-dyed sundress and a silver pentacle around her neck. "Hi. Is there anything I can help you with?"

"No, thank you."

Elia stumbled back to the counter and leaned against it as if her legs couldn't hold her up any longer. "You should've come with me. I needed you to hold my head."

"I'm not your nursemaid."

"You're supposed to help me."

"Holding your head was not in my job description."

Elia scowled. At least her face was now a shade of sticky pale, not a funky sea green, and she was complaining, which meant she was over the worst of the car sickness.

"Do you have a café that serves herbal teas?" Keelie asked.

"The Crystal Cup." The woman pointed across the street with her French-manicured nail. It looked like a fresh manicure. Maybe the town had a nail salon—Keelie could really go for a mani-pedi.

"I need some tea *now*," Elia whined. She rubbed her stomach in circular motions.

Keelie sighed inwardly at her short-lived dream of beautiful nails. "Come on."

They walked down the cobblestoned street. Sean waved

to them from the opposite sidewalk, Knot at his feet. They both appeared to be sober, thank goodness.

"Did you boys have fun?"

Sean shrugged, but Knot's green eyes shone brightly. No one seemed to think a tourist cat strolling down the street was odd. People waved at them. There wasn't a thread of synthetic fiber on anyone; these people seemed to invite nature to join them. Keelie wondered what it would be like if elk, foxes, or maybe grizzly bears came walking into the village and admired the store fronts, went shopping, and ate scones.

She had been in the SUV too long.

There seemed to be a party going on at the colorful maypole they'd passed earlier. Laughing people danced to a fiddle tune, weaving maypole ribbons that echoed the colors of the aurora borealis, which was oddly visible in the sunlit sky above them.

Across the street was a row of shops. Keelie stopped to ogle a shop window that had a display of fairy wings. The wings ranged from silvery snowflakes to a woodland style that had jewel-toned leaves outlining the curve of the wing. These sure weren't like the dollar-store wings her dwarf friend Sir Davey had to wear in *A Midsummer Night's Dream* last week. Those had been sad, but these wings were amazing.

Although Keelie had never been one to want a pair of fairy wings, these wings were like works of art and she was instantly in love. There was even a tiny version with leaves on it, probably for a baby. Or ... Keelie studied Knot. She wondered how he would look with a pair strapped to his back. For all she knew, he had a pair of his own, though he'd never show them to humans. Bet it would bring customers into the booths at the Ren Faires.

Knot rose up on his hind legs and pressed his nose against the glass.

Elia was leaning against the brick wall of the store, looking pale. "Are you through drooling?"

Keelie pulled herself away. She nudged Knot with her foot.

"We'll come back and try them on later."

The stores on either side of the Crystal Cup were crowded, thanks to the overflow of people in the streets. They walked past a mask store called Carnavale. Its window was filled with a variety of masks displayed against black velvet draperies: molded Venetian carnival masks, intricately feathered half-masks, leather masks, and decorative carved wooden masks. The variety was mesmerizing.

"That one looks like Peascod," Keelie said, pointing at a full-face mask with a prominent nose and slyly upturned lips. This one was painted gold, unlike the bone-white one she'd seen Peascod wear. She didn't even know what the jester's face looked like anymore; for all she knew it was hideously scarred, disfigured by his misuse of goblin magic. She shivered, remembering the last time she'd seen him in the Redwood Forest. Peascod had spun in a circle, tunneling into the ground and disappearing—she'd hoped forever. But he said they would meet again.

Just as she was about to walk away, Keelie saw an intricately carved wooden mask. The face was that of the Green Man, the legendary guardian of the forests. Curled wood formed his beard, and oak leaves were intertwined in his beard. His carved eyes seemed to twinkle at her.

The artist had captured the spirit's essence in his creation. She wished she could buy it, but it probably cost more than she could spend. Fascinated, Keelie drew closer, as if the mask were calling her. In her mind, she saw a horned man sitting atop a dark horse. He wore a cloak as black as a winter night sky, and she felt his eyes watching her from atop a hill. Rangy hunting dogs circled him, awaiting his command, and a hawk with black-tipped feathers soared in the sky above him, illuminated by an unearthly red light.

Dogs, hawk, and the elements of winter awaited his command.

Beware.

Keliel felt herself sink, as though the ground had melted, and she was suddenly aware again of the trees around her... millions of trees, all connected to this being. He was real. He was a forest god, and the watching faces in the greenery were his. The Green Man was here, and she heard the unspoken promise that they would meet. The thought chilled and excited her.

Sean's arm draped over her shoulder and his lips touched her rounded human ear. "I'd offer you a penny for your thoughts, but you look like you've left the planet."

Before she could gather her scrambled thoughts to answer, Elia's voice rang out.

"You two are disgusting. Hello? Pregnant woman in need of peppermint tea." She grabbed her middle and looked miserable. "I hope I don't hurl again." She disappeared through the door of the Crystal Cup.

Sean grinned ruefully. "Me too."

"No kidding." Keelie took his hand as they went inside. It was still thrilling to touch him. The crowded café was decorated with First Nations artwork, including a motif Keelie had never seen before—a stag with massive antlers.

She looked closer to make sure she hadn't mistaken it for a moose. Nope, it was a deer all right.

The server came up. "Indoors or out?"

"Outside, please. I need fresh air." Elia was gulping now, and looked a little green.

The server took one look at her and hurried them outside to a tile-topped wrought iron table. Knot took a chair, too, ignoring Sean's glare when he had to move around to the seat on the other side of Keelie.

A cheery waitress wearing a red gingham apron over jeans and a T-shirt gave them all menus, except for Knot. He meowed under his breath.

Elia shoved her menu over to him and closed her eyes. "Order me some tea and oatmeal."

Keelie ignored her. Did the elf girl think she was going to be her personal assistant?

She opened the menu for Knot, and was not surprised when he placed his paws on the fish section. At least he had an excuse—no opposable thumbs. The women at the table next to them did a double take. Keelie glared at them with a *what, you've never seen a cat order from a menu?* look.

"Where's Misery? Maybe we should order for her," Keelie said.

"Misery." Elia snorted and quickly covered her face.

Sean grinned and shook his head.

Miszrial seemed to appear out of thin air. "Saved a spot for me?" She sat down stiffly. "I will presume that you've made an idiotic attempt at making a pun of my name. Miszrial, Misery." She looked at Knot. "It's unfortunate that there are no laws in this town forbidding animals in eating establishments."

Keelie pretended to be happy, since Elia still seemed too queasy to even try. "We're so glad you could join us. I thought you'd still be searching for a car wash."

Miszrial tilted her head. "There is a detail car wash on the other side of the parking lot." If Miszrial had left the SUV, she must be anxious to keep an eye on them.

Goodbye "hiding out in a hotel" idea, Keelie thought. Maybe she could still check out the fascinating shops in the unusual town. She felt a hum of energy threading its way through the street. It felt like magic. She glanced at Sean, who didn't seem to be aware of it.

"Is he really reading that?" The elf guide stared at the cat, who was staring at the menu.

"Of course," Keelie answered.

Miszrial shook her head. "We need to hurry. We're expected at Grey Mantle and I have to return to my work."

"What do you do? Are you a Healer?" Keelie studied the elf guide. She had the disciplined look of a doctor.

"Yes. I'm working on an herbal tincture that will help my

people endure the winter by strengthening their immune system. Now is the time to harvest the principle ingredient, the Hunter's Moon flower." The elf guide straightened, obviously excited by her work. "It grows on the south side of the mountain, and can only be harvested by night, so that the sun's rays don't dry out the delicate stalks."

Keelie felt her eyes glaze over. It was like talking to Risa. A small part of her thought that humans might use the tincture, too.

The waitress returned. "May I take your order?"

Keelie scanned the menu and decided on oatmeal too, Sylvus help her. She was becoming more and more like an elf with each passing day. "Two oatmeals and two cups of peppermint tea." She handed her menu to the waitress.

Sean closed his menu. "A Crystal Cup special with whipped cream." He turned to Keelie. "I've craved fancy coffee drinks ever since that trip to the mall in Los Angeles."

"I was too busy wrestling a tree to drink mine, but I know what you mean," Keelie said. They'd ended up kidnapping the sapling in the food court's concrete planter and giving it a permanent home by a stream near Baywood Academy, her old school.

Knot meowed and placed his paw on the menu.

Keelie nodded. "Good choice. We need a kid's meal of fish sticks and hold the fries."

"Okay." The waitress arched an eyebrow.

"I'm not hungry." Miszrial handed the menu to the waitress, whose name tag said Hannah. "Just peppermint tea."

"Thanks." Hannah took the menu. "I'll bring your drinks back right away."

Keelie opened her napkin and placed it on her lap. She leaned toward the elf guide. "How is Lord Norzan doing?"

"He is better. His time in the Redwood Forest drained his energy, but here in his home forest he is healing. You will see him in Grey Mantle." The elf guide placed dark sunglasses over her face and turned away from Keelie, who definitely got the message: *I do not want to talk to you.*

Knot washed his face, ignoring all the human drama.

Keelie smiled nicely, bit down on her tongue, and didn't say anything—the excellent advice Dad had given her many times over the past months about dealing with cranky elves. She had a feeling she would be staying silent a lot in the coming days.

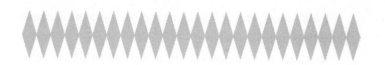

three

As they left the Crystal Cup to return to the SUV, Keelie thought of the Green Man mask and her eerie vision. Despite having witnessed walking trees, angry fairies, and magical unicorns, she'd never seen anything like the dark, horned figure who'd beckoned to her. Or heard a voice like that.

"Keelie, are you all right? You seem worried about something." Elia was wrapping a cloak around her shoulders, shivering in the cool air. Pregnancy was occasionally doing wonders for the elf girl's personality—as in, she'd developed one. Glimmers of niceness, anyway.

"I just zoned out." Keelie smiled at her, still worried about her vision.

"Well, don't daydream in front of my relatives. You'll embarrass me, and since we'll arrive together, I can't pretend I don't know you."

Keelie mentally crossed off the personality upgrade she thought she'd noticed. As they hurried to catch up with Misery the marching elf, they passed the mask shop again. Keelie stumbled when she saw the Green Man mask, and Sean steadied her.

"Something's up with you, I know it," he whispered.

"Later. I can't talk in front of the other elves."

He frowned, but said nothing.

The parking lot was gravel, and on the other side was the detail shop that held their strange little SUV, now sparkling in the northern sun. No crowds here.

"Throwing up made me feel better, but I could use a nap." A long golden curl had come loose from Elia's braid and blew across her face. She turned her head so that the wind swept it back, and stared into the trees. "Do you hear that? Singing."

Miszrial's eyes widened. "Quick, into the car."

Knot meowed scornfully, but Keelie thought that maybe the elf guide had noticed a moose or bear. Or an insane masked jester. She jumped into the back seat and didn't relax when Sean slammed the door behind them.

Miszrial drove as if they were being chased. Elia held on, turning green again.

Sean leaned forward, resting a hand on the back of the

drivers' seat. "Do you want me to help with the driving?" His offer seemed to come more from self-preservation than a desire to help Miszrial.

The elf guide gritted her teeth. "No, I'm fine." Her eyes kept checking both sides of the road.

Keelie's thoughts circled back to her strange experience at the mask shop. She'd seen various kinds of magic in the year since her mother had died, but this vision of the dark rider had been totally different from any of them. Was the Green Man—the forest god—watching her now? His magic had felt deep, old, and very dark, and just the brief encounter had made her shaky. But it intrigued her, too … a tremor ran down Keelie's spine. She'd never dealt with a god before.

She needed to call her father, but she didn't want to do it in front of Miszrial. She was here to help solve a problem for the elves, but it was beginning to look like the situation was more complicated than a simple disagreement over how the magic leak started. Maybe other creatures were involved. Really scary creatures. Whatever was going on, Keelie didn't want the Northwoods elves to think that their ambassador from the Dread Forest was weak, or that she was drawing the attention of old forest gods who felt the need to utter warnings. She didn't know what *Beware* meant, but it sounded alarming.

The elves might be able to tell her about this god, if they even knew he existed. The elves at home couldn't sense lesser fae like the *bhata* and the *feithid daoine*, and they hadn't known about Under-the-Hill beneath them. While it was hard to believe that a being as powerful as the Green Man could be a secret from the local elves, Keelie decided that she wouldn't ask about him until Dad gave the okay.

Elia turned in her seat to look at her. "Are you going to pout all the way to Grey Mantle?"

Keelie made a face. "If being snarky makes you feel better, go for it."

Elia's mouth fell open. "I don't know what you mean." She muttered something.

"Did you just call me a Round Ear?" "Round Ear" was an insulting elven term for "human."

Miszrial snorted. *Laugh it up, Misery,* Keelie thought.

"I don't know what you're talking about." Elia said coolly.

Knot made a disgusting sound and the car filled with a noxious odor.

Elia covered her mouth, eyes wide.

Miszrial shot her a panicked look and swerved the SUV to a shuddering stop on the side of the road. She'd learned her lesson.

Elia flew out of the car and knelt in the tall grass at the road's edge, shoulders heaving.

Keelie sighed and climbed out after her, ignoring Miszrial and Sean, who were rolling down windows and fanning the air. Knot jumped down next to Keelie and trotted, tail held high, to where Elia was being sick. Keelie didn't want to get too close. Instead, she turned to the trees, huge robust pines that seemed to flourish here in the Northwoods. She opened her mind to the trees. Spruce, Frazier fir, and many others. So many.

Tree shepherdess, tales of your deeds precede you. The speaker was a small fir that was straining at the soil, as if it was ready to bound down the hill toward her. She smiled.

Good tales, I hope. I'm pleased to visit your beautiful forest. She might as well practice her diplomatic skills. So far, her visit had consisted of elf vomit and frightening visions. Maybe she could take a moment now to call Dad. She thought of their comfy home, back in the Dread Forest in Oregon. Their house was filled with his beautiful woodwork. She wished he hadn't insisted that she could do this job.

"I feel better, I think," Elia gasped from behind her.

Keelie turned. "You look better." More diplomacy. She was starting to figure out that "diplomacy" was another word for "big, fat, schmoozy lie." The kind of lie that made people feel better, like "You don't look fat in that baggy knit dress."

A blur of movement caught her eye and she spun. She examined the trees, wondering what it had been.

"What's the matter?" Miszrial's voice sounded panicky.

"Nothing," Keelie called back. "Just thought I saw something." She didn't find the elf's fear reassuring.

"Like a snake?" Elia eyed the forest warily.

"No snakes up here." Miszrial sounded calmer.

Then the creature buzzed down, and Keelie gasped in delight. It was a *bhata*, a woods fairy. Two rough-barked sticks held together with stringy moss, full of the spark of life and magic.

It skittered around the tree, almost like a kitten playing. She smiled, the scary mask at the Crystal Faire forgotten.

She knew the *bhata*, and their presence made the forest seem more like home.

"Lady Keliel, we must hurry." Miszrial's voice rang against the trees, and Keelie waved goodbye to the little creature, and to the trees, then hurried back to the SUV.

The rest of the trip sped by, as Miszrial gunned the vehicle around narrow curving roads, climbing into the mountains. They pulled off onto a dirt road which entered the forest. A mile later, the unpaved road widened on the left into a graveled lot with eight cars in a tidy row. Miszrial pulled onto the gravel and parked the SUV.

"Where are we? There's no village anywhere near here." Keelie looked out of the car windows.

"How do you know?" Miszrial said tightly.

"The trees tell me."

Miszrial's eyes widened. "You *are* a tree shepherd, like Lord Norzan. I had a hard time believing it."

"Why, because I'm part human?"

The elf woman reddened and didn't answer. "Let's get on with it. A wagon will now take us to Grey Mantle. It's not far."

Elia and Miszrial exchanged angry looks, and Sean eyed them warily.

Before Keelie could figure out what had gone on between them, they were interrupted by the clopping of hooves. Two large horses pulling a wagon appeared on the road, the elaborate harness beautiful against their glossy hides. A tall, imperious elf held the reins, sitting high on the seat above them.

The horses stopped and the elf looked down over his

axe-blade nose. "Welcome to Grey Mantle. Allow me to move your luggage."

He hopped down from the tall seat and started hauling suitcases out of the back of the SUV and tossing them into the wagon as if they didn't weigh anything. Sean had been ready to help, but instead he shrugged and gave Keelie a look of good-humored puzzlement. She smiled back in agreement. This guy had a serious anger problem.

Keelie grabbed Knot and held the squirming cat close to her chest. Elia stepped out of the SUV and beamed at the wagon driver as he finished loading the wagon.

"Greetings, cousin. It is I, Elia, daughter of Elianard and Cilene."

No expression crossed his face as he stopped and looked at Elia, then continued to pack the wagon. When the SUV was empty, he climbed onto the wagon seat again. Elia stood frozen on the gravel, shock on her face.

"Come on, we've got to ride in the back." Miszrial grabbed a rope that was dangling from the back gate of the wagon and pulled herself aboard. She turned and extended a hand to Elia, who didn't seem to notice her.

Elia wasn't her best friend, nor her worst enemy anymore, but Keelie couldn't stand to see her in pain. She didn't know who the wagon driver was, but when he ignored Elia, it had hurt her feelings.

"Let's rescue Elia," she said to Sean. "Something's not right here."

"I've been saying that since we hit town," Sean muttered. "This is not good, Keelie. Elia is correct in her expectation of a huge celebration in honor of her return to the forest of her mother's people. The baby alone merits much feasting and happiness."

Keelie dropped Knot and went over to the elf, who stared down at her. She glared back, then ignored him as he'd ignored Elia.

"Come on Elia, I'll help you get in the wagon."

Elia lifted an eyebrow. "Why do you think I need your help?" She walked stiffly to the wagon, grabbed the rope, and struggled to get in.

Keelie wanted to give her a swift kick in the backside to help her up, but just watched as she wriggled and flailed her way into the wagon bed, finally accepting Sean's help.

Keelie looked down at Knot. "So do you need help getting in, or are you just going to snarl at me too?"

Knot grinned, showing impressive kitty fangs, then leaped lightly into the wagon. Judging from the distance between the ground and the wagon bed, he must have flown part of the way. Yet nothing surprised her about Knot. Keelie sighed and grabbed the rope and Sean's extended hand. He pulled her up easily, then motioned her to sit on a suitcase as the others had done.

The wagon lurched forward.

"This is fun," Keelie said brightly. "We're starting off with a hayride."

Silence from the elves shut her up. See if she would try to lighten the mood again—if they all wanted to sulk, great. Keelie could tell that this was going to be the worst trip

ever. Elia was watching her, but turned her face when Keelie looked at her.

Keelie examined the passing forest. A huge beetle buzzed past, then swooped around and landed on the suitcase beside her. Knot looked at it curiously, but the others didn't seem to notice it. The beetle stood on its hind legs and nodded its insect head at Keelie, its feelers waving around. Keelie nodded back. The *feithid daoine* were secretive and although she'd seen them frequently, she'd only interacted with them once, when they'd attacked her at the High Mountain Renaissance Faire. She'd been a little leery of them ever since, but they'd left her alone.

This *feithid daoine* pointed up with one pincer-ended leg. Keelie looked up and was amazed to see that *bhata* were following them, leaping from branch to branch overhead. The forest was filled with them. *Whoa.*

"We're almost there." Elia's voice interrupted her. "I must say again that I hope you don't feel slighted, Keelie. As a daughter of the soil and, of course, because of this"—she smiled down at her bulging baby belly—"I'll be welcomed with utmost respect and joy." She smiled at Keelie. "You are a tree shepherdess, of course, so you are due respect as well, but there's that unfortunate, um ..." She touched her pointed ear and glanced at Miszrial, as if pointing out that one of Keelie's ears was rounded.

Keelie rolled her eyes. "Fine. I get it. You're the returning princess. I'm just the mongrel come to help out."

Miszrial's eyes widened.

"Don't you guys watch movies?" Keelie asked. "It's the mongrel who always wins in the end."

"We destroy mongrels," Miszrial said seriously. "Among our animals."

Cold crept up Keelie's spine. She knew she wasn't being threatened, but the fact that Miszrial had said it so coolly meant that these elves were even less compassionate than the ones back home. She couldn't wait to get back to the Dread Forest. This place was seriously creepy.

A deer leaped onto the road, startling the horses, which jolted the wagon. As everyone grabbed the sides to keep from falling over, the driver struggled to regain control of the horses.

The deer didn't run away. He kept pace with the wagon, close enough that Keelie saw her reflection in his liquid brown eyes. His antler-heavy head bobbed with each leap.

Who are you?

The voice went through her head and into her bones, deep and rich like thick chocolate, and strangely familiar. She couldn't move; her hand was frozen on the splintery side of the wooden wagon (pine, from the other side of this mountain). *Who are you?* she answered.

Herne. Herne. Herne. Herne. The voice echoed in her head. The deer sprinted to the edge of the road, then leaped into the forest and disappeared.

Herne. She knew that name. In mythology class she'd learned that Herne the Hunter was the Celtic god of the forest, the Master of the Wild Hunt.

The Green Man.

four

As if she'd been held in thrall by the deer's gaze, Keelie slumped against the wagon's side, her mind whirling with her discovery.

Herne, in this forest. When had he left Great Britain, and what was he doing way up here? He didn't seem scary this time, but she had felt his power. Why was he warning her earlier? What did he want?

"Do not be frightened, Lady Keliel. The forest creatures often come close. They are naturally curious of us. The stag would not harm us." Miszrial's tone was condescending, as if the poor frightened human had never seen a deer before. She didn't seem to know that this was not an ordinary deer.

Elia shot Keelie a murderous look, which Keelie could read well: *don't embarrass me*. The happy Elia who'd left the Dread Forest had been replaced by the paranoid, superior, snot-girl Elia. That was okay. Keelie knew how to deal with them both.

Herne. At least she knew she hadn't been crazy at the mask shop. That Green Man mask *was* Herne, and he'd spoken to her telepathically then, too. If one vision was real, then another could be real as well. Maybe that really had been Peascod on the side of the road. Things were getting interesting, and not in a good way.

Elia was patting her hair and straightening her clothes. They must be getting close to the village of Grey Mantle. Two ancient trees flanked the road, and as they passed, Keelie felt their welcome like a caress on her soul. That was more like it.

A stone-and-timber building appeared on their right, built in the familiar style of the elven homes of the Dread Forest, and then there were more buildings on both sides of the road.

The wagon stopped in a cobblestone-paved square surrounded by gray stone buildings. Two silver-haired elves in long robes stood together. Keelie recognized the symbols embroidered on their robes; these were members of the Elven Council. Keelie was disappointed. She'd hoped Norzan would greet them, too.

Elia's eyes were bright as she stood up. She held her head

high, like a princess, and walked to the edge of the wagon. She looked down at the cobblestones, which seemed to Keelie like a far drop.

What the heck. She jumped down and held a hand up to Elia. She was her niece now, after all. Elia's lips tightened, then she reached down and took Keelie's hand in her own, her grip cold and tight. She's afraid, Keelie thought. All the snootiness was a bluff.

"Let me help." Sean leaped to the ground and put his hands on Elia's waist, lifting her effortlessly and setting her lightly on the cobblestones. Keelie was relieved, and not jealous. The thought of Elia splatting on the ground had bothered her.

Miszrial hopped out of the wagon and walked proudly toward the two elders. She bowed low, sweeping her arms in a graceful arc. "Milords, these are the ambassadors from the Dread Forest. Lady Elia, daughter of Lore Master Elianard, Lady Keliel Heartwood, daughter of Zekeliel, Lord of the Dread Forest, and Lord Sean o' the Wood, son of Niriel."

Keelie kept her eyes on the two men, but wondered what Sean's reaction had been to the mention of his father. Since Niriel's fall from grace, he didn't even have an honorary title.

The two Council members bowed their heads solemnly, and the three ambassadors bowed back. Keelie noticed that Elia's bright, expectant eyes darted back and forth, as if looking for the hidden parade that would greet her.

The taller of the two stepped forward, a beaky-nosed elf with a deeply lined face. "I am Terciel, head of the elven

Council here. I welcome you to the Northwoods and to Grey Mantle. We are grateful to the Dread Forest for sending you to help us to resolve our troublesome conflict."

Keelie didn't think he suspected just how serious it might be. Or then again, maybe he knew exactly who or what lived in these woods with him. How could anyone ignore Herne, the Hunter?

"Lord Terciel, greetings from the Dread Forest." Sean was acting as if Keelie were actually supposed to be standing there lost in thought. She owed him one.

"Sean o' the Wood, son of Niriel, we are pleased that you have joined us. You are the first of your blood to walk here since the old times."

Elia stepped forward. "I too bring greetings."

Terciel looked at her as if she were a bug crawling on his birthday cake, but he bowed his head. "Lady Elia."

Miszrial bowed to them. "Dinner will be in the Council building in an hour. You'll have time to refresh yourselves. Allow me to escort you to your rooms in the lodge."

They followed her through the empty streets. Keelie felt eyes watching them from the windows. "Miszrial, where do you keep the rescue helicopters? I can't see you guys running rescue missions from the human airport."

Miszrial smiled thinly, stopping at a two-story stone building with a small wooden porch protruding from the front like a tongue. "The helipad is on the other side of village, disguised as a barn." She opened the door of the building and stepped aside to allow them to enter first. The inside was almost empty of furniture, but lights glowed high on the walls.

Keelie walked up to one. Not electric, and there was no fire that she could tell. "What is this?"

"Fairy lights," Elia answered, before Miszrial had a chance.

"I've seen these," Keelie said, remembering. "Back home, in Under-the-Hill. Barrow's house is lit with them." Barrow was her dwarf friend whose parents owned the town hardware store. He was currently dating a water sprite named Plu.

"I am not surprised that you have been Under-the-Hill," Miszrial said.

Sean tugged Keelie back when she headed toward the snarky elf. "Easy, tiger. She's saying that to make you angry."

"Why would she want me to be angry? I'm here to help her." Keelie watched Miszrial walk up the stairs that filled the center of the building, followed by Elia. "Grandmother Jo used to tell me that when people were mean like that, it was because they were jealous."

Miszrial was waiting for them at the top of the stairs. She motioned toward a door. "Your room, Lady Keliel."

Elia stood in the doorway next to hers. "Will tonight's dinner be a formal meal?"

"No, it will just be yourselves and Lord Terciel." She bowed and walked to the next door, leaving Elia to shore up her crestfallen face.

"Lord Sean, your room." Miszrial pointed across the hall.

Keelie didn't have a reason to linger in the hall, so she went into her room. It was tiny, which was good, because the warm fire that burned in the fireplace kept the evening chill close to the sole window, which looked more like an arrow slit set deep into the stone wall. A bed with tall, thick posts dominated the spartan room. The only things that brightened it were a colorful woven rug next to the bed and an arrangement, in a glass jar, of twigs bursting with bright red berries. Probably poisonous to humans.

An hour later, Miszrial collected them for dinner. Keelie wore one of her Ren Faire gowns, a long blue linen dress with full skirts and hanging sleeves that swept from her shoulders to the ground. Tight white inner sleeves covered her arms, and she wore her charms on a silver chain around her neck. Miszrial led them out of the lodge and along a leafy path which, as it scaled a small hill, became stone stairs opening onto a small plaza in front of the largest building Keelie had yet seen in Grey Mantle.

"This is the Council building," Elia said, breathless from either pride or the climb. "There's nothing like this in Dread Forest, is there?"

Sean glanced up at the pointed roof of the circular building. "No, nothing like this. Why is the roof pitched so steeply?"

"To keep the snow from accumulating." Miszrial smiled. "Although it's not a problem lately. This year we've barely had two feet of snow. The bears have not slept, either, and they're hungry."

Keelie tried to remember what she'd learned about hibernating bears, but drew a blank. She glanced at the dense forest around them and threw a quick message to the trees. *Let me know if you see any bears near me, please.*

No bears are here, but the fae gather close, came the answer. The trees seemed to speak in a chorus.

"Keelie, are you okay? You have a strange look on your face." Sean leaned closer. "I won't let any bears eat you, I promise."

Before Keelie could tell him that it wasn't bears she feared tonight, Terciel appeared in the arched stone doorway, his figure darkened by the glow of the room behind him.

"Greetings, guests of the Northwoods. Welcome to our forest home." He bowed, and invited them in with a graceful gesture.

Elia strode forward, pushing aside Keelie.

"She's like a kid in first grade who always wants to be first," Keelie said to Sean under her breath.

Miszrial overheard and gave her a frosty smile. "Lady Elia is a true elf, and despite her unfortunate choice of mates, she outranks you. May we speak frankly?" She looked Keelie up and down. "Many of us think it unwise that the elders have decided to summon help from outside, and disastrous that Lord Zekeliel chose you as his ambassador. We know why, of course." She sniffed. "It can't be helped that you are such a sad mongrel, and Lord Terciel thinks you may redeem your family's name if you succeed."

"Redeem my family's name? There's nothing wrong—"

Sean grabbed Keelie's hand, encasing it in his, and she realized she'd drawn back her fist. She took a deep breath and forced herself to relax. She'd never been a brawler. The girls of the Baywood Academy could be snarky, but they never had fistfights.

Lord Terciel's eyebrows rose. "Miszrial, please show Lady Elia to her seat."

Miszrial's angry expression faded, and she bowed to the Council leader before slipping past him into the building. Lord Terciel turned to Keelie and Sean. "You must forgive Miszrial. She blames humans for the situation we are in." His lips thinned out. If it was supposed to be a smile, it failed.

Keelie went in, followed by Terciel. Sean closed the door behind them.

Inside, a small circular vestibule with white plastered walls held doors leading to rooms. The spaces between the doors were hung with tapestries. Elia and Miszrial were admiring them, no doubt aiming their pointed ears toward the conversation.

"So just what is the situation, Lord Terciel?" Keelie asked, then looked quickly toward Elia. The elf girl closed her eyes, eyebrows together in a frown. Okay, so it was probably rude to ask.

Terciel eyed her sourly. "I shall fill you in as we dine. Shall we take our seats?" He gestured toward another room, which held a long granite table with uncomfortable-looking stone benches around it. Five of them had place settings in front of them, although there were eighteen more benches around the table.

Elia stared at the five seats as if they were giant signs pointing out how unloved she was. Keelie watched her swallow hard and turn her face. Sean caught Keelie's eyes and lifted his brows; yeah, he'd seen it too. Elia had hoped that a feast awaited them, a feast where she would be honored.

A small, black-haired elf appeared at the door opposite them, a large wooden bowl in his arms.

"Ah, Saliel is here with our dinner." Terciel waved them to their seats.

"Where's Lord Norzan?" Keelie asked. "I heard he was doing better."

"He's still at the Hall of Healing," Terciel said.

"He is here." A tall figure stepped through the door. He lowered the hood of his robe, revealing a handsome, un-lined face and long, gleaming silver hair.

"Norzan!" Keelie jumped up, lifting her wide blue skirts as she ran around the side of the table to hug him. He hugged her back, holding her close for a moment.

"Keliel Heartwood. We could ask for none braver to help us in our time of need. And Lord Sean, how fare you?" Norzan bowed and Sean, who had stood up again, bowed gravely from his waist, then smiled broadly.

"And Lady Elia." Norzan walked to her side and took her hand in his, looking deep into her eyes with his unusual blue ones. "The very trees rejoice at your news, and greet the new life you bring within you."

Elia's face shone and tears glistened in her eyes. "I thank you, Tree Shepherd of the Northwoods. You do me honor."

Terciel looked as if he'd swallowed a lemon whole.

"I must take my leave to rest again," Norzan said. "I

hope to speak with you again before you travel to the High Court."

Keelie hoped her disappointment didn't show. "You look much better."

"Good night, Lord Norzan," Sean said, echoed by Elia.

The tree shepherd left, and Keelie noticed how slowly he moved.

They sat, Terciel at the head of the table with Elia at his right and Miszrial at his left. Keelie sat across from Sean, who didn't seem thrilled to have Miszrial at his side but tried hard not to show it by making small talk. Elia was quiet now that her sole champion was gone.

Saliel came forward and served each of them a portion of whole grain studded with nuts. It looked like vegetarian cat food.

Elia's eyes brightened, but Keelie poked at hers. Diplomacy did not look tasty.

"You asked about what is happening here," Terciel began.

Yeah, about fifteen minutes ago, Keelie thought.

"The Northwoods elves settled here long before the humans came to this land," Terciel began. "The Shining Ones came to these forests long before we did, as did other creatures of the Other Realm."

Keelie wondered what other creatures he referred to. Talking cats? She'd never heard the term "Other Realm," either, although she was pretty sure it meant places like Under-the-Hill.

Terciel nodded to Sean. "Your grandfather fought the

dragon Avenir in these very hills and defeated him, to our eternal gratitude."

"Dragons?" The little hairs on the back of Keelie's neck prickled to attention.

Sean poked her with his elbow. She'd definitely ask him later.

As Terciel spoke, Saliel served them a salad and giant grilled strips of what looked like steaks. Keelie's mouth watered.

"Queen Vania keeps her people apart from us. In order to speak with her, you must ascend to the High Court."

The High Court always sounded like something from a fairy tale. "So she doesn't come down here?" Keelie asked.

"She has not been seen here in centuries," Lord Terciel said.

"That's a long time not to say hi to the neighbors." Keelie took a tentative bite of the grilled thing. It tasted a little like steak…from a slug, maybe. She swallowed fast without chewing and drank from the goblet before her, then almost spat. Wine. Holy cow. Dad would freak out. She tried to catch Sean's eye but he was wolfing down his dinner as if it was super tasty. Another reminder that she was not an elf, if slug steak appealed to elf taste buds.

Maybe later she could go into town and grab a hot dog.

Terciel was eyeing her expectantly. Right, the questions. "What keeps the elves and fae apart?"

"The High Court engages in frivolous pursuits, while the elves work hard to maintain the forests. Yet the fae have much power. They influence the dwarves, and though they do not see eye-to-eye with the dark fae, they have power there as well."

"How is it that the elves here can even see the fae?" Keelie asked. "The fae in the Dread Forest are invisible to the elves."

"Some of us can sense them. And the High Court has always been visible to us. Their vanity would not let it be otherwise." Terciel sighed. "That does not mean that we agree with the Shining Ones. Over the years Queen Vania has ceased to listen to us, and now, despite the current predicament, she will not see us."

"And she won't come here, so I have to go there?"

"No, *we* have to," Sean interjected. "Your father charged me with caring for your safety."

"What do we say to the queen? I've never met a queen before." Elia seemed excited at the possibility.

"You've met Alora," Keelie reminded her.

"She's a tree," Elia said dismissively.

Keelie wanted to kick her. Alora was much more than just a tree—she was a gift from the Wildewood Forest, an acorn who'd ultimately saved the Dread Forest and become its Queen Tree, as Elia well knew.

Keelie wondered where, exactly, the high fae lived. Not Under-the-Hill, where the dark fae lived in the Dread Forest. The Shining Ones loved light. Maybe at the top of one of the mountains? She didn't do well with heights. Elia would probably thrive there.

"Lady Elia will not go to the High Court," Terciel said, glaring at his guests. "Her child must be protected, and the fae do not get along with elves, as I have mentioned."

Elia looked stricken. She opened her mouth, but closed it again without speaking.

Terciel stopped to turn his scary gaze on Saliel, who had snorted. "Lady Keliel is uniquely qualified to go, since her, er, mixed blood may be acceptable to the fae. Lord Sean, of course, is her protector and must attend her."

"So they'll love me because I'm a mutt?" Keelie took a tentative taste of the salad. She'd kill for a tofu hot dog.

"Mutt." Terciel seemed to consider the word. "Yes, I believe that is correct. The dwarves speak well of you."

There were dwarves here, of course. They lived under mountains and forests. Keelie's heart warmed as she thought of Sir Davey and Barrow. Maybe the ones who lived here knew them.

"Is there anything I need to know before we go?"

Lord Terciel looked at her silently for a long moment. "You are our hope, Keliel. Go, speak to the queen, and ask her to agree to a meeting of all who live in the Northwoods. A summit, if you will. Do not linger at the High Court. It is seductive, and time does not flow there as it does here."

"What dangers might we encounter?" Sean asked.

Terciel and Miszrial glanced at each other quickly.

Not a good sign.

Sean frowned. "We will be prepared to do battle, if need be, to return here."

Terciel nodded. "It would be wise. Do not draw weapons while you are there, unless you are directly threatened. At midnight tomorrow night, you will travel through the portal. Rest now."

Keelie met Sean's troubled gaze. She thought of what the trees had told her. The fae were all around, it seemed. Did that mean the *bhata*, or had Queen Vania sent spies to watch them? Or maybe the *bhata* themselves were her spies. This forest was very different from the Dread Forest, which, despite its scary name, only inspired dread in the humans who neared it. She'd call Dad as soon as she got to her room. This sounded way more dangerous than he'd described.

By the time Keelie returned to the lodge she was exhausted. She punched her father's number into the phone again, but no luck.

"I don't get it," she told Sean. "It's not like it relies on cell towers. This works with forests. Why won't the trees connect my call?"

"Ask the trees." Sean yawned. "I'm going to bed, Keelie. I've got to tell you, I'm worried about what Lord Terciel said. I'm glad I brought my armor and sword."

"Maybe a gun and hand grenades would have been a better choice," she muttered. "Go on to bed. I'll be right behind you. I'm going to try one more time."

"Good night then. Don't go outside alone." Sean kissed the top of her head and went upstairs.

The lower rooms of the lodge were spartan, and Keelie was ready to go to bed, too, if only to give her backside a break from all the stone seats. Apparently the Northwoods elves didn't believe in cushions. She stood close to a window and tried her father's number again. Nothing. With a sigh, she headed up the stairs. Elia had hurried ahead of them and gone to bed without saying good night.

Keelie's room was just as she left it, except that the logs in the fireplace were fresh. Someone scratched at the door. She hurried to open it, hoping it was Sean, but Knot crept in. The hall was deserted.

She looked at the door. The scratching had come from shoulder height. Her shoulder, not the little kitty's. She shrugged. This close to the fae court, there was no telling what the cat would do.

"Where were you while we went to dinner?"

Knot jumped onto the bed, ignoring her.

"You didn't miss much. Slug steak. Turns out it was some giant grilled mushroom, but it sure tasted like slug."

Knot yawned, showing much kitty fang.

"Yeah, me too." Keelie said. "You aren't going to invite all your fairy friends in here to party, are you?"

Knot blinked at her.

"Just a warning. I need sleep." Keelie undressed and slipped into bed, relieved that the sheets were clean and fragrant with lavender. She'd half expected burlap. She closed her eyes, wondering what the next day would bring. The High Court sounded kind of exciting, actually. If she didn't reach Dad tomorrow, she'd have to go without briefing him on Peascod and the Green Man. She fell asleep thinking of the fairies and the trees, and how the elves fit into the mix.

Later, the sound of weeping awoke her. She was pretty sure it was Elia, and as she tried to drift off to sleep again, she felt a pang of sympathy for the elf girl who'd expected so much and received so little.

She couldn't sleep. She got up and opened the door of her bedroom. A reddish light shone into the window at the end of the hall, and she crept toward it, wondering what it could be. In a human town, she wouldn't think anything of it, chalking it up to an exterior light. Nothing like that existed here.

She reached the window and looked out at the thickly wooded view. The trees called greetings, which she answered until she saw the figure that watched her from the ground below. It seemed like a man, but had huge antlers like a deer. Like the hunter she'd seen in the vision. Like the deer that had raced alongside the wagon.

She ran back to her room and closed the door tightly, wishing she could climb into a friend's bed for comfort, but Elia and Sean were not candidates for that job, for very different reasons.

Knot was standing in the middle of her bed, back arched and fur on end. Keelie leaped under the covers and yanked Knot in with her.

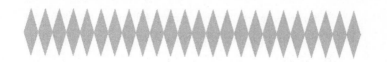

five

"Dad?" Keelie came quickly awake. She wasn't in her cozy bed in her father's timber-and-stone house. She was in the Northwoods elven village of Grey Mantle, and the sound she'd heard was not her father. She lay very still, listening. There. Claws clicking on stone, then breathing close by.

She turned her head slowly, eyes still closed, dreading the monster she'd see. Did Herne have claws? Wouldn't a deer have hooves? She hadn't thought to look.

She opened her eyes and her breath caught in her throat. A coyote stood next to her bed, staring at her, clearly visible in the undulating bands of light from the aurora borealis.

When their eyes met, his mouth fell open, black doggie lips lifting in a pleased grin that showed very sharp white teeth.

"Coyote?" she whispered. "Are you really here?"

"You're not dreaming me." His goofy grin widened and his tongue lolled out of the left side of his jaw, like a damp carpet unfurled over a jagged balcony. "You got anything to eat?"

"Not for a coyote used to eating out of Wolfgang Puck's dumpster in Los Angeles."

The fairy rolled his eyes. "I'm going back to town. At least they have hot dogs there. Probably tofu ones, but I know where they are."

"It *is* you." Keelie sat up. "How did you get here?" She'd met Coyote in her Los Angeles neighborhood recently, and then learned that the fairy had lived there when she was a little girl, too.

He cocked his head. "You have no idea what awaits you. I've been summoned to offer my help."

"Summoned? Who summoned you, and what awaits other than more snotty elves and that forest god? You're the best thing that's happened here so far."

Coyote stared at her for a moment. "You may not be so thrilled if the elves discover me here. I'll try to keep out of sight."

Knot, who'd been asleep on the pillow next to hers, woke up and did a kitty double take when he saw Coyote. The two looked at each other carefully; then Knot nodded, walked to the edge of the bed, and touched noses with Coyote.

For Knot, that was the equivalent of a wild lovefest. Keelie tried not to be jealous. *Who wanted a shape-changing fairy cat to love her?*

"Everyone get to bed. We've got a huge day ahead of us." Keelie crawled back under the covers. Knot settled at her feet, and Coyote turned around four times on the carpet next to her before sinking into a tight Coyote curl. Keelie fell asleep, relieved that she had one more ally. Something was up in this forest, and so far her friends here were few.

When she woke up again, it was still dark but she knew it was morning. The growling she heard was her stomach, not Coyote, who was still asleep, looking innocent.

She, Sean, and Elia were expected for breakfast down-stairs, but even though she was starving, Keelie was dread-ing it. Facing Elia would be the first challenge. The elf girl had sounded heartbroken last night, but Keelie could just guess how much Elia would resent a show of sympathy. Not to mention how hard it would be to cough up any, since Elia had been Princess Obnoxious ever since they arrived.

Keelie dressed quickly in corduroy jeans and a sweater. Coyote stretched and yawned, then thumped his tail on the floor.

"Think we can find food now?"

"With any kind of luck," Keelie answered. She brushed her short hair, then swatted the cat-shaped lump under the rich, leaf-embroidered quilt.

"Up and at 'em, kitty. You'll probably see some *other* real live fairies today." At least, she hoped so. They were here to do a job, and hanging out with Elia's chilly relatives wasn't getting it done.

The lump humped up, then stretched almost flat, then Knot's head appeared outside of the covers, fur sticking up.

Keelie laughed. "Bed head!" She held out the brush. "Come here and I'll groom you."

Knot glared at her, then licked his paw and ran it over his head twice.

Keelie shrugged. "I could have done it better, and without spit. See if I ever offer again." She opened the bedroom door and looked around the hallway. Empty. "I guess breakfast is downstairs." She crossed and knocked at Sean's door, glancing toward Elia's room. Her door was open. Keelie slipped over to it and pushed the door open slowly. Behind her, Coyote slipped down the stairs.

"Hey, come back," she hissed.

Coyote didn't answer. She turned back to Elia's room, which seemed to be empty.

"Elia? You here?" Elia's bed was unmade and a long pink gown lay in a puddle of silk on the floor. Figured. Elf girl probably got tired of waiting for the servants to serve her breakfast in bed. Was that what she'd expected? She'd been independent back home and at the Ren Faires they'd worked together. Maybe "together" was too strong a word for merely occupying the same two acres of medieval-style fun; Elia would hang with the other beautiful elf girls, and Keelie would work her butt off.

Strong hands cupped her shoulders, and she squeaked in surprise.

"Sorry." Sean gave her a quick kiss on her cheek. His grin said that he wasn't sorry at all. "Did you manage to stay warm last night?"

"Barely. Of course, I had Knot with me." She turned, then stopped, chest to chest with Sean.

He smiled down at her, then glanced at the oversized pumpkin fluffball, now headed toward the stairs. "Looks like he knows where the food is."

"Always. Shall we follow him?"

He sighed. "Because you have a job to do, I know."

Keelie laced her arms around his waist and pressed herself against him. "Because *we* have a job to do." She dropped her arms.

"Any luck getting in contact with your dad?" Sean asked.

"No. It's the weirdest thing. I'm going to ask Terciel if he knows what might be causing the blockage."

Knot led them through the first floor to a room at the back of the building. Keelie looked at the bare stone walls and spartan furnishings. If a person could learn about a house's inhabitants from the furnishings and décor, this place screamed "unimaginative and boring." The dining room held a long table (fir) with tall, stiff wooden chairs around it. Coyote was nowhere in sight, thank goodness.

Three of the seats were occupied. Miszrial sat at the head, with Elia next to her, shooting resentful glances her way. At the other end of the table, Terciel had stopped eating to nod at Sean and Keelie.

"Good morrow. We did not wake you, to allow you to rest. You will not be with us long enough to follow our ways."

"Our thanks," Sean said solemnly, bowing his head. Keelie bowed too, but she only moved forward a little. She'd reserve her bows for people who deserved it. She reached out and touched a chair. Fir as well; the wood of choice up here.

Elia said nothing, her eyes on her untouched plate. Breakfast at the elven village seemed to consist of sticks and twigs. Keelie would starve before she got home. Wide, shallow stone dishes on the center of the table held intricately arrayed vegetation.

Keelie tried to smile. "Looks like yummy stuff."

"We care about our health." Elia raised her chin.

Lord Terciel looked at Elia and she quickly dropped her gaze. Keelie was torn between wanting to defend Elia and asking if they could give her lessons on how to get the same reaction.

The Council head turned his icy blue stare to Keelie. "Sit, please."

Keelie took the chair closest to him, and Sean sat to her left.

"First, the ceremony of the winter leaf's passing and the budding of spring." He motioned toward Miszrial, who held her hands out, palms up, and began to sing in a weird, twisty language.

Elia stared at her, then raised her eyebrows at Keelie. This must be a solemn moment, but Keelie could have sworn that

Elia was stifling a laugh. Elia quickly looked back down at her plate.

Miszrial stopped singing and looked at Keelie expectantly.

"Um, that was lovely."

"You're supposed to sing the next verse," Elia whispered, face still down.

Keelie felt a sharp pain through her right sock. Knot, with perfect timing, as usual. Before she could kick him out of the way, she felt the *bhata*, like fingertips on a drumhead, all around them, louder and louder. The elves looked at her, expressions bland. Couldn't they feel it? But no, the elves didn't see the lesser fae.

The *bhata* drummed, and the green sap magic of the trees filtered into her head, and suddenly Keelie knew the song, the ancient song that thanked the trees for their leaves, welcomed the buds in spring, rejoiced in the dance of color that preceded the long winter sleep. The *bhata*'s drumming stopped.

Keelie opened her eyes, although she didn't remember closing them. Miszrial and Terciel nodded solemnly, and Saliel served them tea in small stone bowls. Elia was staring at her, mouth open.

A glance toward Sean showed him just as astounded.

"What?" she whispered, smiling her thanks to the elf for the tea. At least it looked like tea.

"You were singing," he whispered. "In ancient Elvish."

She would have laughed, except that she could see it was no joke.

"You honor us, Lady Keliel," Terciel said. The old elf looked a little teary. "Long has it been since the ancient words were sung in these walls. As your hosts, we may grant you a boon."

"Thank you." She bowed back. "May I think about it and choose my boon later?"

"Of course." Terciel went back to eating his twigs, but then his mouth fell open and he jumped to his feet. "What is that?" he sputtered. "A fairy, in my lodge! Begone." He turned to Miszrial. "Get that foul fairy out of here."

Everyone was staring at him, astonished. He was pointing at the doorway but there was nothing there. Had a *bhata* come in? But wait, the elves couldn't see the *bhata*.

Keelie looked down at the floor and up to the corners of the room. Nothing. Though she felt the tingling magic of the trees and *bhata* outside, there was nothing fairy in the building.

Then Coyote, that wily fae trickster, walked past the door, glancing in as if he weren't really interested in what was going on, and Terciel began to gnash his teeth again.

Keelie jumped up. "A boon. I mean, I've thought of one."

Terciel scowled at her. "Now? Get that fairy out of here and I'll grant you a second one."

"One was very generous, thank you. I wish to take my fae friend Coyote with me to the High Court."

The Council head's silver hair flew out in an arc as he whipped his head toward her. "You brought that fairy dog here?"

"No, he came on his own. And he's a coyote. I'll need all the help I can get," Keelie said. "A fairy on my side can't hurt. I can't take the *bhata* with me, even though they're powerful when they join together. My father told me that the High Court is a thousand times more potent, and cruel as well."

Terciel frowned, his former awe of her forgotten. "You side with the dark fae?" he thundered. "You waste an elven boon on a fae dog? Whom do you serve, Keliel Heartwood, mortal child? I doubt your motives."

"I came here to help you," Keelie insisted. Beside her, Sean rose too. Elia seemed to shrink into herself.

He'd called her mortal child as if it was an insult. The fae sounded scary, but Keelie couldn't wait to meet them, even though she only had a drop of fae blood.

She had no idea how they would treat her, of course. She could end up shunned by both sides. Keelie thought of all the magical challenges she'd faced so far, since her mother had died. She had destroyed the evil Red Cap at the High Mountain Faire, saved the dying unicorn in the Wildewood of upstate New York, and restored the waning curse of the Dread Forest, not to mention that she'd helped cure her uncle of vampirism and reunited him with his family, and the treeling acorn she'd been given by the Wildewood was now the Queen Tree of the Dread Forest. Pretty impressive for a girl who'd just gotten her drivers' license.

She had no clue what she would encounter among the fae. If their queen was as mean and set in her ways as Lord Terciel was in his, she had a hard job ahead. With each challenge she'd faced, she'd changed a little, but she could handle it. Of course, those were probably famous last words.

◆ ◆ ◆

Keelie stood outside of the lodge. She needed to be alone for a moment. After Terciel had stormed out of breakfast, Elia had sobbed all day and Sean, furious at the treatment they'd received, had tried to call Zeke twice. At least she and Sean had been able to spend some time with Norzan, although Elia had not left her room. When Miszrial delivered their evening meal to the lodge, the empty stone walls seemed hung with emotion.

Now, two hours before midnight, Keelie breathed in the crisp night air. Here, the stars were brighter and larger than even in the Dread Forest. Keelie looked up at them, framed by the burgeoning leaves of the comforting trees around the building.

"Are you not cold?" Norzan's voice came from the darkness beyond the lamplight.

Keelie smiled. "Not really. It's been a hell of a day, hasn't it?"

Norzan moved closer, this time holding onto a staff to help him walk. His hair gleamed the color of moonbeams. "I want to warn you of what you face tonight."

"Terciel said we would go through the portal at midnight. The others are preparing. Elia is determined to go, although I don't think she should come with us."

Norzan nodded. "I agree. But she is strong willed. A good thing for the mother of the first elf to be born in almost a hundred years." He looked around, tilting his face as if listening to the night. Satisfied with what he heard, he continued. "The trees say that the fae are on the move. They sense you are here."

"Me? I can't even hear your trees half the time. I have to work at talking to them."

His eyes glinted in the darkness, seeming to shoot blue sparks. "When you reach the portal, you will find that it is only a door in the midst of nothing, but when you step through, you will be in the midst of the Quicksilver Faire, where you will find the entrance to the High Court."

The Quicksilver Faire sounded like fun—the first glimmer of enjoyment she'd had so far in this dreary elven village.

"The Quicksilver Faire is the marketplace of the dark and high fae. It is dangerous, Keelie. Obey all rules, and be on your guard."

"Of course. We'll be careful, I promise."

He regarded her gravely. "You must do more than promise. A misstep would not mean death necessarily, but an immortal lifetime trapped in the land of Fairy."

Keelie's heart sank. She didn't know if she had an immortal lifetime, but it would still suck to be stuck in Fairy and never see her dad again.

six

It was almost midnight, but Keelie could see everything clearly. They stood before the portal, a huge oak door in the forest halfway up Mount Faron, the mountain that formed the backdrop for Big Nugget. Before her, the door's strange silver doorknob glowed as if it had been dipped in moonlight. Life-sized polar bear ice sculptures flanked the door, each holding a revolving model of Earth with fire shooting up out of it like a volcano.

"Weirdest torch ever. It's like something out of a theme park."

Sean leaned close to one of the polar bears and pushed

his metal jousting helmet to the back of his head. He was wearing a mail shirt over a leather jerkin, and a sword belted to his waist. Not full armor, but enough to make a bodyguard statement. "It doesn't seem cold enough to maintain this ice."

"Is this really how we get to the High Court?" Keelie asked Knot and Coyote. The cat shrugged.

"Don't ask me. I'm from Los Angeles. This was the route pointed out to us," Coyote said. He started sniffing around the door. He'd coached them the entire way on their trek up the mountain, after their second strange and inedible dinner.

Do not eat anything while you're there was the instruction that Keelie remembered best. It probably meant that the faire would be full of insanely yummy food. She'd have to be on guard.

Sean examined the sculptured torches. "I've never seen anything like this."

"Fairies, of course," Elia said. "What they do never makes sense."

Keelie glared at her. "Shut up. You're not allowed on this mission. I can't believe you snuck up after us." What she really couldn't believe was that Elia had been so good at sneaking that none of them had heard her until Knot saw her flit from tree to tree and sounded the alarm. Well, the yowl.

"You couldn't leave me back in Grey Mantle. They don't want me there. What if something happens to you?" Elia batted her eyes.

"That only works on guys, Elia," Keelie said dryly. "And

you are so not coming with us. You're pregnant. Uncle Dariel would kill me if something happened to you and the baby. Not to mention, all the elves on the planet."

"None of the local elves seem to care." Elia said it lightly, but Keelie heard the hurt in her voice.

Sean cleared his throat. "We're here on a diplomatic mission, Elia. Try to be nice."

"Thank you, Sean." Keelie wandered around the other side of the door. It looked the same as the front. "What if you went through it in this direction?"

"I don't know. Maybe we'd go somewhere else." Coyote looked at them. "We need to get going. It's nearly midnight, and Terciel said to be there at the stroke of."

"You're right," Keelie said. "I hope he meant human midnight."

"Elves invented clocks," Elia said. "So technically it's elf midnight."

"It doesn't matter to you, Elia, because you aren't going." Keelie stood in front of the door and tried to turn the knob, but it seemed to slither free of her hand.

Sean's forehead crinkled in puzzlement. "Do you say a magic word and it opens?"

"I can try." Keelie stood in front of the door, straightened her shoulders, lengthened her arms, and projected her voice. "Open Sesame." She had seen that in an old movie about Ali Baba and the Forty Thieves. Still nothing.

"You got any more bright ideas?" Elia put her hands on her hips. "You're the one with fairy blood."

"Abracadabra." Keelie said, in a lesser confident tone.

Nothing happened.

Coyote scratched his ear with his back foot. "It will open at the right time."

"So, I thought there was supposed to be a fancy fae town here, maybe a city, and there's only a stupid door in the middle of nowhere." Elia scowled. "And why aren't those polar bears melting?"

"That's what I said." Sean studied the bears. Flames shot higher from the Earth-shaped spheres, and he jumped back. "Obviously, someone is using magic to keep them solid. Could there be a key?" He examined the ground around the door.

"Normally you keep a key underneath a doormat, but I don't see one," Keelie replied.

"A doormat in the middle of the woods makes as much sense as a door that leads to nowhere," Elia said.

Maybe the fairies had hidden the key somewhere around the door. Stepping closer, Keelie touched the wood, and her mind immediately filled with the vision of an old forest, dark and primeval, thick with vegetation and condensation that dripped to the thick, loamy forest floor. It was the first forest, the Great Sylvus' forest.

This door had been made from an ancient oak from the first forest, an ancient oak filled with eons of memories. The tree had fallen when a meteor had crashed near its beloved forest, and the impact had sent shock waves through the Earth, ripping the oak's roots from the ground. Grief for what was overwhelmed Keelie, threatening her with despair. Suddenly, she felt herself thrown back to the here and now.

"What's wrong? What did you see?" Sean's hand was wrapped around her upper arm.

"This is one powerful chunk of wood." She was breathless. She looked down at his hand. "Thanks for bringing me back."

Keelie stared at the knob again, and it seemed different. The metal seemed to be alive with shifting movements within the surface. Could the solution be as simple as opening the door?

Coyote lifted his snout up in the air, and then turned to Keelie. "It's almost time, and then we can pass into the fairy realm."

"How can you tell?" Elia asked. "I don't see a clock on you, and how are we supposed to get to Fairy when we obviously can't open the door?"

Coyote reached into his back leg fur and removed a gold pocket watch. He opened it with one black claw, then closed it. "Time to go." He placed his watch back in his furry pocket.

Elia stared, open-mouthed. Even Keelie had to admit she was impressed. She didn't know coyotes had pockets.

An eerie jangle sounded from the forest. Keelie jumped. "What was that?"

Sean looked around. "I don't know, but it sure sounded familiar."

Keelie shivered. She turned and searched for Peascod, but didn't see him. She hoped the evil jester wasn't watching her from behind his wicked mask, somewhere in the forest. If this was his home, she couldn't wait to get out of it.

In the distance, hounds bayed. Icy dread soaked into her marrow. The Hunter. Was he looking for them? For her? She had the urge to run. "We don't want to be late to meet the queen," she said quickly, stretching her fingers toward the knob and glancing down at Knot. He gestured with his head as if saying *yes, go ahead*.

Keelie touched the swirling knob, expecting it to be cold, but it was warm, and beneath the knob little sparkles appeared. She turned it, and the door began to open. Bright, colorful lights and loud crowd noise spilled out; there seemed to be a party on the other side. She pushed the door farther but it only moved a few inches. Inside, someone yelped.

A frog in a Robin Hood hat peered around the edge of the door. "Watch what you're doing."

Behind her, Elia gasped. Knot scooted through the door, followed by Coyote, who squeezed in under people's legs.

"Sorry, trying to get in," Keelie said. Long, green-webbed fingers grabbed the door's edge and yanked as she pushed, and suddenly, she was in the strangest crowd she'd ever seen. The frog man was talking animatedly with a tall, skinny woman dressed in form-fitting white armor, with a tail whose end was swept casually over her shoulder, its tasseled end flicking back and forth.

So this was the Quicksilver Faire.

A massive woman swept by, yards of multihued gauze floating around her. Tall, iridescent, leathery gray wings sprouted from her back. Others in the excited crowd were more normal looking, if one didn't look too closely. They seemed to be packed into a big wooden gazebo.

She felt Sean squeeze in behind her, the metal of his chest plate hard against her back, and Elia pushed up to her side, eyes wide.

A rabbit was fiddling a sprightly tune while standing on one of the handrails that surrounded the gazebo, and he stopped playing when a man in purple robes raised his hands and shouted "Oyez!"

Silence fell over the crowd, which shifted and shuffled and moved like a living creature that had absorbed Keelie and her companions. The man consulted a scroll, then let it snap back into a circle as he yelled, "Everyone in parade route order and we'll begin shortly. Master Johnny O'Hare will lead us. Are you ready?"

Everyone bellowed at once that they were, and the rabbit leaped high over their heads, landing on a cinder road. He began to fiddle again, and the infectious music made Keelie want to dance.

"Magic," hissed Sean.

"I want to dance," Elia cried, and she bobbed ahead of them, doing a jig alongside a corseted pirate Amazon. Keelie and Sean hurried to catch up, not an easy task since everyone was dancing along behind the rabbit.

As they moved forward, Keelie noted their surroundings like an explorer charting unknown territory. Beyond the stone-and-timber buildings of the town, she saw an enchanted forest of huge trees that glimmered with radiant magic, flowing with waves of light just like the aurora borealis. It was as if they'd entered a version of the Northwoods forest that was hundreds of years older.

The rooflines of the faire's tents and buildings, along with the other odd structures ahead of them, were silhouetted against the dazzle of a beam of spinning light. The beam seemed to be coming from the center of the faire, and it called magic to Keelie like a summons she couldn't resist: *Come to me, come to me.*

She pulled her gaze away and tried to take in the whole faire at once. It was like stepping back in time to medieval market days in London or Paris, only it was a market filled with unimaginable treasures and inhabitants.

A voice in the back of her mind whispered, *Beware of the fairies, for they can hide their cruelty behind their beauty.*

Knot and Coyote ran along at the edges of the parading crowd like fuzzy little kids anxious to get to the fun. Keelie looked back anxiously, searching for a jester hat with dangling, discordant bells, but no one was wearing one, and relief flowed through her. Strange, how she'd rather face the High Queen of the Shining Ones than Peascod. She felt trapped between two dark problems now, when she'd only expected to confront one. Maybe the High Queen would know what to do about Peascod.

Sean had removed his helmet and was looking around as if trying to take in everything at once. "This place is amazing, Elia. We may be the first elves to see it."

"Stay close to me, Sean," Elia whispered loudly. "I smell only fairies."

The man in front of her turned to give her a dirty look.

Elia didn't notice. Instead, she pointed toward Knot and Coyote's bushy tails as they vanished around the corner of a half-timbered building. "Where are they going? Are they going to warn the queen that we're here?"

"They're having fun," Keelie said. "It's good advice to stay close together, though, especially in this crowd." At least at this faire Keelie didn't have to sell furniture, so maybe she could shop when her mission was completed. She didn't know what currency the fairies used. Maybe it was based on magic. A thread of caution formed in her mind, weaving its way in her thoughts—*always be careful when dealing with fairies*. She would be.

Sean walked alongside her, his fingers laced through hers, and she could feel his muscles tense as he resisted the urge to dance to Johnny O'Hare's magic.

She was on her way to meet the Shining One's fairy queen. Images of the deadly Queen of Hearts from *Alice in Wonderland* flashed through Keelie's mind. Echoes of "Off With her Head" swirled in tune with the fiddler's music.

She tightened her grip on Sean's hand. He reassuringly squeezed back. "I'm here," he whispered in her ear.

Knot and Coyote reappeared and paced in front of them, their paws stepping in equal, measured strides as if to present a united front to the fae.

Coyote turned his head to Sean. "Stay with her. Don't let her out of your sight."

"What did you two see? Do you know where we should meet the queen?" Keelie asked.

"The queen won't be meeting us; she's sending an escort," Coyote replied. Beside him, Knot's normally wide eyes were hooded. Not a good sign.

The parade passed the end of a lane where lanterns made of the same sparkling metal as the fairy doorknob floated in midair, illuminating the narrow, crowded streets. Jostling throngs separated from the parade and moved down the street before them, and Keelie grabbed Elia's hand as Sean pulled them free of the parade. They were joined by a group of giggling girls, arms around each other, who looked like any of Keelie's friends on a mall outing—except for the glistening, fluttery wings that arched out behind them.

A stout woman with a basket on her arm, who had her reptilian tail tucked tidily out of the way, passed them. Behind her, a great hulking shape in a hooded robe plodded along, swaying side to side. Keelie was sure she didn't want to see his face; his smell was enough to make her back up a step. Not the image of a medieval English market she'd conjured in her mind.

The bad smell diminished as the creature trudged on, its stench replaced by delicious smells that wafted from a cafe—one very similar to the Crystal Cup in Big Nugget. Red-checked gingham tablecloths covered the wooden tables (rather than wrought iron tables, since most fae found iron toxic), and the café chairs had twisty backs, the wood embellished with crystals. It looked like the furniture Keelie's father made. A woman with fuzzy ear tips, like a cat's, sticking up through her dark hair exited from the restaurant. She carried a tray loaded with glistening pastries, and when she turned around, Keelie saw that she had a cat tail, too. She felt her mouth drop open, and closed it.

The cat-tailed girl turned around and smiled at them mischievously. "Would you like to eat a bite of me cakes? One bite, and you'll never want for food, again."

Knot hopped on the table and glared at the girl, tail whipping back and forth.

"You." The girl's smile vanished and her own tail started to swish angrily.

"Yeow," he replied. They glared at one another.

"You never returned after Beltane. Is she the one?" the cat-tailed girl almost shrieked, pointing at Keelie.

"Let's leave them to work this out." Coyote herded Keelie, Sean, and Elia away from the café and down the path.

"But those pastries looked good. I'm hungry." Elia rubbed her stomach. "I love faire food. Maybe we can find turkey legs like the ones at the mundane faire."

Coyote motioned toward the pastry shop. "My lady, I must remind you once more that if you eat fairy food, you will hunger for it always, as will your child. No human or elven food will nourish your body or your soul, and eventually you will die of hunger."

"Oh." Elia protectively placed her hand over her belly.

Even though she was a major pain in the butt, one thing Keelie knew for sure was that Elia would be a good mother.

"Let's get this meeting over with," Sean said. "I've had enough of this world already."

"Why elf, you've just entered our realm. Is that any way to treat your hosts?" A tall, slender fae wearing a long black robe had appeared before them. His hair gleamed silver and his eyes glowed with an alien tint.

Despite his unusual looks, Keelie felt drawn to the fairy—an immediate physical attraction that made her feel warm and fuzzy on the inside, as if she'd had several cups of mead.

He bowed elegantly. "My Lady Keliel."

She knew she was falling under a spell of enchantment, but she didn't care. It felt so good. "Who are you?"

He rose from his graceful bow. "I am Fala. Your guide to the queen."

The whispers of *beware* floated to the forefront of her mind until Coyote's wet nose nudged her hand. The enchantment lifted.

Fala frowned, as if he knew that the glamour magic he'd spun to entrap Keelie had been broken.

Another fairy laughed as he appeared next to Fala. He turned toward Keelie. His skin was eggplant purple and his gorgeous, long white hair was woven through with strands of silver, which glinted in the light of the lanterns. He carried a quiver of arrows and a crossbow on his back. He reached for Keelie's hand and kissed it. "My Lady Keliel. I am Salaca, your escort."

A frisson of delight skipped up her spine and she had to repress a silly giggle. The drunk feeling returned, but this time she called upon her magic to create a shield. It pushed Salaca's magic away.

His lips formed a predatory smile. "I'm a hunter, my lady, and I've always enjoyed a good chase."

Sean stepped in between Keelie and the elves.

Fala laughed. "She is safe, elf. For now."

"Speak for yourself. I find her quite intriguing for a human hybrid." Salaca eyed her like she was a used car.

"I'm here to see the queen," Keelie said, in her grandmother's "obey me" voice. She doubted it would work on the fae, but it helped bolster her courage as she faced these dangerous and beautiful fairies.

"We ask safe passage to and from your lands." Sean forced the words out past clenched teeth. Keelie could see that it was an effort for him to remain polite.

Knot ran toward them, meowing loudly, covered in icing with bits of cake clinging to his fur. His meeting with the cat girl apparently hadn't ended well.

Coyote stepped in front of Keelie and confronted Fala and Salaca. "Lady Keliel is under my protection as well."

The two fae laughed in unison, and Keelie lost a little confidence in her furry guards.

Salaca stopped his laughter, then lifted his head as if he caught the scent of something, his eyes narrowed. "The Dark Hunt. We need to alert the guard."

Through the door they'd entered, which was still open a ways behind them, Keelie heard the baying of hounds once more. She remembered the horned figure on the horse. Herne. Salaca gestured, and Keelie heard the door slam shut.

Fala grinned at Keelie. "The queen will find this most intriguing. Is it a coincidence that the Wild Hunt rides when the little elf comes to call?"

"Mayhaps Keliel Treetalker has secret surprises for us,

and I'm sure the queen wants to know each and every one," Salaca said as he circled Keelie.

She felt the buzzing of magic against her skin.

Knot stood on hind legs and reached up with his forepaws, as if snagging a thread, and Salaca drew back with a curse.

Keelie had thought her diplomatic status would protect her, but the fairies didn't seem to obey any rules at all. She was suddenly afraid—not for herself, but for her friends. What had she gotten them into?

seven

Keeping her eyes level with Fala's, Keelie called upon her magic to create a shield once again. She wouldn't let him enchant her. Emboldened by her determination, she knew she couldn't let him see fear in her eyes. Dad said that the fae liked to intimidate and force their opponent to submit to their orders and worst whims. If they detected a hint of fear, then their snare was as good as sprung and their victim caught.

Fala bowed. "We shall continue our game later, Lady Keliel."

This was just a game to them. Maybe, instead of fearing

for her elven and fae friends, she should be afraid for her own big streak of mortal.

Elia sighed and rolled her eyes. "Speaking of games, what is that booth over there?" She pointed.

Salaca scowled. "You were not spoken to, elf. Do not speak unless we give you permission."

Elia raised her chin and took a step forward. "I'll have you know that I bear the child of the Unicorn Lord of the Dread Forest. He's part fae and he outranks you."

Fala and Salaca stared at her belly as if a unicorn would pop out and gore them. Then they looked at each other and shrugged.

"Look at all these people," Keelie said. "This faire is much bigger than the human ones I've been to." Crazier, too. Time to steer the conversation to a safe place.

Fala chuckled. "Brother, our guests have not seen the faire, only its sad imitation on the Earthly plane. Let us guide them."

Coyote cleared his throat. He pointed to his pocket watch. "Midnight, boys, and I don't want Keelie to be late for her appointment with the queen."

"If it's midnight, aren't we already late?" Keelie spoke loudly, but the others seemed to ignore her. Instead, Fala motioned to a curious shop across the lane. It was a two-story hourglass, with a door set into the globular bottom half.

"Hello? We're running late. We don't have time for a side trip." Keelie was worried that the queen would be angry at them.

"The Timekeeper can stop time for us. This is an excellent move, Keelie." Coyote put up his pocket watch and led the way.

Keelie remembered her visit to Under-the-Hill. If time passed as strangely in Fairy as it did in Under-the-Hill, then she had a new worry. How much time would pass here, and would she return to her own world a hundred years in the future?

Knot jaunted behind Coyote, tail held high, as the fairies and elves followed.

The inside of the shop smelled like new and old at once. Keelie had entered carefully, avoiding the door's wooden frame, afraid of what she would sense in a shop that was outside of time. Despite being of rounded glass outside, the inside was a normal-looking rectangular room, with a sitting area to the right where a fire burned in a gigantic fireplace. The rest of the room was lined with clocks. The walls were covered in them, and their ticking vibrated through Keelie's body.

A long glass counter ran along the length of the room, and behind it, a golden retriever wearing an apron bent over a counter. He wore a large magnifying glass over his head, held in place by a leather strap. He held a screwdriver in his right paw, and Keelie noticed that he had an opposable paw pad that worked like a thumb.

He was tightening a part inside a small table clock which wiggled and kicked its little peg feet, giggling at the screwdriver that was tightening its innards. "I'll be with you good folks in a moment. Time waits for no one, and everyone waits for time." The dog didn't look up from his work.

Okay, a talking dog. Knot talked occasionally, when he wanted to, with a meowy accent. Like Coyote, the dog sounded human. Maybe it was a cat-and-dog thing.

Sean and Elia were examining the clocks that hung on the wall. There were cuckoo clocks, clocks made of gold, and plain schoolhouse clocks. Grandfather clocks stood in a row like paternal guardians of time.

Knot hopped onto the counter and sat down patiently. His tail twitched in time to the beat of the clocks, which had now softened. Their tick-tock sounded like a mechanical heart, which soothed Keelie. Even Coyote's tail wagged like a fuzzy metronome.

Fala and Salaca waited, tapping their feet in time to the irresistible beat.

When the Timekeeper finished his repairs, the clock stood up and ran back to a shelf and settled itself among a collection of other table clocks. The Timekeeper looked up at them, his doggie eye magnified many times over as his golden gaze took in the room. All the clocks showed five minutes till midnight.

"I have guests," he said. "It has been a long time since a child of Sylvus and a human have entered my shop." He gestured to the fireplace, which was now flanked by cozy chairs. Where had they come from?

Keelie whipped around to stare at the Timekeeper, and he winked at her. The friendly gesture reassured her.

Knot hopped down from the counter and sauntered

over to the fire, and just as he was about to settle down on the rag rug, Coyote ran over and snagged the prime spot, settling in to toast before the flames. He ignored the cat and started biting at his tail as if a flea had just had bitten him.

Knot hissed.

"Let me make us some tea." The Timekeeper bent down and rummaged underneath his work counter, and when he rose, he was no longer a dog, but a man wearing a simple red robe embroidered with silver and gold thread. His eyes were gold, and on his long brown hair he wore a quicksilver crown adorned with an hourglass emblem. He smiled benevolently at everyone. Even Elia seemed to melt under his kindness. Keelie didn't sense anything dark or sinister about the Timekeeper, but she was still wary.

"Coyote, how is that gold watch working for you? I don't often make one from scratch, and it's one of my favorites."

Coyote produced the watch. "Keeps perfect time."

"As it was meant to do." The Timekeeper poured strong tea from a white porcelain Chinese teapot with a blue glazed dragon swimming around its middle. He handed the first cup to Elia. She accepted, but her face reflected the caution that Keelie felt.

"The tea is from India. Nothing fae here. It's safe for you to drink, dear."

Fala and Salaca accepted cups when they were served. Then it was Sean and Keelie's turn. The Timekeeper moved at super-fast speed, then settled into his chair. Keelie watched in quiet surprise as the clawed feet sprouted toenails.

What kind of chair was this?

"What can I do for you?" The Timekeeper asked.

"We've come to ask a favor, Old One," Fala answered. "We are late for an appointment with Her Majesty, and would beg that you stop time for us."

"I see." The Timekeeper turned to Keelie. "You are the daughter of the Lord of the Dread Forest." His intense gaze fell upon her. "The forests speak your name. You are a cherished child of Sylvus."

"Do you know Sylvus?" Keelie asked, her voice sounding squeaky.

"Our paths have crossed." The Timekeeper's lips twitched. "He finds you most entertaining."

The elves swore by Sylvus, the powerful nature god they worshipped. And apparently he truly existed, and he found her entertaining. Keelie didn't know how she felt about that, especially the entertaining aspect.

"The queen is ever angry at those who are late," the Timekeeper added, smiling.

Salaca bowed, hiding his scowl. "Keliel and her friends are guests of the queen. She would do nothing to harm them—she has need of the girl's assistance. We simply ask that you allow her guests the time to visit our faire."

So the queen did want something from her, but what? Keelie liked watching Salaca humbling himself and inadvertently revealing the truth. Bet it didn't happen a lot.

"My Lord," Coyote said, wagging his tail as the Timekeeper turned to him. "I also have a request. I ask that you give Keelie and her companions a boon to allow them to slip back to their tomorrow, not many moons from now." He bowed his head and Knot lifted his paw. Keelie had never seen the cat so supplicant to anyone.

When she looked at the Timekeeper again, she saw that his appearance had changed. Now he wore a dark cloak, and his face was hidden beneath the hood. A skeletal hand came out from the cloak and put the teacup down. Keelie forced herself not to react, although she wanted to step back.

The bony hand went back into the cloak, this time emerging with a wooden hourglass carved with moons and stars, the glass filled with black sand. The sands in the hourglass started to flow backwards.

"A boon has been requested and a boon will be given," the Timekeeper said in a deep voice. "When they return from the High Court of the Shining Ones, Keliel Heartwood and her companions will return to their tomorrow, more or less." He waved his hand, and a holographic image of the solar system appeared, and then it expanded to include the entire Milky Way. Keelie recognized the image from the Elven Lore Book. Who knew? "Keliel Heartwood, Elia Heartwood and her child, Sean son of Niriel, Knot, and Coyote Moondancer will be returned to Earth from Fairy, and all will be as it is."

The image disappeared.

The sand in the hourglass had emptied. The Timekeeper pointed a skeletal finger at Fala and Salaca. "The coyote's boon has been granted, and the travelers are under my protection."

Both fae smiled—forced grimaces that didn't fool anyone.

The Timekeeper leaned forward in his chair and looked at Keelie and Sean. "Stay together, be the touchstone of the other, and you shall travel the realm of Fairy in safety." He turned his gaze to Elia. "Your child will protect you. It is time for me to go."

Then the Timekeeper lifted his hand, and his chair began walking backwards. One of the grandfather clocks opened its door and widened, and the chair galloped through the doorway. The opening disappeared, and the grandfather clock closed its door.

The Timekeeper's voice boomed in the room. "It will stay five minutes until midnight at the faire until you enter the vortex. Anyone who visits the Quicksilver Faire needs a chance to shop." Laughter tumbled all around the room like a booming waterfall, ending in a short bark.

Keelie and the others found themselves outside. She turned around, and all was dark in the Timekeeper's shop.

"What did he mean by the vortex? That doesn't sound safe." Keelie moved closer to Sean.

Fala pointed down the lane. "Let's go this way."

Keelie linked her arm with Sean's. "I think I'll stick close to you."

He smiled, and leaned down and kissed her on the cheek. It was a sweet kiss, and Keelie felt her apprehension melt. His kisses made her feel warm and bubbly inside.

"So what exactly *is* the Timekeeper?" Keelie asked Salaca as he marched past.

"The Timekeeper is the sovereign ruler over time. Neither fae nor elf," Salaca said. "We shall take you to a few shops of our choosing, and then we will meet the queen."

Coyote trotted up alongside Keelie. "The Timekeeper is a god like Sylvus. Queen Vania has to listen to him."

"Thanks, Coyote."

He lowered his head as if he was embarrassed.

"Can I call you Moondancer?" Keelie asked.

"Do not speak my true name here." Coyote moved ahead.

"I like him." Sean said. "He's grown on me."

Elia had been quiet. Keelie hoped she didn't have any bright ideas swirling in her elf head that could lead to complications with the queen.

Salaca and Fala had stopped outside a shop that had a wide front porch with rocking chairs and carpeted cat perches. "Since you're fond of cats and vermin"—Salaca looked over at Coyote—"we thought you might like to see this place." He waved his hand for everyone to enter.

Keelie hesitated. "Are you sure the queen won't mind?"

"We bought time," Salaca reminded her. "And the Timekeeper asked you to shop."

Not shop, she thought. The wise old Timekeeper probably wanted her to get to know the fae before she met their queen.

Keelie touched the wood (aspen, from the ancient forest). She turned the quicksilver doorknob and entered the shop.

Inside it was warm and cozy. Quilts were draped on the

back of cushioned sofas and cats purred in front of a fireplace. Aquariums cast sapphire light on the hardwood floors.

A loud splashing caught Keelie's attention. It was a manta ray. He waved his stinger at Keelie and dived back under the water.

She turned to Fala.

"Sea witches need familiars, too." He looked at her as if she should've known that simple fact.

She looked at the next aquarium and a big eye blinked at her. Then she heard a humpback whale singing. "A whale?"

"It's a dimensional doorway," a woman's honeyed voice said. "The humpback has to be able to view its potential partner. Would you like to fill out an application?"

Keelie turned around and gasped when she saw an enormous lion affectionately rubbing the woman's leg as if he was a big old house cat. He had the most beautiful mane she had ever seen. He had gold ribbons woven through it and in the candlelight it glinted with sparkling perfection. Laurie would've been jealous. She paid top dollar at an expensive salon in L.A. to get that sun-kissed look.

The fairy woman wore a blue corset, with sapphire ribbons laced between quicksilver grommets. "I am the proprietor of this shop. I match magical folk with their magical helpers," she said. "My name is Maemtri." Her eyes were almond shaped and greener than an elf's, as if some verdant light glowed bright from within. The skin around her forehead and down her neck was spotted like a leopard's.

She motioned a delicate hand to the lion, who lovingly beamed up at her. "This is my familiar, Henry."

Henry held out a giant paw, and Keelie shook it as she would a dog's. Henry's paw was soft as velvet and he purred happily. It sounded like a muted chainsaw.

"My name is Keliel." She couldn't stop staring at the lion. She wanted to pet him so badly she couldn't stand it. Knot glared jealously.

Maemtri bowed her head. "You and your companions are welcome, and if you do find a familiar, I think you will find the terms of our arrangements agreeable to all parties. I did not expect a visit from you, Milady Keliel, or I would have prepared. Are you here to purchase a gift for the queen, perhaps?"

Fala bowed slightly. "We're just visiting, Maemtri."

A gift for the queen. Keelie's heart stuttered. She'd never even thought of that. She looked around at the magical creatures, but even here, giving someone a pet was a bad idea. A companion animal was a very personal choice.

Henry was sniffing Elia's skirt, and she'd backed up against a wall. Every cat in the shop was standing at attention, looking at her with their eerily intelligent eyes, like an army of Knots.

Knot yodeled and jumped, sending a box to the ground. Its lid flew off and loud hissing erupted as a dark and icky wave poured out of it.

Keelie recoiled at the sight of huge and angry cockroaches scuttling on the floor. The roaches turned, as if sensing something, and headed straight for Elia. She screamed and jumped against Sean, who picked her up and held her above the floor.

Coyote snickered and then laughed, pointing his paw at Knot, whose fur was bushed out to the max. Henry the lion danced back when the cockroaches came too close to his paws.

"Naughty fairy," Maemtri said. "Serves you right, you curious creature."

The lion lowered his head and cast a menacing glance at Knot.

Maemtri held out the box and snapped her fingers, and the hissing cockroaches all jumped back into their container.

"Who would want hissing cockroaches for a familiar?" Keelie heard the squeak of panic in her voice and tried to calm herself.

"Usually some of the dark fae, maybe a troll sorcerer. If there is a specialty familiar, Maemtri is the one to see." Salaca leaned his elbows against a counter. He seemed bored.

Fala opened the door and gestured toward the bustle outdoors. "Now that we've seen the familiar shop we need to move along. Good luck with any potential clients."

"I will see you at the masquerade tonight," Maemtri said and her eyes held Fala's. Keelie watched as a glance, like a secret, passed between them.

She wondered what that had been about as she and Sean stepped out onto the porch.

"What's next?" Keelie asked. The shop had been interesting, but she wanted to get her mission over with.

Fala turned around and smiled wickedly at her. "You're just going to have to wait and see, but our next stop is going to be educational for Lord Sean."

He and Salaca laughed.

Sean and Keelie exchanged a glance, and she saw a hint of worry in his eyes. She turned away quickly, but she was sure he'd seen it mirrored on her own face. Those two could not be up to anything good.

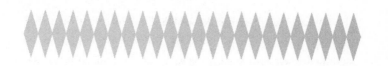

eight

Keelie didn't know how far the Timekeeper's protection of them extended. From what she'd heard, the fae could find a loophole in any rule and exploit it. She didn't like the sound of the fairies' laughter, and she could tell that Fala and Salaca loved to create problems. Given the apprehension in her companions' faces, it was clear that everyone knew they had to keep their guard up.

Led by the tall fae, the group merged into the flow of odd-looking foot traffic, passing shops that catered to the Other Realm's inhabitants. They stopped at a blacksmith's shop, where a hot fire burned brightly in the forge. Three shirtless fae worked inside, not a drop of sweat on them despite the heat, although their red-tinged skin shone as they hammered on a sword. The loud clanging of metal on metal echoed around them. It wasn't a sword of iron and steel these fairies forged—it was quicksilver, the metal glowing as if it were alive and was being formed into a living being.

Sean stepped forward, the siren song of the weapon calling to him. Keelie saw the sword weave its magic upon him.

Fala leaned close to him, his voice a whisper. "Elf, I can hear your warrior heart calling out to the sword. You want it. I will give it to you."

The fairy reached for another sword, which was hanging from a display. He held the blade up and it erupted into flames. Within the flames appeared the alluring outline of a woman, wearing nothing but the flickering fire. She stared at Sean as if she really saw him.

Sean's eyes were glued to the flaming woman's and he drew closer to the sword. "There are legends about swords such as this. My grandfather told me stories about them when I was a boy, and Elianard spoke of it in Lore Class."

Keelie grabbed Sean's wrist as he reached out to take the sword. "Think, Sean. There will be a price. There is always a price when a fairy offers you a gift." She turned to Fala. "Tell him. Fairies speak true, that's what my Grandmother Jo always said."

Fala winked at her, unperturbed. "The price, Lord Sean, is that you freely give up the part of your heart that belongs to Keliel."

The sword flamed once again, and the flaming woman appeared. This time, she tossed her hair back and winked seductively at Sean over her shoulder. When she looked at Keelie, her eyes turned into slits.

"No sword is worth that price." Sean glowered at Fala. "How dare you even think I would trade my heart for a sword."

Fala returned the weapon to its scabbard, the flames snuffing as the sword entered the sheath. "Ho hum. Don't you get tired of being so honorable? Don't you want to let loose and have some fun?"

Salaca pointed at the sword that was being forged. "Put that one on hold for me. I'll be back for it."

One of the blacksmiths nodded and went back to his work.

"I've never seen anything like this. Are these living swords, or do spirits inhabit them?" Elia watched as one of the display swords' flaming edges produced another beautiful figure.

"The swords live. The quicksilver is mined near the volcano, and it has deep magical properties," one of the swordsmiths said.

Elia was still staring at the swords as Keelie dragged Sean away from the seductive weapons to the next open-aired shop. She was surprised to find that the proprietor was a dwarf.

Baskets of gemstones lined the walls, not unlike a store she had seen near the Wildewood Faire. Another dwarf came in from the back. They were dressed in leather leggings and wore tool belts full of tools.

Maybe this is where she would find a suitable gift for the queen. Keelie was sure that the sword shop did not hold anything Queen Vania would want, nor did she want to surrender part of her heart for the purchase.

"Keelie Heartwood, is that you?" asked a familiar voice.

She felt a rush of joy when she saw her old friend and teacher, Sir Davey. "What are you doing here?"

"My girl, this is where I buy my inventory for the Renaissance Faires. Your father told me to keep an eye on you when you came through and to report back to him when I saw you." Sir Davey aimed a nasty glare at Fala and Salaca, who pawed carelessly through gemstones.

"Can you get a message to him? My elf phone doesn't work at all," Keelie said in a low voice. "Tell him I'm safe, that I'm going to meet the queen, and that Elia came along. Her family totally dissed her."

"I think you need some tiger's eye," Fala said nearby.

Sir Davey pulled Keelie away. "I'll let him know, but I'm not sure that I'll be able to reach him either, if you have not. Is it the trees?" His brow was furrowed with concern.

"I have no clue. The trees talk to me, so I don't think that's it."

"How about some rose quartz?" Salaca suggested. He seemed to be deliberately following them. "When you throw one at a troll, it's supposed make him want to climb a tree rather than continue the chase."

"I didn't know that." Fala raised his eyebrows. He glanced at Keelie and Sir Davey, then looked away.

"What does tiger's eye do?" Salaca asked, holding up the banded rock to the light.

"It's supposed to stop rashes." Fala grabbed three rose quartz and a tiger's eye, and handed them to a dwarf behind a table. "Put those on my tab."

The dwarf nodded, removed a leather-bound ledger from a box, and wrote in it.

Keelie would have to remember that little tidbit about how rose quartz affected trolls, if she ever had one chase her. She'd confronted a red cap and a goblin, but not a troll, and she hoped she never would.

Sir Davey walked over to Sean and Elia, who were looking in the baskets of gemstones. His caterpillar eyebrows rose when he saw Elia. "You've changed quite a bit since the last time I saw you," he said. "May I offer my belated congratulations on your marriage, and now I hear you are expecting?"

She proudly patted her rounded belly. "Yes, I am, but I'm ready to leave this place. My feet hurt." She shot Knot a frown. "And I'm still hungry."

Keelie smiled at Sir Davey. "I still need to find a gift for the queen. I'd better go." She leaned low to Sir Davey. "Tell Dad that the Timekeeper stopped time for us."

Sir Davey's eyes widened. "That is a great honor. He doesn't do that for everyone. Your father will be pleased, and I'll let him know when I get back Earthside." He surreptitiously pointed at Salaca. "That one is the queen's eyes and ears," he whispered.

"I figured."

Coyote whined by the door, and Keelie waved goodbye. After Sir Davey's booth, they passed a Poisons and Potions shop. A woman filing her claws cackled when Keelie passed by. She shivered when she saw some of the dark containers that held liquids ranging from ruby red to disgusting, pond-scum green. Janice, the herb lady at the High Mountain Ren Faire, would run as fast as her legs could take her from this place, but her daughter Raven, Keelie's friend, would love it.

Knot was waiting by the entrance. He stood upright and twirled his whiskers with his paw. Coyote lounged against a windowsill next to him, also on his hind legs.

It seemed the more time they were in Fairy, the more the two of them were changing into ... what, she didn't know. Keelie was uncomfortable with the changes.

"Why are you two standing up?" she asked.

"Meow practicing for the queen," Knot answered.

"Meow too," Coyote said, laughing.

Knot growled at him. "Yeow making fun of meow accent?"

Beside them, creatures and fairies wove in and out of the crowd, walking in and out of shops and laughing as they strolled along, singing songs.

Fala and Salaca jumped into the crowd, merging with them behind a group of frog-faced men wearing pirate hats and nothing else. They left behind wet footprints. Keelie shook her head, trying to rid her mind of that image. Maybe they were looking for a shop selling pants. Keelie kept her eyes on anything but their froggie behinds.

As they passed a tattoo shop, Fala noticed that Keelie glanced into the window. "Isn't this a perfect symbol for your life, Keliel? You're always watching other people, and never feeling like you really belong because there are so many different bits of yourself. You're what part elf, fae, and human? Do you ever feel whole?"

Inwardly, Keelie flinched, but she hoped she kept her face a mask of non-reaction. "Shut up," she said. She wasn't going to give him the satisfaction to see how painful his words were.

Fala laughed, as if he knew his words cut her deeply. She glanced at the clock on the tattoo shop's wall. It still read five minutes till midnight. The Timekeeper's magic had worked, but now Keelie wondered how the queen would react to the action, or if she'd even notice.

Below the clock, a dark-haired fairy was getting a tattoo. Wings as black and shiny as a raven's were folded against her back. Salaca tapped on the window, and the fairy girl turned her face to show a flowering vine tattoo twisting up the side of her face. When she turned, real flower petals dropped from her cheeks to the floor.

Fiddle music played nearby, and as they turned up the next street, Keelie saw that it was the rabbit fiddler she'd heard earlier, backlit by a whirlwind of light. The vortex. It seemed close enough to touch, but appearances were deceiving in the fairy world.

She was ready to get on with the mission, but now fear

pulsed through her at the reminder that she was close to her goal. Still, her toes tapped of their own accord in time to the music and the pulse of the vortex. She wondered if the musician wove magic into his melodies.

Beautiful high voices broke into song, and she looked around for the singers who gave words to the fiddler's tune. Many danced, but no one sang.

Coyote scooted up to Keelie and wagged his tail excitedly while stomping his paws in a bad imitation of a tap dance. "Johnny O' Hare's the best fiddler in the realm."

"Johnny O'Hare is a favorite of the queen, but he still chooses to play for the rabble." Fala sniffed.

Around them, the fae had gathered to hear the magical fiddler, but Keelie heard the creatures whispering about her behind their hands.

She's the one.

She's not what I expected.

Pushing her way to the edge of the crowd, with Sean right behind her, Keelie grabbed Elia and pulled her along. The singing grew louder, and she saw a pushcart full of potted flowers. The flowers were singing, their leaves and petals trembling as their tiny magical voices rose to join the fiddler's chorus.

Keelie stopped. "Are those for sale? That's what I want to buy for the queen."

Coyote bounded ahead before she could approach the warty-skinned salesman who manned the cart. "Allow me. You'll probably end up bargaining away your nose."

He bargained intensely with the creature behind the

cart, then motioned Keelie closer. "Choose your plant and let's get out of here."

Keelie looked over the selection and finally chose a pot of red snapdragons with yellow stripes. They looked like they could stand up to a fairy queen. The little flowers sang on, even as she held the pot close to her chest. "They don't bite, do they?"

The warty salesman looked offended. "Of course not. They're singing flowers, aren't they? I left the biters at home."

"Then let's get out of here." Keelie turned to her party, all gathered close to look at the pot of singing snapdragons.

"You've finally shown some sense," Fala said. "Although I don't know why you need flowers. He should have bought the sword."

"I'm here to see your queen, to help her, so let's get on with it." Keelie stopped herself and softened her voice. "I mean, I'm anxious to attend the queen."

She faced the vortex, feeling the hum of its magic run through everything. Why hadn't she noticed that before? She'd allowed herself to be deceived. Salaca was right—she was searching for the one thing in her mixed magical heritage that would make her feel whole, but the real Keelie was turning out to be like an onion, and with each magical adventure she uncovered layers of herself. And with each layer revealed, she felt more exposed and vulnerable.

Nearby, a crowd cheered and the clang of sword on armor was followed by a great outcry, then laughter.

"The joust," Fala said. "The Green Knight must have lost his head again."

"A crowd pleaser," Salaca responded, nodding.

As they moved forward, the rabbit bounced in front of them, still sawing madly at his fiddle and releasing an intricate waterfall of music. The vortex seemed no closer, so Keelie kept walking, the snapdragons singing loudly from their pot. The fiddler followed along, and behind them came the fae who had been gathered around. Before long, a great parade wove through the fae faire of Quicksilver, with Keelie at its head and Sean at her side. She couldn't shake the feeling that she was leading them to their doom.

nine

They finally arrived at the vortex, which shone like a spiraling galaxy of light. Johnny O'Hare lowered his violin bow, but his music played on, flung up by the spinning vortex.

"Time to see the queen." Coyote pulled out his gold pocket watch and clicked the stem. A loud boom shook them, as if something had exploded, but then Keelie felt time move again. It was like taking a breath after holding it for a long time, although she hadn't been aware of holding her breath. Her heart seemed to beat to the rhythm of the clock.

Johnny O'Hare lifted his fiddle up to his shoulder and ran the bow down the strings. He began to play a new tune and everyone began dancing, but under the cheerful melody, Keelie heard the tick-tick of the clock keeping rhythm.

"Okay, what now?" Keelie looked at the vortex, which seemed to vanish into the ground. She did not want to step into a hole into nothingness.

Fala motioned toward the tornado of light. "Just jump into the light. It will carry you."

The vortex pulsed in time to the music. Fala laughed. "Afraid, Lady Keliel? It's the only way up."

Sean grabbed her hand and held it tightly.

Knot walked to the edge, now dressed in the height of Victorian fashion with a velvet coat and floppy black tie above a snowy white linen shirt. He was almost at the edge when a furry brown blur in chaps and a cowboy vest barreled past. Coyote leaped into the light, shouting, "See you there."

Knot bowed to Johnny O'Hare, then leaped into the vortex after him.

Elia stepped forward and clung to Keelie. "If we're going to do this, we're going to do it together."

Sean stood behind Keelie and wrapped his arms around her waist. Keelie clutched the pot of singing flowers in one arm and extended her other hand to Elia, who clutched it tightly. Together they stepped forward and fell.

But then they were flying. She could feel Sean's strong arms around her, and Elia's icy vice grip strangling her free hand. The flowers had fallen silent. The only sound she heard was Salaca and Fala, laughing maniacally behind her.

Keelie came to with a frantic gasp, brushing at whatever was tickling her face. Not spiders. Snowflakes. Shivering, she pushed herself up and looked down at the smooth, cold surface below her. Glass. It was some sort of floor. They were surrounded by darkness, and snowflakes landed softly on her face.

She hadn't expected the world of fae to be cold and wintry. She'd envisioned the Shining Ones as living in sunlit castles surrounded by green meadows and fairy-tale forests. She looked around, but all she saw was darkness except for a small ball of light floating above them. It floated down toward them, expanding until they stood in a silvery circle of illumination. She righted the flowerpot.

Murmurs drifted around them. Beside her, Sean sat up, rubbing his head. At his other side, Elia lay still. Keelie crawled to her, barely registering that she was now wearing a skirt.

"Elia, wake up." She shook the unconscious girl. She didn't dare think about the baby.

Elia's eyelids fluttered, and she moaned. "What happened?"

Relieved, Keelie sat cross-legged. She reached to close her cloak, but there was no cloak. Instead, she wore a burlap corset, and an underskirt of plain muslin stained with mud, and ugly shoes that looked like something she'd bought at the wicked-witch store. Red and white stockings covered her legs. Where was her favorite blue gown? This was not what she'd been wearing when she stepped through the vortex.

Sean's clothes had been transformed also. His hauberk

had become a too-short peasant shirt that exposed his midriff. His nice six-pack was on display, but it looked ridiculous. He had on green hose that stopped at the knee and clunky wooden clogs. His armor had vanished, as had his sword.

Elia now wore a yellow gown with big red handprints on the chest. It was even more hideous than the skirt Tarl the Mud Man had given Keelie at the High Mountain Renaissance Faire. Luckily, Elia was still too groggy to notice.

"Meow."

"You stupid cat. If you would just remove your claw, then we can free ourselves," Coyote growled.

Keelie looked over at Knot and gasped. His fur! He looked as if he'd been to a dog groomer's and now had a fluffy pom-pom at the end of his tail. The fur on his legs had been shaved and he had little muffs by his paws. He was not going to love this look.

Elia lifted herself from the glassy ground and blinked. "Where are we?" She placed a hand protectively over her belly. "I feel queasy."

"I think we're in the court of the Shining Ones," Keelie replied. "And I don't think we're outside anymore." Although she couldn't see it, she felt as if there was a ceiling somewhere far above them.

"What happened to our clothes?" Sean looked down at his new outfit in disgust.

Elia glanced down at herself and screamed. She jumped to her feet and started looking around, as if her other clothes might have been stashed somewhere, but they could see nothing outside the circle of light.

"A sorry jest," Coyote said. His eyes glowed with anger. His motley brown fur had been transformed to black and white with a stripe running down his back. He now looked like a tall, skinny skunk.

"Why?" Keelie asked. But she knew the answer. The high fae—owners of general petty meanness.

Somewhere close, orchestral music began to play.

An announcer's voice began to speak. "Ladies, good gentles, and all who are favored by the queen, please turn your attention to the center." It sounded like Fala.

As if a light switch had been flipped on, light filled the corners and revealed a masked throng dressed in gorgeous clothing. Keelie didn't have a good feeling about this.

Knot hissed.

Coyote narrowed his eyes as a woman in a white feathered swan mask and a crystal-beaded gown strode toward them. She was followed by a good-looking elf who wore a small black mask over his eyes and a sweeping black cloak. He examined Keelie with interest, and she thought there was something familiar about him.

Out of the corner of her mouth, Keelie asked, "Is this lady the queen?"

"Yes," Coyote said, twisting his muzzle the same way.

Keelie stared at the beautiful woman. She could have been any of the gorgeous women who lived in L.A., dressed for an awards-show red carpet—at Mardi Gras. So far, there didn't seem to be anything magical about her.

"Who's the elf? I can't believe he's here after the big deal they made about no elves." Keelie glanced down at Coyote.

He scratched at the huge patch of white fur between his ears that made it seem as if he had a bad toupee.

"Never seen him. You're right. Elves and fairies don't hang out together."

"That is no elf," Fala said. Before he could explain, the queen spotted them.

"My, my. Look what has crawled into our realm," Queen Vania said, looking down at them. Her violet eyes held Keelie's from behind her mask. Dark hair woven with gold spilled down her back. She seemed regal, and waves of strong magic seemed to flow from her, tickling Keelie's skin. This woman was in charge, and she knew it. Woe be unto anyone who disobeyed her, for they would feel the queen's wrath.

Keelie stood up, snatching up the potted flowers. She'd paid her dues—she wasn't about to be looked down on. Of course, she was on a diplomatic mission, as she had to keep reminding herself. She would have to save the sarcasm for when she got back to Grey Mantle.

"Why do you insult me, coming here dressed as beggars and clowns?" The queen looked down her haughty nose. "I don't find it amusing."

Keelie matched her stare with her own. She'd had plenty of practice staring down mall divas back in California. She'd almost thought *back home*, but home was the Dread Forest now, and she wished she was there this very second. The staring contest lasted for almost sixty seconds, and then the queen barked a laugh and looked around. "Who is responsible for this?"

Keelie felt the tense muscles in her shoulders relax a tiny bit. The queen's laughter might be a good sign.

Fala and Salaca looked toward the ceiling and fidgeted. The queen's gaze shot straight to them. "My lords, such petty tricks amused my sister, but Princess Linsa is no more." For a second the queen froze, then she took a deep breath and turned to Keelie. Behind her, the elf who apparently wasn't an elf had turned his face away.

"I didn't invite Keliel Heartwood and her companions here so that they could be humiliated." The queen turned back to them. "Lady Keliel, good folk, be as you were."

The itchy burlap corset morphed into the silky feel of the flowing blue dress she'd worn earlier. Keelie saw that the others were back to normal as well.

Fala and Salaca bowed their heads. "Our apologies to our guests."

Keelie certainly knew who wore the big-girl panties in this kingdom.

The queen walked toward a carved throne. Tall and wide-seated, it seemed more like a small building than a chair. Crystal and white stone polar bears chased each other around the base. It seemed to be made of frost and ice. She sat down, flanked by her knights, and clapped her hands. "Everyone dance while I seek counsel from my advisors." She motioned to Keelie, who approached the throne warily. "Allow me to prepare for our work. Soon you and I must mend the rift."

"Great." Keelie smiled at the elegant and haughty fairy queen. She was glad that Vania was serious, and willing to try to mend the disagreement between the elves and the fairies.

"We will speak again soon." A curtain of mist descended from the ceiling and hid the queen, who was flanked by some of the fairies who had been in the hall.

The music began to play, and this time, Johnny O'Hare hopped in front of the orchestra and began fiddling, and the orchestra played along to the melody. The fiddling rabbit winked at Keelie.

The not-really-an-elf was standing nearby when the queen disappeared. Keelie walked up to him.

"You know, it's not polite to make fun of your guests by dressing up like an elf. Definitely not cool, and it's going to make my job a lot harder."

He turned to her and looked her up and down before bowing deeply. "Forgive me. I thought it would amuse Queen Vania. May I have this dance?" he asked.

Sean was about to protest, but Keelie accepted before he could say anything. She wanted to know more about the fairies, and possibly the fake elf could help her find out what the fae wanted her to do.

"Do not let them scare you," he said as the crowd watched him place his hands around her waist and pull her closer to him. "They do not often see visitors. And you are unique even among those few." He guided Keelie around a dancing couple and then they glided into the twirling throng.

"What a crowd. They're intimidating," Keelie said.

When he swung her under one of the floating lights, she noticed that hers was the only shadow. "Why does no one cast a shadow?"

"The shadow would reveal their true form, so it's best in

many instances for them to hide their shadows. For some it's a habit that is hard to break."

"So why do you hide yours? Are you a troll?" Keelie smiled up at him.

"Vania thinks so." He laughed. "You should see the look on your face. No my dear, I am no troll. I am much like you, I think."

"What should I call you?" Keelie stopped, as did the fake elf, who smiled mischievously down at her. She liked the way his mouth crinkled when he smiled. Behind him, beyond the dancers, she saw Sean's scowling face. Oops.

"Call me friend, and I shall be happy."

"Right. Thanks for the dance. I need to go see if the queen has finished talking to her advisors." Keelie pulled her hand from his.

His black eyes looked down into hers. Black, she thought absently. Not a fairy color, but there were all kinds of fairies, as she'd discovered today. "Do you think you can really heal the rift?" he asked.

"Heal is a mighty strong word. I can get everyone talking together. It'll be a start."

"Talk accomplishes little. The situation calls for quick action and strong magic."

"Strong magic? They don't need to be charmed in order to talk, do they?" Keelie could see herself in his shiny black eyes. Images of goblins, ancient and wrinkled buglike creatures, and red caps filled her mind. She smelled the earthy smell of loam and for a moment felt homesick, until she heard the faint and familiar discordant jangle of a jester's bell. Peascod.

Keelie suddenly felt cold and vulnerable. She wanted to find Sean. She needed him. There was no telling what or who the creature before her really was.

His voice changed, becoming deeper, but kindness was there along with need. "Keliel, you must leave this place. The queen's plans will put you in great danger."

She stepped away from him. This was a trap. The queen wanted Keelie to betray her, to put Keelie in a bad spot so that she would do whatever the queen asked. *Never trust the fae.*

The jangle came closer and Peascod stepped out of the crowd. "Master, I have seen the elves, the cursed cat, and Coyote, but I have yet to find Keliel Heartwood." He stopped suddenly, staring at Keelie.

"As you can see, she is here, with me." Her dancing companion didn't seem to think there was anything wrong with Peascod's presence here, and Keelie stiffened in his arms as she realized that the jester had called him "master."

"Are you following me, jester?" she asked Peascod. "I see you everywhere. Did you come here from the Redwoods?"

"I go where I please, stupid mongrel," Peascod snarled.

Her companion opened his mouth, but before he could speak Keelie whirled to face him. "He called you master."

The mist at the end of the ballroom vanished and the queen stepped out. "I thought I smelled your familiar evil stench, Peascod."

Keelie stared from one to the other.

Queen Vania snapped her fingers and the snow started

up again. Dancers swept around them, and whorls of lights from the aurora borealis swirled through the room.

Keelie felt the room's magic flow through her body, along with the tension of their group, facing each other in the center of the dancing merrymakers.

"Your friends are protected," the queen told Keelie. "They're with Fala and Salaca."

"What about Knot and Coyote?"

Vania pressed her lips together in a tense line of displeasure. "Lesser fae who think they're above their betters. They're with your friends, and as long as they behave, they'll be fine."

Peascod stepped forward warily and stood beside the fake elf. Keelie recoiled.

The queen's eyes narrowed. "Herne, take your pet and get out of here."

"Herne?" Keelie's mind reeled. The fake elf couldn't be the Lord of the Forest.

Then, as she watched, his ears shrank and his form buckled and throbbed, lengthening to become the stag-antlered man she'd seen in the clearing. A thick crown of vibrant green leaves sat on his rich chestnut hair, twining between horns that seemed to sprout from his forehead. He turned his handsome bearded face to hers.

"Lady Keliel," he said, his voice thick as velvety moss and ringing with the echoes of bugling elk, "heed my warning." And then he vanished, taking Peascod with him and leaving Keelie with the Queen of the Fae, who glared at her in displeasure.

ten

So that had been Herne, the *Unsidhe*, Master of the Wild Hunt Herne. Keelie stared at the spot where he'd been. She'd always assumed that Herne was old—like a grizzled wizard, or maybe more skeletal, like the grim reaper or the Timekeeper. And she'd only seen him from afar when he appeared beneath her window in Grey Mantle.

Queen Vania pursed her lips, resplendent and cold in her sparkling gown. She'd removed the swan mask and now wore a crown of quicksilver leaves. In the background, the green and red lights of the aurora borealis glowed brightly, casting an alien light around them. "He knows it annoys me when he comes here," she said. "He's forbidden, of course, but he couldn't resist coming to catch a glimpse of you."

"I'm ready to help, Your Majesty. Where do we start? The elves said they're ready to talk about the magic that's leaking." Keelie thought it was better to get straight to the facts, given that fairies liked to play cat-and-mouse games. She hoped her face projected concentration and unwavering strength, because on the inside, her internal organs quaked in fear. She laid out her agenda, as she'd seen her mother do when preparing a case for trial. "First, we identify all the parties involved. The High Court, of course." She bowed her head to the queen, congratulating herself on her diplomatic presentation. "The elves, the dwarves, and who else? Is Herne one of the parties involved in the rift?"

The queen stared at her as if she were speaking nonsense. "The rift will not be resolved with identification. It will take raw magic and targeted power, and you and I are the only ones who can accomplish it. Follow me."

She whirled and headed out of the hall, her beaded skirts clicking and flying.

Momentarily at a loss for words, Keelie followed, wondering at her words. Herne had said something very similar, about raw magic and power. This had probably gone beyond name-calling, and she was starting to feel outclassed. Maybe Norzan would be a better choice of diplomat.

They passed endless chambers and cold, elaborately tiled halls. Queen Vania suddenly stopped.

Keelie looked around, but the high-ceilinged room was empty. "What are you going to show me?"

The queen smiled and ran a finger in a straight line, down to the floor. A door appeared in the air. "Come to my chamber, and I will show you."

Keelie followed her into a small, circular room lined in crystals that throbbed with the colors of the aurora borealis. A polished stone table stood in the middle of the room, strewn with papers and ink pots. No wood anywhere. Keelie felt very alone.

The queen opened a box and pulled out a quicksilver chain, from which hung a fat crystal with many sides. She reached up to hang the crystal from a hook that protruded from the low ceiling. "Now you will see my pain. Now you will learn what fear is."

She touched the crystal and a view of the Earth appeared before them, real enough to touch. "We cannot mend the rift with talk, Keliel. The rift is not a misunderstanding. It is a crack in the magic that holds the world together. And this is what you are uniquely able to help me repair, the leaking of the magics into the mortal realm."

"I'm just a girl," Keelie said. "You're more powerful than me. What can I do?"

"True, the power I wield is more formidable than most, but power and strength alone will not restore the boundaries. The blood of fairy flows through you, along with your human and elven blood. You, yourself, are balanced in the three, and my counselors tell me that this is what is needed to restore the magic."

"Well that makes sense, but I'm not powerful enough."

"I will show you."

Keelie turned away, overwhelmed. This was not what the elves had led her to expect. She couldn't help with a deep magical problem. She was just a kid.

"If you don't help me, Keliel, the boundaries will collide and Earth as you know it will be gone."

Keelie spun around and stared at the queen. "What will happen?"

"The magic is spilling forth now, and humans who have fairy blood flowing in their veins can feel it. Many have traveled toward it in answer to an unspoken supernatural summons. It's changing them, they will eventually evolve into a different species."

"You're afraid of humans being able to wield magic like the elves and the fae."

Queen Vania frowned. "The elves are bad enough, but to have humans wielding magic is far worse. They are child-like and cannot control their compulsions."

"You mean like changing people's clothes and giving cats pom-poms in their fur?" Keelie lifted her head high and stared directly at the queen.

"I punished Salaca for his disrespect."

"You scolded him."

She shrugged. "He is old, and I cherish that he keeps his playfulness." She looked at Keelie for a long moment. "You did not know about the rift. You thought you were here to parlay."

"Lord Terciel said I was to convince you to come to Grey Mantle, to join him in talking to the elves about who was allowing magic to overflow into the human lands." Maybe

Terciel was truly ignorant of the crack in the atmosphere, but Keelie wondered if she'd been tricked into surrendering herself to the fairy queen.

"Lord Norzan, the tree shepherd, told Terciel of your fae blood. Among the barren elves, the child of a tree shepherd is unique, even if contaminated by human blood. The trees count you among their brethren, and that gives you a deeper connection to the Earth. This connection could be key in mending the crack. Add to that your fae blood, and you are crucial to our solution."

The queen hadn't answered Keelie's question. The fae couldn't lie, but they were good at redirecting conversations. Keelie felt as if her ancestry was taking a beating, too.

"You said if I don't help you, then the Earth as I know it will be destroyed." Keelie didn't know what *she* could do to help mend this crack. To her, the idea seemed preposterous.

The queen pointed to the pulsing lights of the aurora borealis. "Do you know the scientific explanation for these lights?"

Keelie thumbed through her brain for the answer. It had to be hidden deep within her brain cells. She vaguely remembered something in science class. "It has to do with the magnetic fields and solar wind."

"Very good." Queen Vania smiled as if Keelie had answered a question correctly on a test. "If magic keeps spilling out, then the magnetic fields will weaken. The protective atmosphere will be destroyed, and eventually the solar flares will burn your human world. The polar ice caps will melt and flood your coastal cities. Your weather will be unpredictable. Therefore, no crops. Humans will starve, and with their connection with nature destroyed, the elves will perish as well."

Chilled, Keelie thought of Earth with no trees, no people. "What about the High Court and Under-the-Hill?" she asked. "How will they be affected?" She wanted to know what the fairy queen had to lose. "I would think that if humans were destroyed, you could then rule the Earth."

Queen Vania shook her head. "We cannot exist if the others do not exist."

"You need us to survive."

The queen smoothed out an imaginary wrinkle on her dress. "Yes. But we all need each other."

"What if I can't stop the magic from spilling forth?" Keelie's heart raced at the huge responsibility the queen was presenting.

"If we fail, then it is the beginning of the end."

Visions of the end of the world flooded Keelie's mind. She'd seen lots of disaster movies with Laurie.

"Let me show you what I mean." Queen Vania waved her hand, and the image of the sun and the planets whirling around it appeared, in three dimensions, hanging suspended in midair. Keelie wanted to reach out and touch Mars' powdery red surface to see if it was real, or one of Saturn's icy moons. If she squished one of the planets, would her hand go through it or would it explode into small bits? She had to hand it to Vania; she was great at visual displays.

"What does this harmony have to do with Earth?"

Keelie felt like a celestial astronaut gazing at the jewels of the sky.

The queen waved her hand and the Earth zoomed closer to them, making Keelie back up. Something was different about Earth—it was tilting farther on its axis. Queen Vania pointed left, toward the image of the sun. Huge solar flares exploded from the surface and blasted out into the solar system, engulfing Mercury and Venus. But when they hit the Earth, the flares bounced off as if some invisible force held them at bay, then continued on their way deeper into the solar system.

The queen motioned with her hand again, and the image of the wobbly and discombobulated Earth zoomed closer to Keelie. As the solar flares hit the Earth, she could see it was as if the planet was encased in crystal, but in some areas the glassy surface was breaking and flares were shooting through.

"What is that? I've never seen that crystal cover on any Discovery Channel documentary."

"It is Gaia's Dome, the physical manifestation of our combined powers." Queen Vania pointed a long finger at the Earth. "Look."

A great crack had formed along the crystal. Directly below it, on the surface of the Earth, another crack was forming. Keelie could see lava bubbling up, ready to break free and wreak havoc with its destructive force.

"If we do not repair the crack in Gaia's Dome, the rift in the Earth will worsen. This a sample of what will happen," the queen said, her voice was harsh and raspy. She pointed to the sky, where satellites were falling out of their orbit, then to the Earth, where the lights along the East Coast of the United States winked out. Underneath the crust of the Earth, the continental plates shifted, while farther down, at its molten core, the heart of the Earth spun faster and faster. On the surface of the planet, earthquakes rumbled, volcanoes erupted, and hurricanes formed over the oceans in response to the Earth's spinning heart.

"Magic is what protects the planet and keeps the boundaries safe."

Chills formed in Keelie's chest as fear spread through her body. She felt as if she had ice developing in the marrow of her bones. She thought of Dad, and Sean, and Elia and her unborn baby. "What do I need to do?"

"You and I must join our magic and mend the crack in Gaia's Dome. We'll harness the magic from within the Earth to catch the energy of a flare to repair it."

Keelie remembered Risa's greenhouse back in the Dread Forest. The gardening elf had had a problem with herbs she'd been growing there; too much sun was crisping the flowering buds, and the roots had been burnt. The solar panels had been taking in too much energy.

"If we catch the energy of a solar flare, won't it crisp the Earth?" Keelie asked. An image of burnt toast popped into her mind. Burnt toast with cities.

"That is why I need your connection to the trees of the Earth. They will be able to help us if we are connected."

Keelie remembered the solution she'd found for Risa in the Compendium. She'd called upon the energy of the

Earth and a nice lemon tree to counteract the intense heat of the solar power.

"What do you want me to do?"

"I will open the boundary and use my magic to heal the rift on Earth, and the energy from the Earth will draw the solar flare and seal the crack in Gaia's Dome." Queen Vania pointed to the crystal shield. Keelie got it now. The energy from the Earth magic that they summoned would heal the rift in the Earth, and the energy from the Earth would draw on the sun to heal the crack in the crystalline boundary protecting the atmosphere.

"You must hold the image of a tree and its root in your mind when we do this. The Mother Tree, from the great forest, is close by. You need to contact her."

Keelie had never heard of a Mother Tree. "You mean a Queen Tree?"

"No, this is the first tree, the tree that founded the forest. She is said to grow alone at the top of the world, keeping an eye on all the forests. She reports to the Great Sylvus."

Keelie closed her eyes and called upon the ancient trees that populated the mountainsides around Grey Mantle. There was no answer. She opened her tree sense and felt for the rest of the forest. Nothing.

Disconcerted and feeling very alone, she tugged at the cord around her neck and pulled free the charms that dangled from it: rose quartz to keep the Dread away, although there was no Dread here; the Queen Aspen's Heart, which was given to her by a forest when she killed the Red Cap that had been terrorizing it; and the silver acorn bound in silver thorns, the dark fae charm that had allowed her to open the book of secrets that had helped save her uncle and restore the Dread in her home forest.

Queen Vania's eyes widened at the sight of the powerful talismans.

Keelie ignored her and clasped the charred heart of the Queen of the Aspens. She called upon the trees again.

You are the Lady Keliel? The trees seemed to answer in unison.

Yes. I need your help.

Of course.

I need to reach the Mother Tree.

Keelie formed the image of the crack in the atmosphere and sent it to the forest.

Oh!

She felt a swoosh, as if she had formed into a million bits of herself and traveled in a wave of green magic.

She reformed as herself in front of a huge tree, whose branches reached the sky and whose roots sank deep into the Earth. It was larger than the redwoods.

A crackly voice emerged in her mind, and it was laughing. It was the voice of an old woman.

Keelie looked down and saw a bent old woman with branches growing out of her skull sitting on one of the Mother Tree's roots. The old woman's skin was wrinkled like bark, and her gray wisps of hair were like bits of moss. Her eyes were dark green. Darker than an elf's ... earthy green.

Who are you? Keelie asked.

You're young and your sap is juicy. The old woman leaned

forward and clasped a walking stick carved with animals. It reminded Keelie of a totem pole. *What can I do for you, missy?*

I'm looking for the Mother Tree.

The old woman patted the root. *You've found her. Vania sent you, didn't she?*

Keelie nodded. She had a sneaking suspicion this was the human personae the Mother Tree conjured.

Crack has gotten too big for her to fix, so now she calls for help. I've always hated how some people think they can handle something on their own when it's obvious they're going to need help.

I need the help of the trees. Queen Vania and I will call upon Earth magic to heal the rift, but I'll need the trees' help to channel the energy of the solar flare to repair the crack in Gaia's Dome.

The old woman nodded. She rubbed the end of her walking stick in the soft loamy earth that surrounded the Mother Tree's root.

Show me the heart the Queen Aspen gave you.

Keelie offered the heart, bound on its string to her neck.

The old woman arched a gray thin eyebrow. *You're going to need it when you go back to the High Mountain Faire. Keep it with you at all times.*

I will. Keelie wondered how much the old tree knew of her. The High Mountain Renaissance Faire was in Colorado, and she had not spoken of it here.

Mother Tree moved restlessly. *I will help you contact the trees, but this solution may not work. Queen Vania has overlooked the other beings of Earth. She will need to ask for the help of Herne and his dark fae and the peoples under the mountain.*

She thinks I am the answer.

You're part of the answer. And you must go back. Vania is ready. The old woman looked up at the sky and dark storm clouds had formed. *She was never one for patience. She's already captured a solar flare.*

What do I need to do? Keelie asked, panicked. Was she supposed to channel a solar flare?

eleven

Push the extra magic into the Earth, child.

The Mother Tree's words echoed in Keelie's head as the old woman disappeared. Keelie was back, face-to-face with Vania. She was sweating as she held out her hands in an attempt to control the energy surrounding her, and she glowed from within as if she'd swallowed the northern lights, with energy pulsing in and around her.

She closed her eyes and summoned the energy of the trees, but the lights were too bright. Keelie couldn't concentrate. A wave of light energy surged through her. She didn't know what to do—Vania had rushed into this situation, leaving her without any clues as to what was expected of her. The Mother Tree's voice echoed in her mind: *Vania has her own way.* She envisioned the Mother Tree as it stood high on a granite mountaintop. Its roots clasped the stone outcropping, then trailed to the soil.

Push the energy into the Earth.

A trickle of sweat trailed down Keelie's face as more of the solar energy pulsed around her, squeezing the air out of her lungs. She envisioned pushing it deep into the Earth as if the light was a treeling and she was the shovel digging the hole. She hadn't used this much magic since she had tapped into Earth magic to rescue the Wildewood's unicorn. This was much greater.

She heard the voices of the forests of the world all around her, each one unique and different. *We're with you, Daughter of the Forest.*

Lava and molten rock bubbled and reached out with fiery tentacles.

In her mind, Keelie dug deeper, pushing the light into the Earth, willing the crack to close. She envisioned the light as knitting needles and bound the torn edges of the rift together, weaving them closed with the energy and magic. But it was not enough. She could not seal the fissure's upper edges, and it remained open to the sky.

Keelie opened her eyes and looked at the 3-D model of the Earth, where the repaired rift had now turned into an angry red scar. Exhausted, she dropped to her knees. She wanted to press her face against the cool floor and sleep.

Then she heard a loud rumble from the image as a tiny tear formed at the end of the repaired rift.

Queen Vania slumped onto a chair. Her eyes closed. "We have failed. The magic will continue to leak out."

After a long moment, the queen forced herself to stand. "I must use my scrying stone." Keelie noticed that her hands shook as she held up a large crystal. The blue orb of Earth floated in front of them, oceans glowing brightly, then suddenly they saw an expanded version of the forest around Grey Mantle, zooming in until they saw details that proved that this was no map, but an actual view of the world below them. Keelie could see lights glowing in the windows of the rooms they'd slept in, and a tiny figure stomped across the street—Miszrial. Her attention was drawn to the fissure, where the tear was grinding open.

Keelie watched as dwarves poured out of a tear in the Earth, legs pumping, mouths open in fear. They were smoky and their clothes singed, as if they were fleeing a fire in the tunnel behind them. The dwarves scattered as something exploded out of the fissure.

What the—a volcano? Molten lava shot up like a geyser of fire. A bright fireball hurled itself high into the sky and Keelie drew back as if it would burn her. This was no volcano. No, it looked like a dragon.

Dragons couldn't be real, Keelie told herself. Although, why not? Her uncle was a unicorn, and Raven was dating a unicorn. She'd seen all kinds of creatures.

As she watched the tiny scene, the fireball arced up,

then seemed to be on a trajectory headed straight to her. It was coming closer and closer.

"Is that a dragon?"

Queen Vania sat back down in her chair and closed her eyes. "This is worse than I thought. She's awake and we are all doomed." She opened her eyes again and glared at Keelie. "If you hadn't pushed all of the solar energy I was sending to you into the Earth, then both rifts would have been repaired."

Keelie couldn't believe what she was hearing. "Excuse me? You were the one that asked me to help you."

"I assumed you were the answer. Apparently, the human DNA in your blood messed things up."

"You don't know that. And you didn't give me any instructions. I did the best I could, and you—" Keelie couldn't finish her argument.

A shimmer formed and Salaca materialized, wearing fresh clothes and looking worried. "I know you didn't want to be disturbed, but I think your presence is needed to deal with a problem. Several little problems." He sneered, reminding Keelie a lot of Elia.

Queen Vania lifted her head and peered at her subject with glassy eyes. "What?"

"You have several"—Salaca cleared his throat as if he had a hairball hung on the back of his tonsils—"dwarves who would like to speak to you immediately."

"Dwarves? Here?" Queen Vania seemed shocked by the very idea. Keelie wondered if she'd ever said the word "dwarves" before.

"Yes, and they're being very loud. Saying if they do not have an immediate audience with you, they're going to bring their wrought iron garden furniture and redecorate the Great Hall, and hope we all break out in hives."

"Send them off. They are not welcome, and I'm too distraught." Queen Vania waved her hand with a go-away gesture. "This mongrel has destroyed everything."

Great. Now Keelie was back to being a mongrel. One of the few things upon which the fae and elves would agree.

"They're not going to go away. Smoke is billowing off their caps, and they're angry. One of them said he lost his beard because of the fairy magic that blasted through Under-the-Hill."

Keelie turned her attention back to the scrying stone and the approaching fireball. The dragon looked angry.

Fala shimmered into the room, as beautifully dressed as his friend and just as frightened. "Your Majesty, a dragon has been sighted." Apparently, dragons weren't a daily occurrence.

Vania sighed. "Show her in when she appears."

Keelie rose to her feet and dusted her hands off in an attempt to get the blood moving. Having a global mind-meld with the forests of the world had kind of left her limbs numb; she needed to walk around and get some blood circulating.

The queen stood up and jabbed a finger at Keelie. "You will explain to the dwarves and the dragon what you did when you pushed the magic into the Earth."

"Don't blame me. You sent me to the Mother Tree, and she told me to do it."

"Well, it didn't work, and now I have Ermentrude, awake and angry and headed this way. I don't like to deal with dragons." The queen snapped her fingers and her throne appeared behind her.

"Ermentrude the Dragon? You are kidding." It sounded like a kiddy picture book.

Salaca's face darkened and his lips trembled. "You've awakened our doom, mongrel."

Keelie wanted to kick the fairy, but he looked so scared that she almost felt sorry for him. So far, the dragon hadn't done anything but fly out of the Earth and scorch some dwarves. They didn't even seem too hurt. Ermentrude must be really tough if the queen was so affected. She wondered how the dragon's presence would change the situation.

"We're going to have to do this again, so you can't leave until we find a solution to the rifts in Gaia's Dome and the Earth," Vania said as she rose, smoothing down her dress. She snapped her fingers, and her throne was replaced by a mirror that shimmered into existence. Her hair formed into a smooth chignon, and she immediately glowed as if she'd just returned from a full day at the spa.

Keelie felt wilted on the inside and out. She didn't want to remain in Fairy any longer. She simply wanted to leave, have a hot shower, and get some hot cocoa. Snuggling up to Sean would be even better, and if Elia stayed in her own room, it would be a definite possibility.

"Are you ready to explain yourself to Ermentrude?" Queen Vania glared at Keelie.

"But I didn't do anything…"

Before Keelie could finish her sentence, the queen rolled her eyes and snapped her fingers, and next thing Keelie knew, she was back in the Great Hall, where the fairy party-goers still wore their masks. The dancing had stopped and the fae stood in groups, whispering and staring at several dwarves in singed clothes who were huddled together to the left side of the queen's throne. A smoky scent lingered in the air, like burning leaves in a backyard.

The dwarves looked like football players planning their next play, and from the angry expressions on their faces, a quarterback sack was on the menu. Or maybe it would be a fairy queen tackle. *Take her down.*

Sean and Elia were standing at the edge of the crowd. Elia seemed to be counting the candles in the immense floating chandelier, but Sean paced, his forehead crinkled with exasperation. Keelie knew the look and the impatient pacing; he was on the edge, ready to take action. Knot was in front of the throne, sharpening his claws on the queen's rug. Bits of fur floated like dust motes around Coyote, who was scratching his ear vigorously with a back paw.

Sean lifted his head and his eyes met Keelie's. Relief and irritation spread across his handsome features. He took a step toward her, but she shook her head. Queen Vania wasn't finished. The fairy queen glimmered into being, lounging on her throne. At her side were Fala and Salaca, still looking nervous. Their quick eyes took in the room, and they relaxed and glanced at each other.

Uh oh. They were up to something.

The dwarves nodded at each other in unison. They had their plan. They surged forward toward the queen's throne.

A smile broke out on Fala's face, and then he guffawed. "You fellows still here? Not here to cause problems are you, little lords?"

Salaca joined in the laughter. "Little Lords." Fala grinned.

One of the dwarf lords pushed himself out of the middle of the group. "Is this how you offer hospitality to your guests? You insult them?"

Queen Vania waved her hand toward them. "Let them come forward."

The spokesdwarf had a singed hat and his tunic still smoldered. Keelie felt bad. For a moment she allowed herself to gloat at the power that had forced the dragon out of sleep, then forced attention back to the dwarves.

The queen bowed her head slightly. "King Gneiss. What can I do for you?"

Keelie was taken aback. This smoky person was a king? She'd have to ask Sir Davey. Although come to think of it, maybe he'd yell at her first.

"You can explain why a blazing fireball of fairy magic surged through Under-the-Hill and crisped me and my men as we were in the Crystal Caves."

Queen Vania arched an eyebrow. "What were you doing in the Crystal Caves? That area is off-limits to all, including the dwarves."

King Gneiss blustered.

A dwarf with a leather messenger bag over his broad shoulder stumbled forward. He pushed his sagging glasses back up his nose. "My Queen, the magical readings in the Crystal Caves have been off-center for a few days, and we were checking them. It was all purely scientific."

King Gneiss gestured toward the dwarf. "My geologist declared an emergency, a severe threat to Under-the-Hill."

"Then why didn't you let me know there were problems in the Crystal Caves and Under-the-Hill? I might have been able to help."

King Gneiss snorted.

Fala stepped forward and pointed his crossbow at the King of the Dwarves. "You dare insult the queen."

"Put your weapon away," Queen Vania said in a calm but firm tone. "Let the dwarves speak."

"That's better." King Gneiss glowered at Fala.

Everyone seemed to be on a short fuse, and with tempers flaring, Keelie figured it wouldn't be much longer before there was an explosion of dwarves and fairy knights battling it out.

"I want to know what happened. What was the source of the power that surged through Under-the-Hill?"

Uh-oh! Keelie swallowed.

Queen Vania pointed at Keelie. "This is the unique girl whose hybrid blood gives her the ability to wield fairy, Earth, and nature magic. She harnessed the solar energy and pushed it down into the Earth to heal the rift."

King Gneiss turned to Keelie and studied her. "You're the gal Jadwyn, er, Davey, talks about."

"You know Sir Davey?" Keelie asked, attempting to hide the surprise in her voice. She didn't want to insult the dwarves.

"He's my nephew."

"His uncle is the King of the Dwarves? He never said."

The king nodded approvingly. "It's as well. He's chosen the path of a merchant, selling our wares, and he's made a good life."

"He's my Earth magic teacher," Keelie added.

Queen Vania sighed. "Are we through with our mutual admiration? Might I propose we sit down and discuss this in my council chambers?"

Keelie looked up at the queen. Council chambers sounded very official and serious.

Suddenly, the air grew hot. Flames coiled underneath the Great Hall's doors and a loud and furious roar echoed all around, making the fae cover their ears.

Everyone rushed toward the queen's throne as she created a shield of ice to protect them. She turned to Keelie and King Gneiss. "It seems as if Ermentrude has joined us."

twelve

Through the shield of ice, Keelie saw the doors bang open as Ermentrude the dragon entered the room, her goatlike eyes taking everything in. She had to be twenty feet long. Wow! Keelie had never seen a dragon before. Consider her impressed.

Vania inhaled and leaned close to Keelie. "Show the utmost respect, and nod when she asks you a question. Dragons always like to be right."

"What if I don't agree with her?" Keelie asked. "The fae don't lie, and I don't either. I have principles."

"Let's just say principles can get you roasted." Queen Vania nodded and smiled at her unwelcome dragon guest.

"Enough said." Keelie put her trembling hands behind her back.

The dragon reared back onto her massive haunches and swatted at the floating chandelier, which spun, tinkling, to the other side of the ballroom. Her scales clattered against the polished floor and Keelie felt as if all her internal organs had liquefied. Ermentrude's sheer size was overwhelming, and she filled the room with the heavy and distinct smell of brimstone and charcoal.

King Gneiss stepped forward, his thumbs hooked into his pockets. "About time you came out of yer hidey hole, ye ol' wizened windbag. Why don't you do something about yer snoring?"

Was the dwarf king stupid? You didn't call a dragon an old wizened windbag.

"You pitiful excuse for a king, how dare you call me an old wizened windbag. It's a wonder I can sleep with that nonstop digging and hammering that goes on in the mountain." Ermentrude's voice shook the room.

The dwarf placed his hands on his hips. The dragon lowered her head until she was face-to-face with this dwarf with a death wish. Then there was a loud bang, and smoke. Keelie launched herself to the floor. She was expecting roaring and flames, and she didn't want to be in the crossfire of a dragon's fiery breath.

Instead, she heard laughter. When she lifted her head, she was astonished to see that the red-scaled dragon had vanished.

In its place was a middle-aged woman wearing a red gypsy skirt and white peasant blouse. She had long red hair pinned up in a messy bun, and gold jewelry dripped from her ears, neck, and wrists in a tangle of styles and lengths.

"Gneiss, it's good to see you again, ol' friend," the dragon woman said in a sandpapery voice. She sounded like a chain smoker.

"It is good to see you as well, but I wish it was under better circumstances." King Gneiss frowned at the avidly eavesdropping crowd of fae and lowered his voice. "I have felt a major shift in the magnetic energy in the Earth."

"The core is spinning faster," the dragon boomed. Her face darkened. "Many of my dragon brethren in different parts of the world have felt it, too. What happened? Who pushed the strong magic mixed with the solar energy deep into the Earth?"

King Gneiss pointed to Queen Vania and Keelie.

Keelie was still processing the concept that there were dragons all over the world. She saw King Gneiss' stubby finger pointed right at her and gulped.

Queen Vania stood and motioned with a hand. The ice shield disappeared, leaving Keelie and the queen exposed. Keelie wanted to leap behind the throne. The red-headed woman was a freakin' dragon. If she was mad at you, then you were barbecue.

The dragon woman strode toward them, leaning on a crystal-topped cane carved with exquisite quicksilver dragons that looked almost alive as they glinted in the candlelight. Behind her, Keelie saw Sean skirt the crowd, hand on his sword, trying to keep Ermentrude in sight. What was he up to? Unnecessary heroics would only get him killed, and she now felt anxious on top of terrified.

"I should've know you were behind this, Vania, but I felt the power of another." The woman turned her fiery gaze upon Keelie. "Was that you, girl?" She thumped her cane on the floor.

Keelie jumped, and even the queen jumped a little.

Keelie couldn't lie. "Yes. I pushed the magic down into the Earth in an attempt to knit it back together. Maybe things didn't go as they should have."

She couldn't believe she'd said that in front of this woman, who looked almost as threatening as the dragon she'd been only minutes earlier.

Ermentrude pointed a long-fingernailed hand at Keelie. "I heard about you from my daughter. She said to keep an eye on you. Now, I understand."

Keelie didn't know any dragon children, but she didn't ask. One never wanted to upset a dragon.

Queen Vania cleared her throat. "Mayhaps, Ermentrude, you would like to refresh yourself before you return to your caverns?"

Ermentrude lifted her head and leveled her gaze at Queen Vania. Then she smiled, as if she'd discovered something secret about the queen of the fairies that no one else could see.

King Gneiss stepped forward. "You're more than welcome to stay with the dwarves."

"I thank you for your kind invitation, but I think I

would like to visit the elves of the Northwoods," Ermentrude said. "I have an old friend who has been feeling under the weather."

That must mean Lord Norzan, Keelie figured. He was the only elf she could think of who would ever befriend a dragon.

Murmurs traveled through the Great Hall, and Keelie overheard Fala and Salaca whispering to one another. "The dragon would rather stay with the elves than with the fairies. Ermentrude is getting old."

The dragon narrowed her red-gold eyebrows. "Queen Vania, I take insult when members of your court whisper about me behind my back."

Queen Vania turned an angry glower toward Fala and Salaca, who grew suddenly quiet. Keelie tried to repress a smile. It was good to see the two ego-driven fae have their comeuppance.

King Gneiss walked over and leaned close to Keelie. "Ermentrude always had a flare for the dramatic. When she stands on ceremony, she scares the fae to bits."

Keelie wasn't quite sure what to expect. She did feel better being near King Gneiss. However, she wasn't quite sure how the elves were going to take having a dragon as a guest, even if she was in human form. This was going to be pushing their hospitality tolerance to a new level, which wasn't very high to begin with.

Ermentrude walked up to Elia, who trembled under her draconic gaze. Ermentrude reached out and placed a hand on the elf's rounded belly. A protective surge for the child welled up within Keelie. She didn't know what Ermentrude planned to do. She'd never been exposed to dragon magic, and the Compendium never said anything about dragons, but she'd promised Uncle Dariel she would look after his child. Visions of the evil fairy in Sleeping Beauty came to mind, when Maleficent cursed the newborn princess.

Sean moved toward them, ready to step in and protect Elia from whatever would happen. As Keelie was ready to step forward, King Gneiss placed a rough-skinned hand on her arm. "It'll be okay, child. No harm will come to the elf and her unborn child."

Ermentrude turned around and winked at Keelie. "This child will be a blessing to you and your people."

The crystal at the end of Ermentrude's staff glowed, and a stream of magic flowed from it and wound its way around Elia's stomach. Elia looked up with wide, tear-filled eyes and smiled at the dragon. Relief flowed through Keelie as she realized Ermentrude wasn't going to curse Elia or her child.

Elia sighed and placed her hands protectively over her belly. She bowed her head. "Thank you for your blessing."

King Gneiss leaned in close again and held up his hand. "Fairies won't dare do anything to Elia's child. It's now under the protection of a dragon."

Ermentrude bowed her head and walked to Sean, grabbing his chin and tilting his head to the right and then to the left as if she were inspecting a cabbage at the supermarket. "Shadows edge your heart, elf, and you will have to face them before you can have what you desire."

Sean cut his eyes toward Keelie, and she knew that Ermentrude meant her. But what did the dragon mean by shadows edging Sean's heart? Ermentrude sounded like a faireground tarot card reader. The only thing missing was a tent and a crystal ball.

A smile crept over the dragon woman's face and her eyes burned bright as she rounded on Keelie. Sweat beaded on Keelie's forehead and she clenched her clammy hands. She wondered if you could dehydrate because of exposure to a dragon.

Ermentrude looked her square in the eye. "You are the one I wanted to see. You have information I want."

Knot strolled over to the dragon and meowed up at her in a commanding tone. "Meow here."

Ermentrude looked down at the fae cat and scowled. "Well, I wondered where you were keeping your sorry butt. Don't worry about your little charge. I like her."

Not the greeting Keelie had expected for Knot. More like burnt-cat-on-a-stick, because Knot had that way about him.

The dragon turned around and her expression darkened. "He says he's your guardian. How's it working for you?"

Keelie nodded. "He's a good guardian. Sometimes."

Knot scowled, and then he purred.

Snorting, Ermentrude looked down at Knot, who now was washing in between his toes as if he didn't care that he could be insulting a dragon. She turned around and shook her head. "You're too kind in your remarks about him, and I'll give you that, but I should've flamed him years ago."

Knot purred.

"What say we leave and catch up on old times, my fae feline friend?" the dragon proposed.

Queen Vania frowned. "I must insist you take your rest and entertainment with us, Lady Ermentrude. We shall have the finest rooms in my castle prepared for you."

Ermentrude exhaled. "Thanks, Vania, but what I need is an ale, and I think I would like to talk to Keelie on my own and visit my elven friend without bothering your court." She turned her gaze toward Fala and Salaca. "I want to find out what's happening in the big world again."

Keelie didn't know if she wanted to have a conversation alone with a dragon. She might say something that would make her mad.

Vania cleared her throat. "I need Keliel Heartwood here. She can't leave."

"She *can* leave." Flames danced around Ermentrude's walking cane.

Keelie fanned herself, because it was definitely getting hotter in the room. Fairies stepped back as the tension in the air crackled with energy, like the coming of a storm. A fire storm.

Please take note: Don't tell a dragon what it can and cannot do.

Keelie felt a bit like a pawn in a game of chess and wondered if the evening would end. The last thing she wanted to be involved with was a showdown between a dragon and the fairy queen.

A male voice whispered in her mind. *You don't have to stay. Vania has no power over you. But she speaks truly. She needs you. That does not mean it is in your best interest.* Keelie remembered that sweet, dark voice. Herne. She looked around quickly, but he was not in the room.

She was so tired. She'd cooperated with Vania as instructed, and even though she may not have produced the outcome that Vania, or the elves, had wanted, there was no way she was going to stay here. "I want to leave, along with Elia, Sean, Coyote, and Knot, and arrive at Grey Mantle in the same condition we were before." She knew to spell out her wish very precisely.

The dragon turned and smiled at Keelie. "Good. You've got backbone."

"We are not finished, but I will grant you part of that wish," Vania replied. "We still have to figure out what went wrong with the magic. If the magic keeps escaping, then the Earth will quickly grow closer to its end. Do you want to be the reason that humanity will die?" The queen held her shoulders high, looking like an avenging angel bringing judgment.

Keelie glared at her. "I'm only one person. I can't be the only one who has the magic to bind the rift. Don't put this responsibility on me."

The dragon pounded her cane on the ground. The room echoed its loud vibration, and all heads turned to her. "The child is right. Others must step in to help."

Queen Vania stepped down from her dais. "She sealed the rift in the Earth with little help from me. But it did not hold."

Ermentrude frowned at the queen. "What did you expect?"

"And you think the elves can help?" Vania asked, sneering. "What can they do?"

"It seems they can do a lot," Keelie said, indignant. "It seems you need their magic, or why would you need a tree shepherdess?" Stunned, she realized that she was defending the very people who'd snubbed her and treated her as an outsider.

The queen waved her wand, and the vortex of light reappeared in the middle of the court. The fairies backed away for fear of being sucked into it. The sound of Johnny O'Hare's fiddle once more played in tune to the pulsing funnel. Keelie heard the ticking of a clock and the Timekeeper's voice: *Time for you to return to your world.*

The Timekeeper had ensured that all would be as it was when they left the High Court, but Keelie knew much had changed. She looked through her lashes at the dragon woman and wondered how she was going to explain her presence to the grumpy elves.

Sean reached for Keelie's hand and gripped it tightly. "I won't let anything happen to you."

Keelie looked into his leaf-green eyes. "Funny, I was about to say the same thing to you."

"Let's go," he said. "I have something very important to tell you."

Despite the danger she'd been in, the threats that had been casually exchanged by beings more powerful than any she had ever met, Sean's words thrilled her. She wondered what he wanted to say.

Their hands clasped, and Keelie prepared to jump. She saw Elia, with Knot and Coyote close at either side, leap into the light and vanish. Just as she and Sean were about to jump, he wrapped his arms around her waist and kissed her. She leaned into the kiss and put her arms around his neck. "Don't let go."

"Never," he swore. And they jumped together.

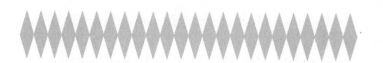

thirteen

Keelie and Sean landed lightly next to the others. Once you knew what to expect, the vortex ride wasn't so bad.

Apparently Keelie was the only one who thought so, because Elia was bent over, being sick a few feet away, and Ermentrude stood in the middle of a wide, sloped meadow, weaving around on unsteady but human legs. Smoke trailed from her ears.

"Where are we?" Keelie thought they'd be in Grey Mantle. Hadn't the queen promised? The fairy's words came back to her—she'd said that only part of the wish would be fulfilled. Keelie shivered, wondering what else might be different.

The dragon tucked stray wisps of her red hair behind her ears. "What a ride."

In the blue sky above them, the aurora borealis shone more brightly than ever. Waves of crisp greens, pinks, and purples had replaced the hazy bands of color that ebbed and shone the night they'd left. Keelie wondered if this was a side effect of increased magic, or if she had caused it when she'd tried to bind the rift. She stumbled at the proof of her power, and Sean's arm tightened around her waist. "What have I done?" Keelie whispered.

Coyote trotted up to them and butted her hand with his head. She scratched his ears.

"Only what you were asked to do," Sean assured her. He held her close. "We'll fix it, Keelie. Your father sent you here because the Northwoods elves and the fae asked for you. They can't blame you for doing your best. You're still our best hope." He looked around. "What we need to worry about is getting a ride back to Grey Mantle. From the position of the sun, I'd say we're on the other side of the mountain from Big Nugget."

"I need to call Dad. I'm not sure Sir Davey got through to him, and there's a lot more to tell him now. If only I knew what to do. The Compendium didn't mention dragons." She pushed away from him reluctantly.

"I still have something I have to tell you, Keelie, but not here." Sean looked around, then froze when he saw Ermentrude standing close by. A slow smile spread across her face as she looked him up and down.

"Go on and tell her."

Sean hesitated. "After Herne and Peascod left, I heard two fae say that "he" had been in the queen's chambers. I think Herne is in league with Queen Vania."

"No way." Keelie frowned. "That makes no sense. She hates him."

Sean shrugged. "It's what I heard. Just keep an eye out for strange alliances."

Ermentrude elbowed Keelie's ribs. "Don't be upset. Go back to kissing him. After witnessing that clinch, I feel like I need a smoke." Eyes still on Sean, the dragon reached into an oversized bag made of some leathery stuff and beaded with sparkling dragon scales. She pulled out a homemade cigarette and smiled at it happily.

A scream made them whirl to see Elia, arms wide, staring at her belly, which seemed to have grown considerably in just a few minutes. "What's going on?" she cried. "The fairies have cursed me and my child!"

Ermentrude rolled her eyes. "No, they haven't. Your baby's just grown the way it should have in the time we've been gone. Now that we're back, it's caught up."

Keelie felt a chill go down her spine. "There shouldn't have been any time passage between now and when we left, according to the Timekeeper." She tried to remember exactly what the Timekeeper had said. "And we should have arrived at Grey Mantle, but instead, we're here. Wherever *here* is. The queen did this because I didn't heal the rift!"

"You think so?" Ermentrude seemed surprised. "The High Court has never been able to channel that much magic."

Alarmed, Keelie looked around. "We don't know how much time has passed."

"Well, obviously not too much, or there would be a grown elf-man next to Elia instead of a baby in her belly," Ermentrude pointed out.

Keelie thought of the elves who had sent them on their mission. What did they think had happened to them? She looked at Elia. "I don't know anything about pregnancy. How far along do you think you are now?"

Elia's eyes were wide. "It's hard to tell. And as far as I know, I'm the only pregnant elf that's ever gone to Fairy."

"And you wouldn't have gone at all if you hadn't snuck after us," Keelie accused.

Elia burst into tears. "I didn't want to be alone," she wailed. "I need my husband. I want to go back to Dariel."

Keelie hesitated, then went to the weeping elf and put her arms awkwardly around her. "It'll be okay. No one's hurt your baby. Just hurried things up, that's all."

Ermentrude frowned, waving her cigarette. "Are we near any cows?"

Puzzled, Keelie shook her head. "I haven't seen any cows since our plane landed." Was Ermentrude having a snack attack? She shivered at the thought of a dragon swooping over Big Nugget. It would certainly give the crystal gazers something to talk about.

"There are cows in Grey Mantle. Not many." Elia sniffed. She looked much better.

Keelie shook her head to clear it. Too much fairy. Too much magic. Too much dragon. She angled her gaze toward Ermentrude. "Why do you need to know if cows are nearby? You aren't hungry, are you?"

"Honey, if I am, I can eat a burger, same as you. But methane and dragon fire, a very combustible mixture. I just wanted to be sure this big meadow isn't a pasture." She puffed out her cheeks. "Cow comes near when I'm having a hot flash, ka-boom!" She stuck the cigarette between her lips, flicked her thumb, and lit her rolled cigarette with her flaming fingertip. She shook her hand to put the fire out, then took a puff and exhaled with a satisfied sound.

"You'd better not do that around the elves," Keelie said.

"Why not?" The dragon inhaled. Smoke leaked from her nostrils and ears, twirling down to surround Knot, who was back to his normal size. He looked up at her from Elia's feet and purred loudly.

"Because elves don't care for fire." Keelie sounded confident, but inside she quivered. No one had gone over dragon etiquette with her, but repairing the rifts in the Earth and dome and stopping the leaking magic was going to take the cooperation of everyone, including the dragon. They were all going to have get over their differences and work together for the greater good.

Good luck with that.

An herby cookout smell wafted from the dragon, like a rosemary-infused barbecue. Ermentrude fixed a sizzling glare on her, and Keelie wished she was wearing fire retardant clothes in case Ermentrude blasted a fireball at her. Maybe she couldn't do it in her human form, but Keelie wouldn't put it past her.

Instead, Ermentrude just arched an eyebrow and snorted. "The elves are going to love me. Everybody loves me. I'll win them over with my charm and grace."

That was news to Keelie. "Have you met any other elves?"

"Besides Norzan?" Two little spirals of smoke trailed out of Ermentrude's nose. She chuckled. "Elves, fairies, humans, dwarves—they're all the same to me. They all eventually do as I say."

Sean's face darkened. Knot purred even louder as the herby cookout scent increased.

"I think it's time we get to Grey Mantle," Keelie said in a forced cheery tone, the kind tour guides use on the last tour of the day. She decided it was safer not to say anything else to Ermentrude. Knot blinked up at her as if he knew what she was thinking. He winked.

"How are we going to get there?" Ermentrude asked, smoke rings still drifting out of her ears.

"We hike. That's how we got to the door to the Quicksilver Faire."

Ermentrude looked uncomfortable. "This is why I have wings."

Keelie glanced at her watch. At least the hands were moving again.

"I can ask the elves to come get Elia," Ermentrude added, looking down at Knot. "Want a ride?"

Knot nodded.

"Wait. You aren't going to, um, change, are you?" Keelie wondered what the elves would do when a dragon flew overhead. For one, Dad would call.

"You got a better idea? If we do it your way, we'll just walk around in circles until we see an elf." Ermentrude rolled her eyes. "That could take years."

"Knot can't ride on your back." Keelie said.

"Why not?" Ermentrude wrinkled her forehead as if she was insulted.

"He might fall off."

"Hey, I have a great safety record. I haven't lost a cat yet."

Knot turned his head. "Meow."

"Fine, fly with the dragon, but if you fall, don't expect me to put a Band-Aid on your fuzzy cracked head."

"He's a big boy. He can make his own decisions." Ermentrude motioned to Knot and walked away from the group.

So the dragon thought she could charm anyone? Ha. She'd been less charming every minute Keelie had known her. Since Knot seemed to be on her side, maybe Coyote had an idea of what to do to keep the dragon from terrorizing the locals. Keelie looked around, but Coyote wasn't anywhere to be seen. He had a way of showing up and then disappearing. She hoped he hadn't gone back to Queen Vania. She hadn't been too happy with them.

"If you can get us home, then do it fast." Elia sat on a rock and closed her eyes. "I feel really weird."

Ermentrude looked at Keelie and grinned, exposing teeth that lengthened as Keelie watched. In seconds, Ermentrude had super-long fangs and her back was hunched.

Keelie watched, fascinated, as Ermentrude turned back

into the huge dragon who'd first crashed into the High Court's great hall. Going from red-haired woman to flame-throated, scaly monster lizard took a matter of seconds. In dragon form, Ermentrude stretched her throat and roared fire into the sky.

Keelie felt the trees around them recoil in horror. *It's okay, she's a friend*, she said in tree speak. *She won't hurt you.*

The trees weren't convinced. The entire mountainside seemed to tremble as if a small earthquake had struck.

An orange blur streaked past her and leaped onto the dragon. Knot dug his claws into Ermentrude's scales as she extended wings the size of picnic pavilions and launched herself into the sky. The dragon flapped her great wings until she was high in the sky, then wheeled around and disappeared over the other side of the mountain.

The roar of a motor sounded behind them, and Keelie turned to see the SUV that had picked them up at the airport. It stopped and the driver's side window slid down. Miszrial stuck her head out and stared open-mouthed at the dragon flapping out of sight.

Good thing, too. With their personalities, Ermentrude and Miszrial would have hit it off like a lit match and a stick of dynamite.

Miszrial jumped out of the car and ran toward them, still staring at the sky. "Was that a dragon?"

Duh. "Yes, she's helping us. How long have we been gone?" Keelie noticed that Elia was standing still, listening intensely.

"Almost a month. Things have not gone well while you

were in the High Court." Miszrial looked unhappy. "Your father is here, and he blames Lord Terciel for endangering you. He is meeting with the Council now, to prevent Lord Terciel from destroying the doorway to the fae world." She glanced around nervously. "The forest lord alerted me that you were here. The dark fae have never contacted us before. I came as soon as I could."

If Herne had told Miszrial where they were, then he was certainly connected to this mortal plane.

"The town of Big Nugget has been evacuated," Miszrial continued.

"Evacuated?" Sean had been listening closely.

"There have been earthquakes, and some of the buildings are unstable. Plus, the humans say its been overrun with rats, but it's really goblins."

"I don't understand." Keelie wanted to shake her, to get the whole story out at once. Her father and Sir Davey would be frantic. Uncle Dariel was probably beside himself.

"Much has changed since you left." Miszrial looked around nervously. "We must hurry. Please, into the car."

Elia waddled quickly toward the vehicle, looking scared. Keelie followed, with Sean behind her.

"I think we need to get Elia out of here," Sean said in a low voice. "I think she needs to return to Dariel, not go to the Healing Hall."

"I agree. I need to connect with the trees and my father, since he's close enough to hear me now."

Sean hugged her, then strode over to Miszrial. She smiled, or what would pass as a smile, at Sean.

Keelie opened her tree sense. *How is the forest? Are you well?*

All is well in the forest, but things go badly for the walking creatures. The goblins have come from the deep, summoned here by the watcher.

Who is the watcher? Keelie had never heard of a watcher.

He who watches. He watches you now. The trees sent Keelie an image, relayed over the forests. She saw a meadow, with a tiny creature standing next to a car. It was her, as the trees around saw her. She saw the green of her tree magic surrounding her, and in the forest at the other side of the meadow, a dark smear. She'd seen darkness like that before, in the Redwood Forest, where the tree Bloodroot had been contaminated by goblin blood. She pulled the image closer and saw a familiar figure.

Peascod. Just fabulous.

She hurried to the car and climbed in. "Elia, we've only been gone a month. That's a good thing, right?"

Elia turned haunted eyes to her. "But I'm so much bigger. What has fae magic done to my child? With Dariel being a guardian of the forest, I'm afraid that the baby is going to ..."

"Have some unicorn traits?"

Elia nodded.

"Do you think Ermentrude's magic did something to the baby? Or the trip through the vortex?" Keelie felt bad for bringing it up and she didn't want to make Elia worry, but they had to make sure the baby was safe.

"I don't think it was Ermentrude. She gave the baby a

blessing. There was no malice intended, or I wouldn't have let her come near me."

Keelie knew that good intentions mixed with magic could have disastrous results. At least they did in fairy tales.

"I do think the baby is much further along, though. I may be close to my time." Elia bit her lip. "What will I do? I need to get back to the Dread Forest. I need Dariel."

Keelie wondered if the baby was in unicorn form inside Elia. She wondered if it could shapeshift in utero. The Compendium didn't have anything on cross-species reproduction, pregnancy, or delivery.

For the trip back, Elia crawled into the back seat and slept, and Sean sat next to Keelie, his fingers intertwined with hers. Keelie yawned and put her head on his shoulder, thankful to have him here with her. When this was over, she'd sleep for a week. She hoped Coyote was safe, and that Knot hadn't fallen off the dragon…although knowing Knot, he might sprout wings. He was always a surprise.

As they drove into Big Nugget and through the remains of the Crystal Faire, the change that Miszrial had warned about became apparent. Many of the shops were empty, and the raucous party atmosphere had vanished. Instead, it was like a ghost town, although Keelie felt a strong surge of energy all around her. They passed the mask store, where she was startled to see eyes form behind the open sockets, watching them as they drove past. Magic haunted the streets, and except for a hand on a twitching curtain in an upstairs window, Keelie saw no sign of life.

"Why are we driving so slowly?" Sean seemed anxious, too.

"I don't want to draw attention to ourselves." Miszrial's voice shook.

Keelie looked out the window. Ahead, she saw frantic movement by the maypole, but it wasn't humans who were dancing around it.

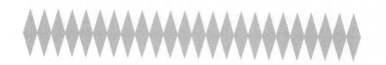

fourteen

"Goblins." Miszrial failed to keep the fear in her voice under control. She stopped the SUV and popped open the glove compartment, rummaging frantically. A look of relief crossed her face as she pulled out a baggie full of chopped green herbs.

At Keelie's raised eyebrows, she said, "We've started to keep some of this mixture about. It will cloak our presence, keeping us invisible to the goblins as long as we don't get too close."

Sean leaned closer to look at the bag. "That's enough for the entire vehicle?"

"Let's hope so." Miszrial hung the bag from the rearview mirror.

Keelie shivered. In the Redwood Forest, she'd dealt with Tavyn, a half-goblin elf who'd told her they'd make a wonderful pair. Maybe he'd made his way up here, where Herne protected his dark fae.

"This is the doing of the fae. It's all their fault the wild magic is loose and the goblins are attracted to it." Miszrial glanced accusingly at Keelie, who cut her eyes toward her, then turned away, troubled.

"It wasn't the fae, just their queen," she said, unsure of how much she should tell Miszrial before speaking to the Council. "We must all work together to heal the rift in the Earth, so that the magic will be contained once more." Keelie felt wearier than ever.

Goblins ran up and down the streets, lounged in the shop doors, and looked down from rooftops. Luckily, Elia was still asleep in the back seat. The sight of the goblins would have panicked her.

Sean clenched his fists. "Why are they here? What do they want?"

"They're attracted by the magic, just like everyone else." Keelie said, rolling down her window for a closer look.

The armored goblins danced, and despite their gruesome black eyes and avocado leathery skin, they seemed almost comical in their revelry. But there was a dark danger about them as well. It was in the air, as unpleasant as their music, which sounded like bad heavy metal. Even in the magically protected SUV, Keelie felt it. It was as if their dance was some ritual, and by dancing it created more magic. She thought about Johnny O'Hare's fiddle playing, and how it had made her want to dance a jig.

In the street next to the dance, market stalls had been set up. Armor and swords were for sale. She glimpsed huge horses breathing flames standing next to their goblin masters. Then Keelie heard a discordant jangle and grabbed her head. Pain lanced her mind with each repeated shake of the jester's magical bells.

"Keelie, stay still." Sean reached over to roll up the window.

She waved her hand toward the macabre scene of frolicking goblins. "Peascod is out there."

"How do you know that?" Sean asked, peering through the window.

Keelie blinked as if it would clear away the pain. She needed aspirin and a nap.

"It's because she has fae blood flowing through her veins," Miszrial said.

Sean turned to her. "And by the end of all this, you and yours will be glad that she does."

"Terciel thinks she'll be influenced by them. How can we trust her?" Miszrial asked.

"Because Norzan trusts her, and I would think that would be enough," Sean answered grimly.

They were moving away from the goblins, and the dance was over. The discordant jingling faded away. Keelie knew from experience that Peascod was up to no good, but she didn't want a face-to-face with the jester.

"Herne rules over the goblins?" Keelie asked. "He was scary, but he didn't seem evil. I need to talk to him." Maybe he would know what had gone wrong with their attempt to heal the rift.

The car stopped suddenly. A dragon was blocking the road, wings tented to either side. Knot was perched between her eyes, claws clutching the scales on her forehead.

"Great Sylvus!" Miszrial cried, awed or frightened, or maybe both.

Keelie opened her door and hopped out. "Ermentrude! Just in time. Did you see goblins while you were flying?"

The air shimmered around the dragon and it disappeared, leaving behind a rumpled redheaded woman with a cat on her head. She batted Knot off and he jumped to the ground, hissing.

Ermentrude's eyes were glowing bright red. The barbecue smell was back in full force. "The woods are lousy with them. These aren't Herne's people, either. Armed and armored, as if they're ready to do battle. And the humans are gone." She sniffed the air. "Not eaten, though. I don't smell blood."

"Would Herne know where the goblins came from?"

"I'm sure," the dragon said. "The dark fae answer to him alone. Which makes these goblins all the more dangerous. You should speak to Herne. He's got a soft spot for you."

"No way." Sean had come out of the SUV and was standing beside Keelie. "She's in enough danger as it is. I don't know why the elder elves are relying on a sixteen-year-old human with limited experience and little knowledge of the power she wields. Why aren't they here at her side to guide her? Instead, they send her into danger—and put me in charge of her safety."

Ermentrude frowned. "Most elves are not my friends. They fear me and my kind, but you are right, Sean. They must be desperate to rely on a child to save us all. Listen to me, young Sean. Your passion could be the undoing of the elves."

"You always speak in riddles," Sean said. "Keelie is not safe around Herne."

Keelie wanted to kick him. "Excuse me, sixteen-year-old with limited experience standing right here listening to you. The elves *are* desperate. Dad is monitoring the other forests of the world, and so is my grandmother and Uncle Dariel. All of them are connected, as are we all, and that's the point they're making. I'm supposed to be an ambassador, not a tool kit."

Ermentrude interrupted, exasperated. "Arguing out here is only going to draw attention to ourselves."

Keelie put a hand on Sean's arm. "We need to stay focused on repairing the rift, and I trust you to keep me safe, but we have to take risks."

Sean tensed. "Taking risks and safety don't go together. Nor do goblins and elves."

Elia sat up as they got back into the car with Ermentrude. Miszrial, who had stayed in the driver's seat, stared at the dragon woman wide-eyed.

"What? I promise not to smoke in the car, okay?" Ermentrude sat back and dragged her huge purse into her lap.

Knot leaped into the car and rubbed against Elia's belly, purring loudly.

Elia jumped. "The baby moved. Wow."

Ermentrude looked at Elia. "That's a very special baby you've got there, missy."

Keelie pulled Knot into her lap. "Leave her alone, bad kitty. She's been through enough." Knot drooled and stretched, making biscuits on Elia's clothes, still trying to get close to her belly as they drove on.

In the Grey Mantle parking lot, elves in cloaked hoods stood to one side, looking like monks. Miszrial exited the SUV and ran to the elves, leaving everyone else in the car.

Ermentrude's attitude changed from happy-go-lucky to listen-to-me as she faced the others. "The goblins were doing a battle dance back there, but I didn't want to let you know in front of that Northwoods elf. The goblins are getting stronger, and they will attack the humans and the elves."

"How do we stop them?" Sean seemed battle-ready.

Ermentrude looked at him. "You have to patrol the area with the other elves. And eventually, you will have to coordinate with the fae."

Sean frowned, but Keelie interrupted his protest. "What about me? How do I contain the magic?"

"The magic can't be contained by one person. It will take the cooperation of all the magical beings. We have to unite to repair the rift in the Earth and the crack above. That's where Vania went wrong. She thought she could take a shortcut using you."

"Why can't *you* convince everyone to cooperate?" Keelie asked. "A flaming dragon seems like a good incentive to listen. And the elves already know about the goblins in Big Nugget."

"And that is exactly why you need to talk to Herne about helping us."

"Me?"

"Herne will find you. And you can't delay." Ermentrude glared at Sean. "No complaints. She must do this."

On the other side of the clearing, Miszrial was pointing to the van. The elves lowered their hoods, and scowls formed on their faces.

"She can't meet with Herne," Sean nearly shouted.

"She has the blood of the fae and he looks upon her as one of his kind. Herne does not trust the high fae, nor the elves," Ermentrude replied. "It is time to join the others."

"What about the elves? Can you convince them to join their magic with the fairies and dwarves?" Keelie asked.

Ermentrude placed a hand on the door handle. "It's like I told you earlier—the elves will find me charming."

Keelie wondered if it had anything to do with the barbecue smell. The elves might find the scent irresistible. Whenever elves tried to persuade someone to like them or see things their way, they used a charm, a glamour that was accompanied by a cinnamon smell.

Ermentrude strode over to the elves, and Miszrial gestured to them to come over, too. The dragon and the elves bowed to each other, and to Keelie's surprise, the elves' scowls soon transformed into huge, goofy grins.

"I know Ermentrude says you need to meet with Herne, but I don't want you to," Sean muttered.

"I'm going to let you two love birds work this out. I'm desperate for some goat cheese. It was total misery not to be able to eat at the faire." Elia waddled off. She seemed to have recovered from her shock.

"Sean, I'll be fine. I'll take Knot with me. You'll be patrolling the area for goblins, right?"

"If I can talk the Northwoods elves into it. They may already be doing it."

Miszrial had stepped aside from Ermentrude and was watching Sean and Keelie like a huntress.

"Come on, we can discuss this later. We need to join the others."

As they walked up, all conversation stopped. One of the elves glared at Keelie. "Can we help you?"

Keelie's cheeks burned. "I thought…"

Ermentrude winked at her. "Keelie, I think you'll find what you're looking for in the woods behind Norzan's cabin, toward the north. Knot will go with you."

Sean began to follow her.

"Lord Sean, you'll need to turn to the east because the elves who volunteered as border guards are awaiting your instruction." Ermentrude smiled benevolently at him.

Sean bowed his head, but Keelie swore she heard some not very nice words being quietly uttered.

Honestly, she didn't relish the idea of meeting Herne by herself, in the woods, with goblins about. She had no idea how she was going to convince him to help with the repair of the rift. If Herne was angry with Vania, then Keelie didn't know what she could do. But she had to try. Ermentrude really was persuasive.

Dragons!

Purring thrummed against her leg. Keelie looked down to see Knot trotting along beside her.

"Glad you're doing your guardian job."

He turned his head away as if she didn't deserve any acknowledgment from him.

"Are we heading in the right direction?"

He crooked his tail forward.

"You could talk to me."

He kept walking.

"So, you want to have a mead sometime?"

He stopped and washed his butt.

"I take that as a personal insult. I'm sure you meant it that way."

He started walking again.

"Fine, I don't want to have a mead with you." Keelie wasn't even old enough to drink mead. She trudged past the village's stone buildings to the trail heading north. It went straight up a hill, through thick pine trees.

She reached out to the trees. *Do you see Lord Herne?*

He waits for you, the trees replied as one.

Suspicion stung her, and Keelie didn't know who to trust. Terciel, Herne, Ermentrude, King Gneiss, and Queen Vania were all powerful beings, and they probably all wanted a piece of the wild magic. She would have more information after meeting with Herne, but she was going to talk to Norzan and Dad. If any of these beings had made secret alliances, there was no point in trying to get them to work together. This was way out of her league. What she needed was a magical United Nations peacekeeping force.

The faintly marked trail that led up the hill was springy with fallen pine needles, and every step released their aromatic scent. The silence was unnerving. No birds, no rustling leaves. And no *bhata* followed her, as they had since she'd arrived.

A twig snapped behind her. She jumped and spun around, heart racing. "Who's there?"

Branches rattled in an unnatural breeze.

Is someone in the forest?

Yes, the trees answered.

Is it a goblin?

There was no answer.

Another twig crackled, and Keelie whipped around, ready to face the goblin. Her hand went to the charred heart that hung around her neck, and it warmed as its magic was released. Keelie's heart raced, pounding against her chest as adrenalin fired her muscles.

A deer stepped delicately into view, its head crowned by a huge rack of antlers. Keelie's fear quickly became awe. Strong muscles clenched under its sleek hide, and its powerful neck arched. It turned, pinning her with its blazing obsidian eyes.

"Do you fear me, Keelie?"

fifteen

She'd expected Peascod or a goblin, not Herne himself. Keelie backed up as the deer stepped closer to her. She shielded her eyes with her forearm as a flashing swirl of light blinded her, and when she lowered her arm, she saw that the deer had transformed.

Cloaked in dark green, Herne seemed a part of the forest. Green blanketed the ground around them, and the nearby hardwoods sported fresh leaves. Flower petals drifted in a warm, sweet-scented breeze. He exuded power, far more than any fae she'd met, and the dark fae magic she'd absorbed in the Dread Forest responded to his presence.

"That was impressive." Keelie tried for a light tone, to hide the fear he'd seen.

She remembered gazing into his black eyes when they'd danced in Queen Vania's ballroom. He was just as irresistibly handsome now as he'd been as an elf. Herne was trouble, but he was also the key to keeping disaster from striking. She had to stay.

"I didn't mean to frighten you." His words seemed to be wrapped in warm caramel.

"I need answers. I came to help the fae and the elves talk to each other, and instead I find that the problem is something else entirely, and that there are dwarves here and even dragons. And you. The situation is a lot more complicated than I was led to believe. Please help by being part of the solution."

Herne's eyes twinkled. He seemed amused by her little speech.

Keelie examined the forest floor for Knot. He'd better not be off having an ale with Ermentrude when he was supposed to be her guardian. She glanced over her shoulder, and saw a curtain of leaves forming a barrier between them and the rest of the world. She realized how quiet it had become, hearing just the sound of her own breathing. "Where's Knot?"

"He's been detained." Herne smiled wickedly. Keelie shivered. The plot to a horror movie popped into her mind: *Shapeshifting deer stalks elf girl*. She wasn't sure what the King of the Dark Fae wanted with her, and she didn't like feeling vulnerable in front of him. Now would be a good time to make a retreat, but… Keelie wanted to stay. She sniffed. No cinnamon.

"Do you smell something that offends you?" Herne arched an eyebrow, unsure of what she was doing.

Keelie blushed. "No, it's just that whenever elves use magic—" Should she reveal this information to him? The fairies might not know about the elven charm.

"Ah! You were wondering if I have charmed you."

Relieved, Keelie figured that by now, the fairies and elves up here knew a lot about each other. "I need you to come back with me. You must speak with Terciel and Ermentrude, and then we can go to Queen Vania once more." She tried to sound like Finch, the Wildewood administrator who certainly knew how to be blunt-spoken. She wanted a straight answer.

"You get right to the point—I like that about you," Herne said. He snapped his fingers, and a big red apple appeared in his hand. He brought it to his mouth with a flourish, then stopped and raised an eyebrow at Keelie. "Would you like one? I love a snack before making a big decision."

Keelie didn't know if he was aware of the symbolism of producing the apple. She wouldn't take a bite. It hadn't worked out for Snow White or Eve.

He bit into its glistening red peel with a loud crunch.

"Are you going to have a snack, or are you going to discuss what is going on? If not, I need to go."

He grinned. "Patience is not one of your virtues."

Keelie rolled her eyes.

"Mayhap a cup of tea to help you with your mood, and a more substantial offering."

Herne clicked his fingers, and two mushroom-shaped chairs with big poofy cushions appeared, along with a table laden with delicious cakes and a hot teapot filled with fragrant tea.

"I don't have time for a tea party, and I'm not in a bad mood."

Herne sat down on one of the chairs. He waved a hand over the table. "I have always found it easier to negotiate business terms over a meal. It keeps everyone at ease. In fact, this is my own blend. I grow it myself."

"I was warned not to eat fairy food." Keelie sat on the edge of the chair, but as it started to tip, she moved back and found herself trapped in its comfortable depths.

"You're part fairy, so eating fae food won't hurt you. Anyway this tea will help you see things more clearly." Herne poured her a cup.

"Conversation can do that, too." Keelie took the cup, bone-white china painted with acorns.

Herne chuckled. "Then let's talk."

Keelie took a sip of the tea. "Are you going to help me?"

Herne snorted as he served himself. It wasn't a reassuring sound. "All in good time." He settled himself more comfortably in his chair.

"Sean and the elves will miss me if I'm gone too long. They know I've come to see you."

"I think your young Sean won't know you're missing for a while." Herne reached into his cloak and produced a gold pocket watch, the kind that railroad engineers wore during the Wild West days. Keelie had seen a similar watch recently.

"Did you get that from the Timekeeper?"

Herne shook his head. "I got it from a friend. Sometimes it doesn't work the way I intend."

"My day in the High Court lasted a month. Meanwhile, the rift widens. Herne, I can't afford to stay here more than the few minutes that normal time allows."

"I'll do my best."

"Why couldn't we meet back in Grey Mantle, or in the forest where we first met?"

"Because the rogue goblins are at large. We must go to Under-the-Hill."

"We're not in Under-the-Hill now?" Keelie looked around at the now-summery scenery. Maybe this Under-the-Hill was different from the one back home.

"No, this is an alternate reality I've created that will last only as long as I need it. We must speak privately." Herne leaned forward to gauge her reaction.

She sniffed the tea before taking another sip. The scent of jasmine and apples was indeed soothing. She glanced at Herne, who was watching her over the rim of his cup. So maybe he grew his own apples and tea plants, or perhaps these were imaginary refreshments, part of his alternate reality. Keelie hoped he'd grown them, since he was more connected to the Earth than court fae like Fala and Salaca. People who worked with plants were mellow. She knew dealing with trees had given her a different perspective on the world.

Herne stared down into his teacup. "What has the dragon

told you? She hears everything." His voice was very serious, and his gaze held hers.

Keelie swallowed. "She only said I needed to talk to you, and that all magical beings need to work together to heal the rift. I tried to do it alone with Queen Vania, and failed."

He nodded. "I respect Ermentrude. She gives good counsel."

"So you'll work with Vania?"

"That's another matter." Herne frowned. "The High Court has always held itself apart. And the queen's sister, Linsa, died not long ago. The queen mourns, and blames me for her sister's death."

Keelie stared at Herne. She wanted to go *huh?*

"She was found slain next to the rift," Herne said. "Vania thinks that I talked Princess Linsa into trying to overthrow her, and then murdered Linsa when she would not go through with the plan. But believe me, that is not true. I think that Linsa was trying to prove herself worthy to her sister, who never showed her love, and was killed by one of Vania's slavish minions. Vania killed Linsa, even if she did not do the actual deed."

Keelie listened, shocked. The fairy queen had shown no sign of sorrow, and there hadn't been much mourning going on at the party. "Why would she blame you?"

"Because Linsa and I loved each other, and Vania didn't approve of our relationship."

Keelie had to remind herself that this being was not a man. That he ruled over the underworld, the dark fae. Even so, stray threads of compassion escaped. "I'm sorry."

Herne shrugged. "Have you ever heard of dragon magic?"

"I never even thought dragons were real until Ermentrude crashed the party last night. Er, last month."

"You've probably noticed that dragons are enigmatic creatures. Perhaps I can help you understand them better." Herne plucked a book from the air and handed it to her.

Keelie took the heavy book, but she couldn't read the rune-like symbols of the title. Its cover sparkled like Ermentrude's scales, and its thick, deckled pages were age-spotted, and written in the same strange script. "I already have to read the Elven Compendium of Household Charms. I feel like the homework fairy has cursed me."

"I don't know him." Herne pointed to her cup. "You need to finish your tea before it gets cold."

Keelie wrapped her fingers around the cup and let its warmth soak into her body. She took another sip, then drained the contents. Her vision clouded, and objects began to seem strangely elongated. She didn't feel dizzy, more as if she were being propelled forward on a rocket through space, but at the same time still sitting in her chair. She seemed to be able to see another layer around her, a different dimension that affected everything. She'd experienced something similar when she'd used dark magic.

Herne smiled mischievously. "It's the fairy in you responding to the tea."

"Have you awakened the dark magic? What have you done to me?" Panic welled up in Keelie. She had struggled so hard to control the dark magic now dwelling within her.

"You're fine. It's just kicked up your abilities a notch or two. Look at the book."

Keelie blinked, and realized that she could now read the title of the book. "It's called *Into the Minds of Dragons*."

She thumbed through the pages. The strange letters rearranged themselves on the paper, and Keelie understood what she was reading.

When speaking to dragons, utilize utmost respect, and know that the dragon will not be fooled.

She looked at Herne, reminding herself that even if he wasn't like the Shining Ones, he was still a fairy.

"Why are you helping me?"

Herne stared at her. "You asked for my help and said we must all work together. This is the key that you can use, because dark fae magic flows through you. It's time you met others of your kind."

Her kind? A little magic did not make her kin to the dark fae. "I hardly think—"

The cocoon of leaves shielding them from the world disappeared, and the colors of the aurora borealis undulated strangely against the bright sky. Keelie's head began to whirl.

Herne reached for her. "Steady. Call upon the fae magic within you to control how you see things."

"I'm not going to Under-the-Hill." She'd had enough tours of fairyworld to last her quite a while. She felt a homesickness for the Dread Forest surge through her.

"It will open your eyes to another layer of the world and

help you see things from a different perspective, which is what we're all going to need if we're going to repair the rift."

Yes! Herne's power would be a great help. Keelie didn't want to go with him, but when she closed her eyes, she saw the gaping wound in Gaia's Dome that protected Earth from space. The planet seemed so vulnerable. She could not walk away.

She met his warm gaze. "I'll come with you."

"Spoken like a brave fairy." Herne reached for her hand, and she placed hers in his.

When she looked up at him, his eyes had darkened. She turned away. She had seen Sean stare at her with the same intensity, and she knew it meant that Herne was interested in her. He was a being of power and magic, and he found her attractive.

She liked it.

Maybe the tea had bewitched her, or the fairy magic within her was calling to him. Whatever it was, she found Herne incredibly handsome.

"Are you ready?" His voice was a forced whisper.

"Yes."

A sharp jangling of discordant bells interrupted them.

Peascod spun up from underneath the ground, dirt spewing everywhere, spattering them with pebbles.

The Lord of Under-the-Hill didn't seemed pleased with his jester.

Peascod's burning glare bore into Keelie. "Insolent faker. Mongrel. You dare seduce my king? My liege, you must not take this creature to my realm."

sixteen

"*Your* realm?" Herne said softly. Then his face reddened and flames erupted in his eyes, flickering against the black. "You dare speak so to me?"

Keelie stepped back, ready to run. She'd known Peascod was dangerous, but not that he was stupid enough to confront Herne.

"Yes, I dare. You've never listened to me when I've advised you." Peascod juggled his glass spheres and threw one up into the air. Light surrounded it, and in the deep reflection of the glass, Keelie saw the image of a beautiful woman who resembled Queen Vania. Princess Linsa.

Herne inhaled sharply and his face paled. "You dare show this to me."

Peascod laughed behind his mask. "You allow your desires and feelings to interfere with your role as our king," he hissed. "Yes, I question your decisions. Many of our brethren gather in the human town waiting to hear your orders, yet you call them rogues. We're ready to claim the power that is rightfully ours. We have been held in submission by the High Court for thousands of years—now it is time to rebalance the world. If you bring the mongrel elf-lover Keliel to Under-the-Hill, then we'll know that our king does not support us."

Herne seemed to grow taller as he looked down contemptuously at the jester. "These goblins are not mine. They are rogues indeed, the wild things of the cities of men. You have gathered them in my name, but they obey you, and have offered me no fealty."

Peascod juggled on, but his eyes seemed to narrow. He turned his angry gaze to Keelie, then back to his former master. The scrying sphere descended, and the jester didn't attempt to catch it. It landed on the hard, cold ground and shattered, the image of the woman exploding into many jagged images. Herne dropped to his knees and stared disbelievingly at the woman's face, reflected over and over in the shards. He picked one up, and in a soft whisper spoke her name.

Then, tilting his head back, Herne lowered his cloak and it dropped to the ground like cloth wings. His cry of pain shredded Keelie's heart.

She feared for her life. If Herne lashed out in his grief, and Peascod, who was just as dangerous, reciprocated, she'd die right here. She didn't know where to run. She reached out to the trees.

Can you hear me?

Yes, Lady Keliel. We hear you. Your heart beats fast. We hear it all through our sap.

I need your help. Lend me your magic.

A wave of green magic enveloped her, creating a shield. She could feel the power flow through her body, awaiting her summons. She would defend herself, and she would return to Dad, to Grandmother, and to Sean.

Peascod looked at her, raw hate poisoning his gaze. He pointed at her with the needle-sharp fingernail of a goblin. "She will bring this pain to you again, Your Majesty. She will make you feel a mortal's death. You can't let it happen again." His tone was smug, confident that he'd convinced his lord of Keelie's evil plans.

Herne reached down for his cloak and draped it around his shoulders, then stood with slow, precise movements. He didn't look at Keelie. He didn't look at Peascod. Abruptly, the Lord of the Dark Fae spun around, his cloak whipping out, making him look like Lord Death coming to collect for his realm. He waved a hand and Peascod was lifted from the ground and held in midair, face up, so that his limbs flopped awkwardly from their sockets. His two remaining glass spheres dropped and clattered against each other on the ground like oversized marbles.

"Please, Lord Herne, I speak the truth. Do not hurt me. It is the elf girl that does this to you," Peascod yelled.

"You dare show Linsa's image to me? You invade my lands with rogue goblins, then dare suggest you need more power?" Herne rasped in anger. He reached out and grabbed Peascod by the throat. Dark mists of magic seeped from the ground, rising to encircle and bind the jester so that he couldn't move his arms. He dangled his legs back and forth like a puppet as he struggled to free himself. His eyes bulged, and the green veins in the whites of his eyes grew larger.

Although Peascod deserved to be punished, Keelie didn't want to see him strangled to death. On the cop movies she'd watched on television with Mom, hostage negotiators remained calm and kept a neutral tone of voice. "Lord Herne," she said gently.

"Keliel." Herne seemed to return to the present. He tightened his grip on Peascod, whose eyes bulged even bigger. He wrapped his hands around Herne's, trying to pry them off his neck.

He wasn't kicking out as much now, and Keelie could tell that if she didn't stop Herne, Peascod wouldn't be long for this world. She walked up to him and touched him on the shoulder, trying to quell her shaking. "Let him go. He's not worth it. You don't want his blood on your hands."

"He would have me kill you," Herne said. He squeezed Peascod's neck even tighter. It was now a lovely shade of purple and brown. When asphyxiated, goblins must turn brown from lack of oxygen.

Keelie looked down at the image of the woman in the crystal shard. She lifted her hands up to Keelie, as if beseeching her to stop Herne. Keelie picked up the fragment, and held it in her palm, then held it out to the dark fae lord. She was taking a big risk, but it felt right.

"Linsa wouldn't want you to kill Peascod."

Herne slowly turned his head, and his black eyes filled with bloody tears as he gazed at the shard. Like an animation, the image of Linsa smiled and nodded at him.

Herne closed his eyes. Red tears trailing down his face, he dropped Peascod to the ground, where he lay, writhing and gasping for breath. The fairy lord took the glass shard, and the image of Linsa smiled. Then it faded, leaving behind empty broken glass.

Silence blanketed the area, broken only by Peascod's ragged breath.

"She was very beautiful," Keelie said softly.

"I never thought I would love. Five hundred years was too little time with her." Herne turned, his face a mask of forced concentration. It was as if the tears and pain she'd seen seconds ago had been packed away, deep in a hidden chamber of his heart. "Don't be surprised, Keliel Heartwood. The fae can love and lose just as humans and elves can. Pain is not exclusive to mortals."

"Lord, forgive. Forgive, forgive," Peascod beseeched as he crawled toward Herne.

The dark lord blasted the jester with silvery waves of magic, propelling him back ten feet. Peascod hit a beech tree's trunk with a loud thud, and the snap of a cracking bone made Keelie wince. "Milord!" She placed her hand on Herne's shoulder.

As if sensing what she was about to suggest, Herne looked down at her. "He would have had me kill you to further his plans. Would you not have me do the same to him?"

Keelie shook her head. "No."

Peascod lifted his head and spat at her. "I don't want your human charity. You're below me."

"Do not speak to her like that." Herne lifted his hand.

"Do not banish me from your sight, my lord, I am the only thing saving you from this madness." Peascod rose to his knees and cradled his limp arm, which hung from his shoulder like a well-worn dishrag. "You must see reason."

"Reason?" Herne laughed. "You have acted out my suspicions, Peascod. If I were to let you stay, then my kingdom would be in danger. Bringing Keliel here will save us all. From this day forward, you are banished from my sight and from Under-the-Hill, never to return."

Peascod glared at Herne, and an understanding passed between them. Keelie didn't know what it was, but it was apparent that a conflict had been building between them for a while now. She was only the catalyst that prompted the banishment; still, she wasn't comfortable with that idea.

"You can't banish me, milord. Under-the-Hill is my home. I will be doomed to roam the Earth without home or clan." Peascod got to his feet, still cradling his arm.

"Then you will feel the pain of its loss for the remainder of your days upon Earth." Herne motioned for Keelie to join him.

"You would send me away for *her*? For a mere human, so she will be your consort?" Peascod spoke each word with venomous hate.

Consort? Keelie racked her brain for the definition. She'd heard that word. Where? It wasn't a car ... then the image of a woman dressed in a tight, revealing corset at the High Mountain Faire came to mind. She had been introduced as the king's mistress. The king's woman. Whoa.

Keelie was sixteen. She wasn't ready to be any man's consort.

Peascod stumbled closer, his face lined with pain and anger. He glowered balefully at Keelie. "This is all your fault. You will pay for your interference. If I were you, Keliel Heartwood, I would sleep with one eye open, because I will always be near you."

She stared at him. "I'll be waiting for you." She tried to sound brave, although she was so scared she wanted to pee in her pants. The green magic within her wove a shield as fear pulsed through her body.

The trees whispered to her. *Lady Keliel we are here for you.*

Wait. Let me know where the jester goes. I want all the trees to watch for him.

Yes, Tree Shepherdess.

Herne raised his hand, but before he could summon his magic, Peascod spun round and round, and descended back into the ground. Keelie hoped he would tunnel his way into the depths of hell, from where she was certain he came.

The discordant jangle and Peascod's voice echoed in her

mind. *Till we meet again. Enjoy what's left of your life. It will be short.*

His threat seemed real. She turned to Herne, who offered her his hand. "Come with me to Under-the-Hill," he said.

Keelie could see the shimmers of magic rolling off him. In the back of her mind she heard herself say no, that she had to go back to Grey Mantle, to Sean, but she could not speak. Herne waved his cloak and, like a storm cloud, it billowed out behind him and shrouded her in its voluminous material.

And when he took her into his arms, everything went dark.

seventeen

Air whooshed past her ears. Keelie wrapped her arms around Herne, eyes closed against the hot wind, struggling to keep upright as the ground vanished beneath her. The darkness intensified her fear, and she screamed. Then, with a lurch, she was on solid ground again. But was it just a ledge? She kept her eyes shut tight.

Muffled against him, she could feel only his powerful arms and the woodsy scent of his clothes. She grasped the back of his leather jacket, just in case.

"We're here, Keliel," Herne said in a soft voice. "Open your eyes and behold the wonders of Under-the-Hill."

Still reeling from the wild ride, Keelie held tighter, trying to find a better handhold on the solid wall of his back muscles. "I don't think so. I'm okay with my eyes closed."

"Much as I'd enjoy carrying you, you'll need to walk."

At the thought of being carried by Herne, Keelie's eyes flew open. She was enjoying his muscular presence a bit too much. What had gotten into her? She stepped away from him and looked, amazed, at the vast world before her. A dim, reddish light, the eternal dusk of Under-the-Hill, illuminated rolling plains and rocky hills, with roads cutting through them and sometimes disappearing underground. In the distance, a dark castle with burning towers illuminated the area with its bright flames.

The air was rich with a dank, musky scent, part wet soil, part vegetable rot, with a faint reminder of the reptile house at the zoo. She moved away from Herne, as if distance would help her control her thoughts and feelings. She missed Knot, who would have clawed and drooled on her if she was glamoured. Some guardian he'd turned out to be. Here she was, being tempted by Herne, and she was on her own. She would have to protect herself against her desires.

Keelie blinked in the dim light, wondering, as she had in Under-the-Hill in the Dread Forest, how creatures lived their whole lives below ground. She didn't think she could stay in this dusky realm for very long. She had too much elf in her. She needed the sun.

Cold air brushed against her skin and Keelie wrapped her arms around herself. Far away, she could see what seemed to be tall dark trees, their branches reaching upwards although there was no sun to warm them. She threw her tree sense toward them. The energy that touched her in return was not the familiar green energy connected to light. It was Earth magic. Deep, deep Earth magic. She could feel the energy of various crystals and rocks intermingled within their amber sap. These trees were different from the trees above. They seemed wilder, more primal and in tune with a long-ago version of Earth.

Intrigued, Keelie greeted them. *Hello.*

Who are you? They seemed surprised that she'd spoken to them. They replied as one, like a hive of bees.

I am Keliel Tree Talker. I have been called Forest Friend. She had learned to be formal when greeting a new forest.

You're the Tree Shepherdess. We've heard stories about you from the Mother Root.

That was a new one—Mother Root. The Mother Tree got around.

She's the one.

A chill went down her spine as she wondered what this strange forest could want from her. She wasn't sure what stories they'd been told about her, and these were dark fae trees. And something wasn't right. She couldn't put her finger on it. Maybe Herne knew.

"Trees need sunlight, but I sense these are using another source of energy." Keelie gestured toward the strange dark forest. She wondered what their bark was like. Would it have a different texture?

Herne arched an eyebrow as if her question took him by surprise. "They tap into Earth magic."

Keelie was pleased that her analysis was correct. She closed her eyes and connected with the trees. She wanted to know what species she was dealing with. She'd found cultural and personality similarities among different varieties of trees back home. Maybe these were different. She would have to add this information to the Lore Book when she updated the tree sections. This was all new knowledge.

"I feel like they might be oaks, but I'm not sure what else." She turned to Herne, seeking an explanation.

"Linsa and I brought acorns back from Earth long ago, and I planted them in soil from the primal forest, but Under-the-Hill transformed them. When the grove developed a consciousness, it sought out energy from the crystals to take the place of the sun." Herne frowned. "Lately, this has changed—one of the troubling differences in the Northwoods and Under-the-Hill. I feel an emptiness here, as if something is gone, or blocked away from me. I thought that you could speak to the trees and find out what it is."

Everyone wanted something from her. Keelie sighed. Maybe if she helped Herne out, she'd get him to cooperate with the others.

She moved closer to the grove, savoring the mix of magics that had created it. She was a lot like these trees, a mongrel mix. She stumbled, then turned to stare at the smooth soil behind her. No holes, no roots. Had the ground moved?

"I'm pleased a tree shepherdess finds my trees interesting and is welling to help." Herne reached for her hand and tucked it into the crook of his elbow. He didn't seem to have noticed anything strange. "Would you like to take a tour of my world? There is someone you should meet, who knows something of your family's past."

A thrill of excitement shivered down Keelie's spine. Who here might know of her family? There were no elves here. "You've got my attention. Let's go."

She took a step forward, and then realized that her feet were no longer touching the rocky ground. Instead, she was hovering inches above it. She flapped her arms and skidded sideways before righting herself. She was flying.

"Yes, we're going to fly there. Quit flapping around as if you had wings. You'll get yourself killed."

Now she knew what the wings at the Crystal Faire were for. Controlled flight. Keelie desperately wanted a pair. "Where are we going, exactly?"

"Markettown. It's our marketplace—our Under-the-Hill version of the Quicksilver Faire."

Keelie didn't know if she liked the sound of that. On the other hand, maybe she'd find some wings, although she had no idea of what passed for money down here. Going to Quicksilver had been enough for her. And she didn't like the sound of rogue goblins. But before she could respond, Herne waved his cloak.

Keelie rose like a bubble in a glass of Coke. "Oh no. Not again. I can't do the whoosh." She saw the ground far below her; she was hovering like an alien spaceship.

Herne chuckled. "We won't whoosh, as you put it. Flying is different." He took off, his hands at his sides, looking more like a surfer than Superman.

Keelie glided in the air behind him, her hair blowing back from her face. She looked down. Mistake.

Herne grabbed her arm. "Looking down is not recommended." He pointed ahead. "There's my home."

They were close to the castle, and now she could see that a small town had sprung up around its base.

"We'll walk in," Herne said. "Flying disturbs some of my people."

They landed outside the stone gate entrance into the town. Keelie was relieved when her toes touched the dirt, pleased that she could still stand without wobbling. She realized she'd quickly acclimated to Under-the-Hill, more easily than she had to the Quicksilver Faire. Funny how much she liked being here, despite the gloom and the reptilian-basement smell.

Loud voices sang from an ale house inside the gates. She almost knew the words to the song, and felt herself drawn to it. She knew she should talk to Herne about helping her with the rift, but curiosity overcame her. This was the largest gathering of dark fae in the hemisphere. If Knot were here, he would've already found the alehouse.

As they entered the stone gates, a bug-eyed creature was suddenly right there with them, watching every move Keelie made. He made her uncomfortable and she walked faster, giving him plenty of room. It could be that it was protective of Herne, but maybe it blamed her for Peascod's absence.

Unlike at the Quicksilver Faire, the market stalls here were close together. Crowds filled the narrow lanes. Some of the residents looked almost human, while others were fantastically different. They talked and bargained and laughed. Keelie had not heard any good-natured laughter in Quicksilver. Although strange, this town seemed friendly.

Herne walked ahead, then stopped and turned to her. "Are you coming? I'm sure you'll find Markettown as unique as Quicksilver."

Keelie followed, watching out for the tiny goblins who scurried everywhere. Strangely, she didn't feel out of place.

She stepped aside as two huge trolls in long robes shuffled past, tusks protruding from their lower lips. They released a stench that Keelie recognized from Quicksilver—the hooded creature there had been a troll. A group of stork-legged men with little fat bodies, like bowling balls on stilts, scrambled to get out of their way. They cursed as one of them got his legs tangled and they all fell into a produce stand. The stand's owner was a three-mouthed man, and he used all his mouths to curse them impressively.

She was comforted at the sight of dwarves. At least she knew how to deal with them. Unlike the abandoned feeling of the Under-the-Hill beneath the Dread Forest, this Under-the-Hill seemed very much alive. Maybe Herne's presence made the difference.

And despite the gloomy light all around them, Keelie couldn't help noticing how different this Under-the-Hill was from the High Court. The dark fae seemed happier than the Shining Ones. They were more real, or maybe just more like her ... they seemed to accept each other regardless of appearance or power. Keelie wondered if her sense of belonging was genuine or part of some glamour.

She crashed into Herne, who helped her and wrapped his arm protectively around her. "What's wrong?"

"It's—" Keelie stared at him, her tongue was tied. She loved the feeling of his arms around her. Was she under some kind of spell?

"It's a spider. I'm afraid of spiders," she stammered, lying. She was afraid of her attraction to Herne.

He put his other arm around her, gathering her close to him. "You're safe with me." He brushed his face against her hair. "Your blood calls to me. I find you enchanting."

"I'm sixteen, Herne. I haven't even had a boyfriend for even a whole summer yet, and your last relationship lasted five hundred years. I can't process that."

He smiled at her. "I can wait a long time for the right consort." He ran his arms down to her waist, then kissed her hard and fast on the lips—a drive-by smooch. He released her and stepped back and bowed. A crowd had gathered and burst into applause.

Keelie blushed, though she determined not to be embarrassed if he wasn't. "Aren't we supposed to find out about the rogue goblins?"

"Yes, and we are meeting someone in Markettown, as I told you. She may have helpful information." Herne looked down at her as they walked along the dirt path. "Heed me in this town, Keelie. If rogue goblins are here, you, more than any, will be in peril. Your humanity is like a beacon."

"Of course. That makes sense." Keelie hesitated. "I wonder, though. You said you would help heal the rift, and you're friendly with the dwarves ... so why can't you and the dwarves just join with the elves?" She figured she'd leave the High Court out of the conversation until later.

"The elves trust no fae, not even the Green Man, who shares their love of nature." Herne cut his eyes over to her. "Doesn't your own elven grandmother distrust the fae?"

Keelie reddened. "She doesn't trust anybody. Believe me, it's an issue."

"How do you feel about that?"

"What do you expect me to say? I have fae blood, too," Keelie said. "It's in me, and I can make up my own mind. But my family knows that I'm stubborn and opinionated."

"Linsa was like that. You remind me of her." Herne stared toward the darkness, lost in thought.

"I hope I don't hurt your feeling by asking, but if she was murdered, why isn't anyone looking for her killer?"

"I know who killed her," Herne said. "A goblin wizard has arisen who gathers power as he seeks to usurp my throne. I don't know who he is, but he will reveal himself, and I will be waiting for him."

Keelie reeled. "Just like that? You'll wait? You're fae. You're immortal. It could take centuries."

"I can wait." He smiled at her. "Your human side is showing. You're so impatient."

"Maybe I can hear that big clock ticking," Keelie retorted. "I'm so sorry Linsa died."

"Thank you. We thought we had forever. We always pursued our own interests and spent time apart because we thought it kept the relationship fresh. We didn't want to take one another for granted. Tread lightly with Sean, Keelie. You will live as long or longer than he, and you must be certain of your choices."

Keelie looked up at Herne, astounded by this revelation.

"Ah, we're here." He stopped before a huge arched doorway studded with silver nailheads. No iron here. He opened the door and entered. "Now we'll find out about our rogue goblins."

Keelie started to follow him, still thinking about what he'd said to her. *She was destined to live as long as Sean.* It could have been bluster—or perhaps the Green Man, the King of the Dark Fae, knew something about her that she didn't know.

Her heart rushed with hope. Death had taken so much from her, and she'd been resigned to living a normal human span even though her father and other relatives would live for centuries more. If life was dealing her a better hand of cards, she would joyfully accept them. Maybe she wouldn't be immortal, but she would be happy with hundreds of years to learn, to be, and to love.

Most importantly, she could freely love Sean. She'd held back, thinking it was unfair to ask for love when her own life would be so brief. Now she'd only have to worry about Sean loving her in return.

eighteen

Still abuzz with Herne's revelation, Keelie stepped into the shop. She was immediately assaulted by familiar animal shrieks, growls, and howls, and the indescribable smells of dozens of unusual creatures. She was somehow back in the familiar shop from the Quicksilver Faire, or else its twin. A slimy hand reached out and touched her hair. She shoved the hand away and faced its owner, a blue-furred monkey wearing a jester's suit.

Keelie stared at its eyes, wondering if it was Peascod in animal form, but it had soulful, purple eyes.

"What are you?"

"That's a plimikin." Maemtri's voice answered. She wore a long green dress covered with an paisley apron that could've come from the Vera Bradley collection.

"Wait. How did we get to Quicksilver?" Keelie looked around. Yep, same place. The basket of hissing roaches sat on the flimsy table, and Henry the lion snoozed in front of the fireplace.

Maemtri's eyes followed her gaze. She leaped over to the basket and pushed it back to a safer location. "Don't want a repeat of that tragic accident. You aren't in Quicksilver, Keliel. We're in Under-the-Hill right now, a dangerous place to be if you don't know where you are."

The plimikin jumped up on a counter to a glass jar filled with what looked like chocolate chip cookies. He removed one, then stopped and eyed Keelie. "You want one? They're very good." He plunked the cookie into his mouth and screwed the lid back onto the cookie jar.

"No thanks." The talking blue-furred monkey's slimy hand was an appetite killer. Plus, the no-eating rule probably applied here, too.

Herne noticed and laughed. "You're safe here, Keelie."

Maemtri dismissed him with a wave of her hand. "He's right. And I'm glad you're back. I wanted to tell you something when we last met, but that dreadful cat knocked over my cockroaches and caused a scene. I knew your Grandmother Josephine." She paused, choosing her words carefully. "People have been keeping secrets from you—for what purpose I know not, except that elves have always distrusted the fae. Your grandmother is one of those secrets. I want to tell you about her."

The world was getting smaller and smaller, but weirder and weirder. This fairy woman who rescued familiars knew her kind-hearted Grandmother Jo?

"What secrets? I recently learned that she had fae blood. But my grandmother never left Los Angeles—did you visit her there?" Keelie asked.

Herne raised his eyebrows at Keelie as he removed his cloak and draped it over a coat tree. The coat tree exited the room, its little feet tapping on the wooden floor.

"I have a lot to tell you. Have a seat?" Maemtri gestured toward a velvet sofa with a carved backboard. Keelie sat down, sinking into the cushions. Herne lowered himself beside her and sank against her. Then Keelie grabbed the back of the sofa and pulled herself up. The wood sang at her touch. It came from the Under-the-Hill forest, and she saw the image of the first forest. In the distance, a stooped and wrinkled woman was standing underneath a tall tree that grew as high as the clouds, its roots sinking all the way into the Earth.

It was the Mother Tree. The old woman turned to Keelie and spoke, her voice whispering like dry dirt falling on rock. *Knowing your roots is important to help you determine your true home.*

Plummeting back to the here and now, Keelie looked at Herne, who was still slumped into the Victorian cushion, looking relaxed and talking to Maemtri as if they were old friends catching up. No one had noticed that she'd zoned out. She didn't know what that had been about, but it reminded her that Maemtri hadn't yet told her about Grandmother Josephine, and she needed to turn the conversation back to that topic. Maybe that was what the old woman in the vision meant.

Herne looked at her with concern. "Are you okay? You seemed lost in thought."

"Just wondering about where Maemtri saw Grandma Jo."

Maemtri smiled at her. "You are mistaken when you say your grandmother never left Los Angeles. She was born to the High Court, and she was a friend of mine." At Keelie's look of surprise, she continued. "Your grandmother was a fairy who fell in love with an injured mortal man she'd healed. Healing was her gift, but Queen Vania grew angry when she heard that a fairy had fallen in love with a human. It had happened too often, and if too many fae mated with humans, soon there would be no pureblood fae."

Blood pounded in Keelie's head. If Grandma Jo was pureblood fae, that meant that Keelie had way more than just a little drop of fae blood. She fought the urge to jump up and scream "no way." Rubbing at her eyes to stop the burning, she turned away from Herne's inquisitive eyes.

Herne leaned in closer, interested. "I've never heard this tale. Keelie, you have many secrets."

Secrets Keelie hadn't known, either.

Maemtri snapped her fingers at Herne. "I'm not finished." The Lord of Nature pressed his lips together and frowned.

"Queen Vania decided to make an example of your grandmother," Maemtri continued.

"How?" Keelie asked.

"She turned your grandmother into a brownie. She banished her from the High Court."

Banished. Was that how Gran ended up in California? "What exactly is a brownie? I don't think we're talking about a chocolate dessert or a little girls' service club," Keelie said.

"It's a wrinkled creature that likes to do housework. Brownies are transformed creatures who have displeased the queen at one time." Herne pushed himself into a straighter position. "Under-the-Hill is crowded with them."

Keelie gasped. "That's horrible. My grandmother didn't look like that."

"The meaner ones are boggarts. They are usually wizards or witches who have abused their power," Maemtri said. "They're very mean to their familiars."

The plimikin ran to Maemtri and hid its face in her skirts. "Once they've been transformed, I rescue the familiars." She patted the blue-furred monkey, and Henry the lion stretched and came to her too, rubbing his big face against her knees.

Guiltily, Keelie thought of Knot. Maybe she shouldn't call him snotball anymore, or push him out of bed when he licked her hair at night. She just wanted her cat back. She shook herself. What was she thinking? Two minutes in the naughty cat's presence and all this love talk would vanish from her head.

"Willow, whom you knew as Josephine, was distraught,"

Maemtri said. "Even as a brownie she mourned her human, whom she loved so. Linsa took pity on her and transformed her into a human, too. She'd been a brownie long enough to be affected by brownie ways, but even as a human she kept her fairy healing power. Such transformations are tricky that way." She paused. "One thing was certain, however. As a human, Willow would live a human lifespan. But she chose it anyway, to be with that boy. No one expected her to have children, and that the fae blood would breed true."

Keelie was stunned at the news. She'd struggled with not knowing how long she would live, but her grandmother had chosen the shorter life for love. It was as if Keelie and Grandma Jo were living parallel lives with some paradoxical twists. Luckily, she hadn't inherited her grandmother's compulsive need to organize closets, but apparently Josephine—Willow—had been a Healer, so maybe that's where she got her own satisfaction at healing trees. Her fairy past, working with her elven present.

Queen Vania was something else, though. She'd transformed her Grandmother Jo into a wrinkled and pitiful creature because she wanted to make an example of someone. And now she needed Keelie's help to get out of trouble. Indignant, Keelie clenched her fists, and the skin on her chest felt hot. "How dare Vania ask me for help? Doesn't she know who I am?" Dad was going to get an earful.

Herne gave the familiar's shop owner a stern look. "Oh, she knows. I suspect she didn't want anyone telling you about your grandmother."

Keelie lifted her chin. "I'm glad Maemtri did."

"Vania still needs your help," Maemtri said, her warm eyes holding Keelie's. "The realms all need to cooperate, if we're to solve the problem of the rift and the wild magic."

"That's what I've heard." Keelie's head was still spinning in reaction to what she'd just learned.

"You've seen what has happened, and it will only get worse," Maemtri said.

"Leaking magic and a rift aren't your only problems," a booming voice bellowed from the fireplace. The rocks that backed it were grinding aside, exposing a drafty opening.

Herne chuckled, and Maemtri didn't seem to find anything strange when King Gneiss appeared in the fireplace like it was a front door. He stepped over the crackling logs, then wiped his feet carefully on the rug before stretching back to his full four feet right in front of her eyes. Long gray hair flowed from under the quicksilver crown on his furrowed head, an interesting look with his dirt-encrusted clothes. "Goblins be yer problem, and they're growing stronger."

Keelie felt a chill in her blood, and pictured the armored goblins in Big Nugget.

Herne straightened, and bowed to the King of the Dwarves. "Tell me something I don't already know."

The king's hard expression turned even more stony. "When the shaft collapsed in the rift, we discovered that wild goblins have been mining the quicksilver, the dirty devils."

Herne started in surprise and his face twisted with anger.

"My goblins are forbidden in the mines. Are you certain that they are not mine?"

King Gneiss nodded grimly. "These are wild ones, Green Man. And they seem to be banding together."

The plimikin pushed its face deeper into Maemtri's skirts at the mention of wild goblins.

"This does not bode well." Herne's mouth pursed as he stalked back and forth. "Wild goblins have always been few and solitary. Last one I've heard about was chased from the Redwood Forest many years ago."

Keelie started at the mention of the redwoods. "If it's the one I think you mean, he died there, and poisoned one of the great trees. And another came. I saw him."

Herne and King Gneiss stared at her. Maemtri had gone pale.

"Goblins in the redwoods?" Herne looked at Maemtri. "Did you know of this?"

Maemtri shook her head mutely.

"Norzan was with us in the Redwood Forest. Didn't he tell the High Court?" Keelie had grown uneasy at their reaction. Maybe the elves should have been more worried. Then it struck her that they had been, and that was why Grandmother Keliatiel had stayed behind. The most powerful elf on the continent was guarding the most ancient forest.

"There's more. The goblins are above, in the human town." Maemtri patted the plimikin.

King Gneiss growled. "Yes. They are breeding in the cities, where they live off the debris of humankind."

Keelie nodded. "I saw them dancing as we drove through Big Nugget."

"Yet they have not entered the forest," Herne said, looking troubled. "Peascod was my eyes and ears in the mortal world, but I am no longer surprised that he did not speak of it. Let us go investigate." He whistled sharply and the hall tree trotted into the room. He snatched his cloak off the hook.

"You should not trust that masked ninny." King Gneiss' eyes were as hard as flint. "Always prancing and singing, but behind the jokes and juggling he is cruel. Tell him Maemtri, what he did to your cat."

Maemtri's eyes filled with tears. "Poor Purrington. He was a trickster, too, but he didn't deserve such a sad end."

Keelie's heart clenched. She did not want to hear this story. "Peascod killed your cat?" She turned to Herne. "Didn't you suspect? Haven't you heard any stories about him?"

"The dark fae are full of trickiness and cruelty, but we don't hurt each other much. And we have centuries to heal." Herne sighed. "Peascod is a traitor to me, but he seemed no different from some of my darker subjects, the ones who relish blood as much as laughter."

Keelie resisted the urge to roll her eyes. "You're mad mostly because he's tricked you." Typical.

Herne glowered at her. "Do not forget, sweeting, that you are here because you've involved me in your game. You don't seem very grateful at the moment."

"If Peascod is behind the wild goblins' presence, where

did he get such magic? It would take great power to hide it from you," King Gneiss said. "Perhaps as much as an origin's point would muster."

"What's an origin's point?" Keelie asked.

"The vortex in Fairy is an origin's point. A new one would be impossible to create without access to my library and books of magic. But Peascod had that access." Herne seemed to have grown taller.

"An origin's point to Under-the-Hill," Maemtri said, voice squeaking. "He could control the magic coming to this realm."

Peascod in control of the Under-the-Hill magic. Keelie had a sudden vision of everyone in Under-the-Hill bowing to Peascod's warped ideas. Surprised, she realized that she was offended, and that her indignation arose from a feeling of kinship with the dark fae, one that she hadn't been able to understand before. Now she had her answer. Their blood flowed through her veins, too, and explained why Under-the-Hill felt like home.

No one messed with her home. "How do we stop him?" she asked.

"We find him and destroy him." Herne clenched his fist. "Keelie, come with me back to Grey Mantle." He turned to King Gneiss. "I will send trolls to help you secure your borders against the goblins."

Keelie clutched her rose quartz. She wanted to be out of here before the trolls came.

Gneiss bowed his head and began to shrink until he was small enough to fit through the fireplace. "I shall return to my people and my mines. We'll take care of the goblin nest we found, and await the trolls."

Herne had draped his cloak around his shoulders as the fireplace rocks reformed themselves into a solid wall. "Come with me, Keliel." He held out his hand. "Your work starts here."

"But I still have questions."

"Later. We have pressing work to do."

The tension in his voice told her how concerned he was. Maybe almost scared. She put her hand into his, surprised anew at the slight shock of his skin against hers. She really didn't have a choice. It was the only way to stop Peascod.

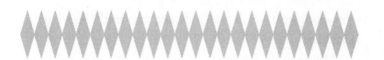

nineteen

The shop vanished and its animal noises and smells faded, turning to bright light and the putrid smell of garbage. Keelie blinked, clutching Herne's hand. She didn't like feeling vulnerable while her eyes adjusted and drew closer to Herne's warmth, wondering where they were that smelled so foul.

Gradually, she saw a sooty brick wall and a big green industrial dumpster. Above the dumpster was a row of steel windows, the glass painted over from within. The sky above was pale blue. Keelie let go of Herne and took a step toward the dumpster, which had a sticker that read "Big Nugget Hauling."

"We're in Big Nugget!"

Herne cursed. "This is not where I meant to take us."

"What is that smell? It's not coming from the dumpster."

"Goblins. Keep your voice down." Herne walked quickly to the mouth of the alley and looked up and down the narrow street outside.

Keelie shrank back against the peeling paint on the old brick wall. She remembered the teeth on the goblins who had danced around the dark maypole.

She jumped as a loud clang came from the dumpster. But it wasn't a goblin. Knot was glaring at her from the dumpster's lid—he'd leaped onto it from the roof of the building. He hunched on the edge of the lid and hissed. "Yeow had me worried."

Keelie was glad to see him, but she didn't want to show it. "Herne took me Under-the Hill. How did you know I'd be here?"

A bright light zoomed overhead, like a flicked match with a purpose. It turned and dive-bombed the cat like a tiny missile and he swatted at it, his brow furrowed in annoyance. "Pixies. Meow called in lots of favors to get them to look for yeow." He glared at her. "Yeow owes me for four days of swatting."

The pixies barely registered as Knot's words sank in. "We've been gone four days?" Keelie whirled to face Herne. "Why didn't you warn me?"

He shrugged. "Don't complain, sweetheart. I wanted you

to see Under-the-Hill and speak to Maemtri." He glanced back down the road to the left. His shoulders tensed. "We don't have time to argue. The goblins will scent us soon."

"A month in Fairy, and now four days in Under-the-Hill. My dad must be frantic." Keelie glowered at Herne. "And I'm not your sweetheart."

He smiled mischievously, eyes twinkling. "Not yet."

Herne was so full of himself. Keelie knew she had to steel herself against his charms and stay focused on a resolution for the rift.

Knot jumped to the ground and stalked to the mouth of the alley. He looked where Herne had been looking. For a second he was very still, and then his ears flattened against his skull and the fur along his spine stood on end.

Keelie hurried to Knot's side. The streets seemed to be deserted. "What do you see? Is Dad here yet?" Reminding Herne she had a father might deter the nature god.

"Your father is not here," Herne said. "I would've sensed his presence by now, as would the goblins."

"Can they sense me?" Keelie asked in a low whisper.

Herne shook his head. "You confuse them. We need to go."

"Why can't you stop them?" Keelie wanted to know. He was the all-powerful Herne. "Can't you control all goblins?"

"Someone else controls them, but I can try to sway them."

Keelie and Knot followed Herne, slinking from one doorway to the next on the street. She felt exposed, as if every goblin could see her, and her ears ached from listening for the jangling of the bells on Peascod's jester hat.

Knot hurried at her side. "Yeow be careful."

"I really need to call Dad, but I left the phone with Sean. Is he nearby?" She looked at an empty playground across the street.

"Will you two keep quiet?" Herne said through gritted teeth. "Keelie, follow me closely. If goblins attack, go up. They're afraid of heights."

They scooted from store front to store front, resting in the doorway of a crystal shop. Herne pointed out a steel ladder on the side of the building.

Keelie nodded, wishing she knew of a stone or crystal that served as goblin repellent. She was definitely going to be asking Sir Davey the next chance she got. If there was a next chance. She racked her brain, trying to remember the goblin charms from the Compendium.

She'd noticed some stray, scrubby prairie grass growing next to the wooden storefront, and it reminded her of the hay-fever charm, which she could strengthen by infusing it with Earth magic. It might give them some form of defense. While it wouldn't repel the goblins, it would annoy them and maybe slow them down. She tugged and pulled the clump of grass up by the roots.

"What are you doing?" Herne asked, his brow creased with worry. "You'll alert the goblins to our whereabouts if you use the magic."

Keelie thought she noticed beads of sweat forming on his forehead. "It's Earth magic, and I need some way to fight them off," she told him, clutching the grass tighter in her hands. "You're stronger, and you should be able to stop the goblins. I mean, they're from Under-the-Hill, aren't they? I don't understand."

Herne lowered his face and studied the ground as if he sought the answer in the dirt. He looked at her. His expression serious. "Something is wresting my power from me. I am weak. Very weak."

"What? You're a nature god. You can't be weak. You've transported us from Under-the-Hill to here." Keelie refused to wrap her mind around the possibility that Herne couldn't stop the goblins.

"I meant to take you to Grey Mantle. My magic hasn't seemed as strong lately. I thought the grief I felt at Linsa's death was the reason, but it wasn't until we were in the alley near the maypole that I realized how frail I truly am. I have not felt this way in a millennium."

"How could you not know?" Keelie asked. "The dark fae depend on you for protection."

"I know. I must find a solution, and quickly—it seems the more wild magic escapes, the more fragile I become. I wonder if this is how humans feel." He opened and closed his hand in a fist, as if trying to find his lost strength.

Knot sniffed the air around him. "Meow goblins come."

Keelie's back stiffened with fear as she gripped the green grass tighter. If she couldn't pull on a thread of Earth magic, she would summon the trees to help her. She reached out to them, but something blocked her communication again; it was a stilted consciousness, dull and heavy. *Dim-witted* was the impression she received.

Herne turned around and stared at something farther down the street. "I think we should move on."

Keelie recoiled when she saw the goblin. He looked just like Tavyn did when he exposed his true nature, shedding the skin of the handsome elf he'd shown the world. Maybe Tavyn really was here with his kind.

The goblin carried a rusty and blood-stained battle ax. He stepped closer and sniffed the air, and his eyes widened when he caught the scent of prey. He knew she was here.

Knot puffed up, his fur maxed out, his claws exposed, ready to do battle.

Maybe Keelie was out of her element, but she couldn't count on Herne to blast the goblin to pieces. She was going to have to go ninja and take it on herself. The goblin was as tall as she was, but she could grab his greasy dreadlocks and let Knot scratch him up. Knot lifted his head and nodded, understanding.

The goblin approached, raising his ax as if about to chop wood. Just as Keelie and Knot were about to charge the smelly creature, Herne's hand shot past Keelie's shoulder and snapped the goblin's neck with a loud crack. Keelie shivered. The goblin's eyes rolled up in his head and he flopped to the ground like a dead fish.

Herne collapsed against her. Keelie held him up, leaning against the building to support his weight. Despite the danger, she felt a special thrill being so close to him.

"We need help, Knot, but I think the best thing is to get Herne to a safe spot and then you can go. I'll watch over him."

"Neow way. Goblin prophecy says you're the target. Meow stay, yeow go to dragon and elves." Knot blinked up at the sky and a swarm of bright lights came down and landed all over Keelie's arms and shoulders, like cordless Christmas lights. "Pixies will watch and tell."

The pixies suddenly shot up in a fireworks display and swarmed into a nearby tree. Some help they turned out to be.

"Knot, I don't think that's going to work."

The cat growled, and his tail twitched back and forth like a furry cord. He could've been sending the pixies a telepathic message.

They came back down, and with them a flurry of flying sticks. The *bhata* had come to Keelie's aid. The tiny stick fairies gathered under Herne's arm and lifted him from her.

Herne grimaced. "I really don't think this is necessary."

"I don't think you have much of a choice. They want to help you." Keelie felt a strong wave of magic flowing from the *bhata* to Herne, who was able to stumble down the street.

"I hope this doesn't ruin the image you had of me as a charming, all-knowing being," he joked weakly.

"I don't think you need to worry about me. It's them." Keelie looked behind her. More goblins had come and were gathered around the dead one, licking their lips. The *bhata* swarmed over Keelie and a surge of strength flowed through her.

The little fae helped her while they helped Herne. They made their way to a pharmacy at a place where three roads intersected. Keelie propped Herne against the shop's doorway.

He leaned against the wooden frame, his face pale and his mouth drawn in a straight line as he fought off some pain.

"Knot, keep guard."

He saluted with his tail. "Meow."

Inside the pharmacy, Keelie saw a lunch counter with old doughnuts and pies under glass. Her stomach rumbled with hunger. She hadn't eaten or slept in a long time; no wonder the fossilized treats were looking good.

A piercing shriek behind them signaled that the goblins were after them. Fear pulsed through Keelie's heart, and she inhaled deeply to calm herself and salvage any remaining courage. They were doomed. There was nowhere to go.

"We'll have to run." She turned to Herne.

He shook his head. "I'm too weak. The *bhata* can't lend me their strength anymore."

More waves of power flowed from the *bhata*, and their berry eyes glowed with adoration. They smiled as Herne absorbed more from them. Then Keelie watched in horror as the stick creatures came apart, their twig-and-moss components bouncing to the ground.

"Can you summon the trees?" Herne whispered, hoarsely. "I cannot." He was fading fast.

"I'll try," Keelie said. But the trees gave no response.

"If I can get back to Under-the-Hill, I will be restored. You must mend the rift, Keelie, and cut off the goblins' source of power."

More shrieks and ululating cries, like claws on chalkboards, rent the air.

Knot jumped out and ran ahead, bottlebrush tail at full mast.

"I'll help you walk." Keelie pulled Herne's arm over her shoulder and stepped out of the doorway just as the gathering goblins ran toward them.

"Keelie, get out of the way!" Sean was standing in the street, sword drawn, with Sir Davey at his side holding a shorter but deadly looking blade. Both were in full armor, at the head of a group of armed elves and dwarves.

"We have to get Keelie and Herne to safety," Sean barked to Sir Davey.

Keelie reached down to grab more grass growing from a crack in the sidewalk. She gave it a mighty yank and then said the words that formed the hay-fever charm. The first goblin started to sneeze and veered away from her, followed by others. Sean had enough time to reach them, crowding them back into the doorway and protecting them as the two armies met with a clang of weapons and the screams of dying goblins.

Keelie reached for a rock and threw it, breaking the window of the pharmacy. A *bhata* climbed up onto her arm and touched her face. She felt warmth and energy flowing from the fae creature. With the extra magical boost, Keelie was able to haul Herne inside.

Sean followed. "What are you doing?"

"This is not necessary," Herne said. "Just leave me here, and I'll be able to take on a hundred rogue goblins."

"You heard him." Sean motioned his head at Herne. "He can take on a hundred goblins."

"He's been zapped by something and he doesn't have any power," Keelie said.

Sean frowned at the horned man.

"You can't keep a secret." Herne scowled at Keelie.

"Let's head to the roof." Sean reached for Herne and pulled him over his shoulder. He climbed the stairs, the forest god's antlers rattling as they scraped the wall. Keelie blocked the door with old furniture and then followed them.

The flat rooftop was a patchwork of shingles lined with roofing tar, surrounded by a low wall. From below came the clash of metal and the screams of the injured.

"I need to join the others," Sean said, releasing Herne. "Stay here and stay out of sight."

Keelie didn't want him to go. "Stay with me—you'll be safe. Or I'll come with you."

He grabbed her shoulders and kissed her. "You don't know how to use a sword."

"I took lessons. You practiced with me!"

"Which means you know just enough to get yourself killed." Sean glanced at Herne. "I know you'd cheerfully join the battle, Keelie—you're fearless. But you have a greater job to do, and you'd best do it from here."

"Herne said that goblins hate heights." Keelie's heart pounded at the thought of Sean getting hurt, but he was right. She had to stay, and his job was down below.

He left, and Knot, grown to human size, helped her block the rooftop door with an old metal cooler. Herne eased himself over and sat on it, adding his weight to the blocked door.

The battle below looked bad for their side, as goblins poured in from every street. So far, none had looked up and seen her. Knot pulled out his sword and nodded to Keelie, then leaped into a nearby tree and scooted down to join the battle.

Keelie watched the fighting, horrified. Sean and Knot—she loved them both, and they were in great danger.

Behind her, Herne spoke. "Keelie, look."

He stood, weak but without help, as hundreds of glowing lights surrounded him. They landed on his skin until he looked like a Christmas display.

"The pixies will lend me their power. I will return with an army." Herne and his pixie escorts winked out of sight.

Knot, back to normal-cat size, scrabbled to the top of the roof and walked toward her on his hind legs, picking bits of goblin out of his teeth.

Minutes later, the door to the roof started to crash in and Keelie mentally prepared herself for a goblin attack. When the door finally banged open, she was relieved to see it was Sean.

His bloodied face was tense. "Where's Herne?"

"He left." Keelie didn't try to explain.

"Good," Sean said. "We need to get you out of here. The town is overrun by goblins. The elves are returning to the village to regroup for another attack. I've come to lead you out."

"Where's Ermentrude?" Keelie asked. She hoped the dragon would appear and flame the goblins.

"I don't know."

Keelie stumbled to the edge of the roof. She'd been so worried about the elves and dwarves and Herne that she hadn't thought about Dad, but he was in danger, too. *If she lost Dad.* She couldn't even think about it. She wanted to fight the goblins, but she had no power. Everywhere she looked the goblins lurked behind cars and in doorways, or marched boldly in the middle of the street. From the safety of this building, all she could do was watch.

Battle shrieks from the goblins drew her attention. A small group of elves was surrounded.

Then a roar filled the valley, and a hot wind smelling of Juicy Fruit scented the air. A dark shape flew overhead, and Keelie felt the buoyancy of hope lift her for the first time since she and Herne had popped into Big Nugget.

Ermentrude had arrived.

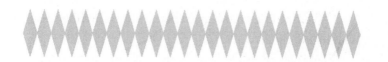

twenty

Ermentrude swooped down over the valley, wings outspread like two scaly green awnings that caught the air and made her soar, her long reptilian neck outstretched and her mouth trailing smoke and flame. She roared and attacked the goblins, flame rushing from outstretched jaws lined with jagged teeth. Oily smoke rose from the patch where the goblins had been.

The great dragon bellowed in triumph, wheeled up, then paused in midair to attack again. She arched her neck and took a breath, her great sides inflating, ready to do her flamethrower trick again.

"We win! Dragon to the rescue!" Keelie grabbed Sean and kissed him.

He kissed her back, hard, then broke off their embrace and pointed to the street below. "We haven't won yet. Look down there."

Keelie looked, and saw the loping, skittering shapes of fleeing goblins racing toward the forest.

"We'll have to chase them all down and make sure they don't regroup to attack." Sean headed toward the stairs.

Keelie froze as she saw a lone figure making its way against the tide of goblins. "Peascod."

Sean came to her side and stared at her. "That power-mad jerk really is here? I thought he was human. Why is he with the goblins?"

Below, Peascod leaped onto an abandoned car's roof and screamed out the goblin battle cry. Oh good. Now Ermentrude would spot him and turn him into a little pile of ash. But Peascod turned his masked face up toward them, pointed, and laughed. "Elves," he shouted, "you have met your doom. No dragon can vanquish us." He turned his arm, aiming his finger at Ermentrude.

She vanished, leaving a small red-haired figure plummeting through the sky.

Sean cried out, "No!"

Horror made Keelie's breath stop. Time itself seemed to stop as she opened her tree sense. She reached out to anything that would answer, and the branches of the surrounding trees began to wave madly. A swarm of *feithid daoine* flew toward the falling figure, a dark cloud outlined in light by pixies. The swarm reached Ermentrude and surrounded her as well, slowing her fall. Keelie did a frantic mental review of the Compendium's pages, trying to think of anything that would save the dragon. She was sure that in human form, Ermentrude would die from falling such a great distance.

Shouts in the street signaled that Peascod had rallied the goblins, who returned to attack again. She felt Sean leave her side and head down the stairs, but Keelie couldn't take her eyes off Ermentrude and her fae escort. She ignored everything around her, concentrating; she'd thrown her power before. Keelie imagined the air turning thick, like pudding, every molecule suspended. Her right hand closed around the Queen Aspen's charred heart and she stretched her left hand out, as if to grab Ermentrude from the sky.

The small, falling figure suddenly stopped, hanging suspended in the air, unconscious, her red hair like tangled yarn. She was surrounded by a cloud of unmoving *feithid daoine* and pixies, which looked like pepper specks around her. A breeze blew by and the floating group drifted along with it.

Shouts came up from the streets as the elves and dwarves reacted to the sight.

Keelie stared, both pleased and horrified. She'd saved Ermentrude, but how could she get her down from there? As she watched, her magic broke apart and the dragon and her fae escort fell in slow motion, like deflated helium balloons, to land out of sight on the other side of one of the buildings.

Several elves ran in that direction, and from the concerned

looks on their faces, Keelie knew that the landing hadn't been light.

"Impressive, little one." Herne suddenly stood beside her, looking restored. His great antlers branched skyward, as broad as his shoulders.

"They're hurt." She wasn't sure about the *feithid daoine*, but Ermentrude must have hit with a big thump. "How are you?"

"Still somewhat weak. I put all my power into my personal appearance to show the goblins that I am here."

The sound of fighting drifted up and Keelie ran back to the waist-high wall around the roof's edge. Below, a thin line of elves was battling the goblins, bright swords flashing. Her heart thumped as she saw that Sean was with them.

A trumpet sounded behind the pharmacy and more elves ran to join their brothers. Keelie gasped. The elf leading the charge was her dad. She'd never seen him wear armor, but now he strode, tall and fierce, with a long sword in his right hand and a shield that was emblazoned with a single green tree strapped to his left foreman.

Dad! She sent a telepathic call to her father. This close, it couldn't fail.

Stay there, Keelie. Can you distract the goblins so that we can get Ermentrude out of here?

Keelie looked around wildly, wondering what she could do to get the goblins' attention. She'd seen trees walk before, dragging their roots out of the earth to shuffle forward. It had been a frightening sight, maybe scary enough to freak out a goblin. She called on the trees, and they responded. But they weren't strong enough to move.

Keelie reached for the wild magic that billowed and eddied in the wind like drifts of pollen. She grabbed up as much of it as she could, pulling it through herself, using her body to funnel the magic to the trees. The pines across from the pharmacy began to vibrate, their leaves shaking violently, but they didn't walk. Instead, slender figures stepped out of their trunks.

"Dryads." Herne's voice was husky with emotion. "You've called forth the dryads."

The elves and goblins stopped fighting for a second to stare at the creatures.

Dad turned his face up to Keelie, clearly astonished.

The dryads lifted their pale arms and screamed, then rushed the goblins.

"They'll get hurt," Keelie cried. "What have I done?"

"Magic," whispered Herne. "They'll come to no harm. Watch."

She felt the green magic anew, coming from the rushing horde of dryads, and realized that the weirdness she'd felt in the forest had come from them. They were neither male nor female and were only vaguely human-shaped, with arms and legs and torsos. But they were scaring the goblins.

The ground shook, and Keelie grabbed at the black-tarred roof to hold on, but this was not an earthquake. Below, the trees lifted their roots and started to move, using their great limbs to smash the goblins against the buildings and into the street, guided by the dryads. The elves followed warily, swords at the ready, shields lifted.

Keelie shifted her vision, looking at the scene through tree sight, and watched the wild magic flow around the dryads and seem to do their bidding. The goblins fled, unable to fight the trees.

As soon as the fight got to the end of the block, Keelie ran down the stairs and into the street, Herne and Knot behind her. Outside, the Healer elves were performing first aid on the fallen. The dryads had all disappeared but one, who seemed to be waiting for Keelie.

"Viran and your grandmother send greetings," the dryad said, its voice papery and thin. "They heard your call for help, as we did. We have answered."

Viran, the old tree shepherd of the Redwood Forest, had grown weary of life outside of the woods. After the goblin threat there had passed, he had melded with one of the Great Trees and was now helping Grandmother Keliatiel, the new tree shepherd of the redwoods.

"You heard them all the way from California?" Keelie asked the dryad. That was some reception.

The slender figure nodded what seemed to be its head. "I will remain, to represent the tree spirits at the meeting of the Councils."

Keelie looked at Knot, puzzled.

One of the Healer elves turned to her. "We couldn't find you and called upon the dwarves and the dragon to help us. We meet tonight at the Council building."

"The dark fae will be there too," Herne promised. He

turned to Keelie and bowed. "You are indeed a warrior." He vanished.

A green tickle in her mind told Keelie that the Mother Tree would be there tonight as well. Maybe not in person, but seeing through Keelie's eyes.

The Mother Tree. Keelie wondered where the withered old woman kept her roots. Was she part of the Mother Tree itself, perhaps a more physical manifestation of the tree spirits Keelie had met in the past? Or was she like a dryad, the creatures who lived in the trees? "Will Queen Vania come too?" she asked.

"She has not answered the call." The elf on the ground moaned and the Healer elf's attention turned back to him.

Keelie ran to see if Dad and Sean were unharmed. Her racing heart slowed when she saw Dad holding up an elven woman as her leg got bandaged. He seemed relieved to see her, too. He nodded at the Healer elves and stood, just in time for her hugs and kisses.

"Where were you for four days, after you returned from Fairy?" he asked. "I heard it rumored you were Under-the-Hill, but that cannot be true." Keelie's blush told him it was.

Dad pulled her away from the medic's area. "Are you mad? I send you with a warrior and your fae guardian, and you leave them behind to help Herne, alone? And what about Elia? She bears the hope of our forest, but she is alone among strangers in the Northwoods. These elves have no love for her."

"I noticed. But it wasn't my fault, Dad. You don't say no to a forest god."

Dad didn't seem to hear. "Dariel is upset—he abandoned his forest to come here to his wife's aid and found her alone in the elven village. Do you know how often a unicorn leaves his forest? Never."

"Elia was always with us in the beginning," Keelie said. "But I tried to ditch her when we went to the Quicksilver—" Oops. She realized her error when Dad turned hot red.

"You did what? You took Elia? To the High Court?" He tugged on his long hair, eyes wild. "Where's Davey? Why didn't he stop her?"

"Davey's related to King Gneiss, the King of the Dwarves. Did you know that?"

"Don't change the subject. Once you step into Fairy, you cannot control your fate. How did Elia come free of the place? What was the price?"

"I'll tell you everything, Dad. Knot came with me." Keelie told him about the rift and trying to mend it, and when he started to get angry, she told him about the Mother Tree. He seemed to relax. A little.

Miszrial appeared at their side. "We've counted one hundred and fifty dead goblins. Many have escaped."

Dad frowned. "And our wounded?"

"Twenty wounded, two dead. The wounds are mostly bites."

"That's good, right?" Keelie looked from one to the other.

"Not good," Dad said. "Goblin bites fester quickly."

"I'm not surprised," Keelie said. "They're so gross."

Dad straightened and looked behind her. "How could

you allow her out of your sight? She went to Under-the-Hill with Herne. Alone."

She turned to where Sean stood, his face pale, and rolled her eyes. "Guys, I'm right here. I'm in one piece, virtue intact. And we need Herne's help as much as he needs ours. You sent me here to get us to work together and I was doing my darndest. If you want to get mad at someone, get mad at Queen Vania. She does not play well with others."

"We'll address that at the Alliance Summit." Dad looked at Sean. "We're not done speaking. Don't lose her again."

Knot walked by, once more in his regular cat form, and Dad glared at him. "You, too."

Knot purred and rubbed up against his leg.

A Healer elf came running up. "Ermentrude's awake and asking for the tree shepherd."

Keelie and Dad turned to her, both answering, "Yes?" Dad looked at Keelie. "My turn. Go get cleaned up. Take her to Grey Mantle, Sean, and don't lose her."

"Come on, Keelie." Sean began walking away, his hand on the hilt of his sword, as he did when he was upset.

She ran after him, matching his pace. "We can't go back to the village yet. I need to find out where Peascod went. He's planning something, Sean. He wants to defeat Herne, and Herne's weak enough that he might lose. He's seriously weak."

Sean stopped abruptly and turned to her. "Everyone is meeting in Grey Mantle. Herne promised to be there. You should let other people help now. This is not the mission you were sent to accomplish. It's much bigger, and you can't do everything alone."

Sean was right. Herne would be at Grey Mantle; in the meantime, she could talk to Ermentrude. The old dragon might have an idea about how to stop the leaking magic without involving Vania.

In the treetops above, Keelie sensed the presence of dark fae. When she lifted her head, afraid of what she'd see, she was relieved that it was only a *bhata* waving to her. It had something in its sticklike hand that looked like a small present. The *bhata* moved to where a large limb branched off into smaller ones, and it pointed at another creature in the tree.

"Knot, you can't eat the *bhata*," Keelie said. Knot swished his orange tail, eyes fixed on the little creature. "I think it has a package for me."

"See, what did I tell you?" Sean said, waving his hands. "What are you talking about?"

"Knot, come back down here."

"Meow." Knot jumped down and stomped over, sitting down next to Sean.

Keelie held out her hand and the *bhata* climbed down to her. Clasped in its little stick fingers was a tiny red book. It held it out to Keelie, and she accepted it.

"Thank you." She studied the tiny book, then felt a tingle in her fingertips. The book began to grow. Its binding lengthened and its cover widened until Keelie recognized the title.

It was the dragon magic book. A piece of parchment

was stuck in between the pages. She pulled it out, and read the strange, rune-like handwriting.

You left this behind. Thought you might need it.

Keelie smiled, then frowned when she lifted her head and saw Sean scowling at her. "It's a book on dragons," she explained. "To help me understand Ermentrude."

Sean arched an eyebrow. "From Herne?"

Keelie nodded slowly, dreading Sean's reaction to that piece of news, although it was kind of cool that he was jealous.

"Let's go." Sean stormed away.

Angry about his elven stubbornness, Keelie stomped after him and grabbed him by the arm.

He stopped, but wouldn't look at her. "What?"

"You wanted me to be honest."

"I want you to be smart, too. And Keelie, encouraging that dark beast to befriend you is not wise."

He said "befriend" as if it were a bad word. He turned to look at her then, and she saw the hurt and fear in his eyes. Then he hurried off.

"Mmm, mmm. That is one hunk of handsome elf flesh. If I were you, I'd hang onto him. He's got a good heart, and a lot to learn, but it would be fun to teach him." Ermentrude was leaning against a nearby wall, her cane at her side. She winked at Keelie. "I heard old Herne is sweet on you."

"He asked me to be his consort, but I told him I'm too young."

"I notice you didn't tell him no. And for the record, Sean is right."

Knot padded up to the Keelie, but stopped, his back arched, when he saw the dragon.

"Yeow!" he hissed.

"You!" Ermentrude bellowed.

Keelie saw flames erupt from the dragon-woman's eyes and quickly stepped out of range. "Knot," she hissed, "run!"

Ermentrude closed her eyes and started to chant, then took a deep breath and exhaled. "It's a challenge to keep control over my temper, especially when sneaky cats get into my bag." She pasted on a false smile when she looked at Knot, her lips pursed as if she were biting down on her tongue. "Knot, the next time you want to play in my yarn, please ask me."

"You knit?" Keelie asked. That Knot had tangled her yarn was no surprise.

"Yes, I'm making a scarf, and when I changed colors and looked through my yarn bag, I found orange cat hair everywhere."

Knot turned his face away and whistled. He refused to look at Ermentrude.

"Stay out of her yarn," Keelie warned. She put the book under her arm.

Ermentrude's eyes widened when she noticed it. "What are you doing with a book on dragon magic?"

"Herne gave it to me." Keelie didn't want to offend the dragon, but there was no magic here except for the way the book had grown in her hand. She held it out. The spine read *Understanding Dragons*.

Keelie stared at it, confused. "The title used to be *Into the Minds of Dragons*."

"Magic is arbitrary between worlds. Objects can be one thing in Fairy or Under-the-Hill, and quite another on Earth," Ermentrude answered. "It's a handy book to have. Be careful with it." She puffed on her cigarette. "I'm flattered. You're wanting to know what makes me tick. When you're finished, I'd like to read it. Might help me communicate with my daughter."

Keelie wasn't sure she wanted to know Ermentrude's daughter. She pictured a girl like her friend Laurie, only scaly with long ropes of red hair, garlicky dragon breath, and a bad temper.

Miszrial came striding over, not seeming happy in her new role of errand girl. "You're wanted in a Council meeting. I told them that as soon as I found you, I'd bring you."

"I thought the meeting was tonight," Keelie said.

"This meeting is for the elves only," Miszrial replied.

"Then I don't know why you want me there."

Miszrial's lips thinned out. "Terciel warned us that you favor the fae, even though you are a Lord of the Forest's daughter."

Keelie reminded herself that, as the daughter of an elven lord, she needed to conduct herself with every bit of elven dignity that she could muster. For her father's sake.

She looked down at Knot. "Ready to go to the Council meeting?" She thought of Dad, and how he always had to trudge to meetings at all hours of the night and be a diplomat when dealing with prickly elves. Ruling the elves was at the bottom rung of her career wish list.

Knot shook his head. "Not meow again."

Her sentiments exactly. Council meetings were boring, and you couldn't leave early because it was considered rude. It never failed—as soon as a meeting started, she needed to go pee. She turned, hoping for a few words of support from Ermentrude, but the dragon was gone. Keelie tucked the book back under her arm. It would make for good reading during the boring parts of the Council meeting.

"Are you ready?" Miszrial was tapping her foot impatiently.

"Yes." Keelie watched Miszrial start up the road to Grey Mantle. "Is there a reference book on elves? If not, there should be. Maybe I'll write one. *The Human's Guide to Elves*."

"It's forbidden to tell humans about elves," Miszrial said stiffly.

"Right. And it's forbidden for elves to have a sense of humor, too." Keelie trotted after her. She looked back at Knot. "You're coming, right?"

"Meow have to?"

"Yes, yeow has to."

"You're talking to your cat," Miszrial snapped.

Keelie smiled. "Yes, I'm talking to him. Don't you talk to your cat?"

"I don't have a cat."

"You need to get one. It would improve your personality."

"I don't see how having a cat would improve my personality. Everyone finds me charming."

Whoosh! Comment sailed over her head.

Dad was waiting for her at the foot of the stairs when she left her room in the lodge. Uncle Dariel and Elia were sharing a room, and Dad was bunking with Sean, so Keelie still had her own space.

Dad smiled appreciatively when he saw her. She was wearing her elven robes, which Grandmother had presented her with last winter, and she'd put on some eyeliner and lip gloss, stuff she never usually bothered with. The elves preferred a natural look, and today Keelie wanted to highlight her human side. The alliance included the dwarves, the dark fae, and the elves, but the humans got no say at all.

"You look lovely." Dad wore one of his elven robes, too; it was long and richly embroidered, with wide sleeves over a tight-sleeved jacket. His long hair was loose and hung down over his shoulders.

Keelie tripped over the hem of her robe and Dad caught her. "Oops." Her knee-high Ren Faire boots gave her steady footing, but the long clothes took some getting used to and she'd only worn them once before.

The forest was full of armed elves on the lookout for goblins. Keelie and Dad started up the path to the Council building. In the Dread Forest, the Council met in a stone circle, but the weather must get intense here in the winter. Keelie couldn't imagine meeting outside when it was twenty degrees below zero.

"I'm proud of the way you've handled yourself." Dad looked down at her and smiled. "It hasn't been easy, I know."

"Thanks, Dad. It's nice of you to think that, even if I did mess the rift up even more." Keelie lowered her voice although the path was deserted. "These elves are really un-friendly. You should see how they treat Elia. It broke her heart."

He sighed. "They fear change, and Elia married Dariel. A unicorn. They could probably forgive his past disgrace, but anything not elven … as you say, not so much."

"I guess that's what makes me the angriest. That they're mad at her because of Uncle Dariel."

"Queen Vania will not be here tonight," Dad said, abruptly changing the subject. "Do you think she would welcome another visit from you? Without Elia, of course."

"You'd be okay with that?" Keelie thought about the angry, powerful queen. "I'm not sure it would do any good."

Dad patted her back. "None of us knew how dangerous the situation was when we sent you, Keelie. We heard only that it was a disagreement between the elves and the High Court about how the humans were getting access to magic. We knew you would gain admittance in the High Court as no elf could."

"They let Sean and Elia come, though. No one stopped them." Keelie thought of the strange faire at Quicksilver. "We saw some weird things and met some really outrageous people. If you can call them people."

She stopped talking when they arrived at the Council building. Just off the main vestibule was a huge room. Long benches surrounded a fire pit, and the walls were covered by cloth hangings embroidered with elven symbols. Keelie felt a mix of elven and Earth magic around her and realized that the symbols held some sort of charm.

A group of elves in blue robes were seated around the circle. Elves were big on meeting circles. Maybe they needed some drums. They could pound out some good beats, although Keelie didn't think these uptight elves could produce a drum circle like the ones at the Ren Faires she'd attended. Maybe a keg of mead and some nachos would help.

She spotted a familiar, friendlier face and headed over to Norzan. "I'm glad to see you up and about, Lord Norzan."

"Good evening, Keelie." Norzan bowed his head. "Thank you for the help you've given us. We have put you in grave danger, I fear." He looked tired. Keelie knew that the drama among the elves, on top of the injuries he'd received in the Redwood Forest, must be exhausting for him, but she was so glad he was here.

Dad clasped Norzan's arm in his, and the two tree shepherds looked into each other's eyes for a long moment. Keelie had no idea what that was about.

"Now that everyone has gathered, we can begin." Miszrial stood to one side, hands lifted, palms up. She looked regal, but spoiled the effect when she tossed her hair behind her shoulder.

What was she doing on the Council? She didn't have the people skills for a leadership position.

Miszrial smiled at some of the other elves, and they returned her smile. One big happy family.

Keelie didn't have a good feeling about this meeting. She sat with Dad and Norzan. Terciel sat across from them.

Then Terciel stood up. "We must discuss the goblin invasion. Soon the dwarves will join us, and Herne and his dark fae brethren. But first, we must meet as elves." He turned to Keelie. "Keliel Heartwood, leave the meeting until such time as the others join us."

"What?" Keelie felt her mouth drop open. Talk about an unexpected action.

Dad's face paled, and Norzan stood shakily. "What is this outrage? We sought out Keliel Heartwood. She came here at our invitation, to help us speak with the High Court."

Miszrial leaned forward. "And if you remember I disagreed with that idea, and all of my predictions have come true. She didn't help us speak with the queen—she followed the queen's orders to repair the rift and made it worse. More magic is spilling out. We are battling goblins in our own forest. The only good thing to come of this, in my opinion, is that the humans have fled."

"And how is this Keliel's fault?" Dad spoke quietly, but his voice seemed to ring against the walls.

Miszrial gave him a pitying smile. "The elves of the Dread Forest are ancient, but you sent a poor representative. Her blood is tainted with fae and human elements that cause her great conflict. She knows not where her loyalties lay. Who can trust her?" She turned to Keelie. "Leave us now."

Keelie stood and put a hand down on Dad's shoulder to keep him from joining her. "What happens here affects the whole world. I'll wait outside until the others may enter."

She left, chin up, and wished she weren't so well-bred. She was trying to be dignified, but she wanted to give the haughty elf a middle-finger salute.

Outside, a few dwarves had already arrived. The dryad was there too, standing next to Ermentrude, who was wrapped in blankets and sitting in a chair. Sean, who was not invited to participate, was sitting at Ermentrude's feet.

As Keelie headed toward them, Sean stood. "Have you come to ask us in?"

"No, I got kicked out for being a mongrel." Keelie shrugged, trying not to let her hurt show. "I thought my mixed blood was what got me invited up here in the first place."

One of the dwarves, a female warrior, turned to her with a frown. "The elves evicted you from their meeting?"

Keelie nodded.

"I am Topaz. You know my cousin Jadwyn."

"I know him as Sir Davey." She looked over her friend's cousin. Despite the peaceful nature of the talks, the woman was wearing two knives and a sword.

Topaz smiled. "He speaks highly of you, unlike others." She shot a look of dislike at the Council building. "Excuse me." She rushed to the other dwarves and spoke earnestly. The group glanced at Keelie and talked more.

Great. Now everyone was gossiping about her.

"They're outraged, Keelie." Sean stood next to her. "As am I."

"They can do whatever they like," Keelie said. "Besides, Dad's in there. He and Norzan won't let the elves come up with any weird plans."

Sir Davey arrived and waved cheerily at Keelie, but he was stopped by the grumbling crowd of dwarves. As he listened to their words, his eyebrows rose and his eyes widened, and Keelie saw his hand tighten on the dagger he wore on his belt. He glanced toward Keelie.

The doors of the Council building banged open and Miszrial stepped onto the plaza. Behind her were Dad, Norzan, and Terciel, as well as some of the other elves.

"Forest peoples, welcome to the Alliance Summit. I am Miszrial, and I welcome you on behalf of the elves of Grey Mantle." She motioned to the others. "The elves welcome you."

The air changed, growing warmer, and with a dramatic thunder clap, Herne appeared, horned and majestic. He must have timed it. Sean frowned and Ermentrude laughed at his theatrical appearance, but it seemed to work on the elves. They gasped. The dryad straightened, then bowed. Keelie slipped behind a tree. She didn't want to add to the drama.

But Herne had other ideas. His stern gaze took in the assembled forest peoples, and he frowned.

"Where is my consort? Where is Keliel Heartwood, Forest Daughter?"

Keelie banged her forehead against the tree (a birch). *So much for waiting. Thanks a lot, Herne.*

twenty-one

Keelie stared at the dingy yellow wall of the No-Tell Motel, an abandoned motor court halfway between Grey Mantle and Big Nugget. The ride there, in the elven SUV on treacherous roads constantly watching for goblins, was bad, but not as bad as the Alliance Summit. Which hadn't even gotten started.

The motel walls were a fly-spotted, mildew-streaked yellow, all that was left of a once-soothing white. Keelie knew she had to calm herself. Her father and the other Dread Forest elves had left Grey Mantle shortly after Herne's disruptive entrance, and it was decided that this motel was easily defended against goblins. Uncle Dariel and Elia were in the next room, and their voices rose as they argued.

Knot sniffed the musty shag carpet. "Meow stinks!"

Dad paced back and forth. He was thinking, and Keelie didn't want to disturb him; he had the I'm-going-to-lose-my-temper look on his face. He had maintained a persistent beet-red glow ever since Herne had announced that Keelie was his consort.

Coyote was back with them, having mysteriously reappeared after they found rooms in the motel. Keelie hadn't yet had a chance to talk to him, and now wasn't the time. Coyote dug between his toes with his teeth, avoiding eye contact with Dad. Tension hung in the room like sticky cobwebs.

Above the beds hung a framed photo, a stag pose majestically in front of a stand of trees. Even this disgusting motel was reminding Keelie of Herne. She was so mad at him. How dare he show up and break up the meeting she'd worked so hard to arrange?

She hadn't really taken all of this consort nonsense seriously. Maybe she should have, but figured she'd find a way to handle the nature god. And part of her had *wanted* to be with him. Keelie recalled how strong and muscular he'd felt when they flew next to each another in Under-the-Hill. She'd felt safe.

Dad stopped and stared at her, as if he was picking up on her thoughts.

Keelie smiled, forcing her mouth muscles to work. "I was thinking of going to get some ice," she said, pointing toward the faux-wood plastic bucket on the even more faux-wood dresser.

Shaking his head, Dad began walking back and forth again. "You're staying right here." He was going to wear a hole in the carpet, which in her opinion would definitely be an improvement. Knot washed his tail, and Coyote was now working on cleaning out the toes of his other paw. No help from her guardians. She was on her own with Dad.

"I can't believe I chose to stay here. When we first arrived in Big Nugget, I wanted to stay in a motel instead of the elf village. Be careful what you wish for."

She missed Grey Mantle. She missed the stick-and-twig granola. She even missed Miszrial. Dad didn't reply.

Loud, deep singing replaced Uncle Dariel and Elia's arguing. The motel was crawling with dwarves, who had taken it over after Ermentrude's appearance. They were excitedly preparing for war, which consisted of consuming large quantities of beer and singing bad songs.

"Off on the road to the shores of Bagadoom, we'll march through the dark and the gloom ..."

The door opened and Dariel and Elia entered, both scowling. Elia plopped down on the shiny nylon burgundy bedspread embroidered in sparkling thread. Her rounded belly stuck out like a mound.

Keelie watched as something moved within. Startled, she realized it was the baby. Eek. This was the first time it really hit home that there was a child growing within Elia. It would be here soon.

A sense of urgency filled Keelie. The cataclysmic images

she'd seen at the High Court rushed back to her. In her mind's eye, solar flares baked the surface of the Earth. They had to find a solution to mend the rift, and soon, or all would be lost.

Elia placed her hands on her belly. "Dariel, come quickly."

He ran to her side and placed his hand over hers. His face melted with love as the baby seemed to move even more, as if it knew that Dariel was nearby.

Dad smiled and he looked at Keelie. "I remember when I first felt you within your mother." Keelie's chest clenched.

"I want to go home, Dariel. I don't want to give birth here." Elia lifted her hands to indicate the motel room.

Dariel smoothed back Elia's hair. "We'll go home soon, but right now, we're safer here from the goblins."

Keelie felt bad. She wouldn't want to give birth in a motel room, especially this motel room. They needed to re-solve everything so they could go home. But she knew deep down that there wasn't going to be an easy solution. Like an apple with a rotten core, Peascod was at the center of the situation, working his manipulative evil. It was imperative she discover the identity of Peascod's new master, if Herne was right about him finding one. Peascod alone couldn't have weakened Herne.

She looked at Dad, and he met her gaze and frowned. It was as if he knew she was thinking about Herne.

"Why did you go to him? Why did you put yourself in peril?" His voice cracked, as if he had to force the words out.

Dariel strode over to Dad and placed his hand on his

shoulder in a brotherly gesture. He turned to Keelie. "Help us understand how this all came to be."

She flicked her eyes over to the photo of the stag. "I don't know what the big deal is. I needed help rounding up allies to help me with the rift. Herne offered his help."

Keelie watched as Dad and Uncle Dariel exchanged glances. Perhaps she could lighten the mood in the room. "It's extremely inconvenient to have a god fall in love with you."

Crickets chirped, the only sound other than the dwarves singing, "In the dark moon of the night…"

Dad lifted his head toward the ceiling, as if it might open wide and Sylvus himself would descend and offer advice. "This is serious, Keliel. You didn't see the way he looked at you."

"How did he look at me?"

Dad's eartips flushed bright pink, which was a nicer shade than the beet red on his face. "It was enough for Terciel to accuse you of favoring the forest god."

"Are you on their side? Do you agree with Terciel that I'm conspiring to bring about the downfall of the elves because of my fae blood?" She glared at Dad.

He threw his hands up. "I didn't say I agreed with Terciel. Didn't you see Uncle Dariel hold me back from punching the arrogant elf when he accused you of being a mongrel?"

Keelie had to repress a smile. Dad had come to her defense, and it had made her feel wanted and loved when he threatened to put a balding charm on Terciel.

"You're my daughter, and I don't want anyone or anything harming you. That includes a forest god who wants to claim you." Dad's voice rose again. His eartips now matched the rest of his face. Keelie wondered if he was yelling so that Herne, wherever he was, could hear him.

Elia moved the pillow over her head in an attempt to block out the conversation.

"What happened in Under-the-Hill?" Dad stared at Keelie. His once-livid face was a dark gray, as if asking the question had drained all of the blood out of him.

"My virtue is still intact, if that is what you're wondering," she reassured him.

Dad sighed. "Good." Uncle Dariel looked away, and Elia lowered the pillow.

Keelie didn't know if she wanted Elia to hear all of this, but she didn't have a choice. They were holed up in the motel whether they liked it or not, and she had to make Dad understand they all had to work together.

"There's a lot more going on than goblins going to war and trying to collect more magic," Keelie said.

"I know the wild magic is caused by a rift in the Earth," Dad said. "What else do you know?"

"There's also a crack in Gaia's Dome, and the Earth's atmosphere is at risk. If we don't find a way to repair it—"

"Then the Earth will burn up," Elia interrupted in a soft voice, embracing her rounded belly. Her eyes were wide with horror. "Dariel." She reached out her hand to him, and he sat down on the bed beside her and held her.

Dad's gray face became even more so, and his green

eyes clouded with understanding. "Norzan didn't mention this to me. The High Court was supposed to keep him informed as to what was happening."

"Vania refuses to talk to the elves." Keelie shrugged. "I don't think most of the fae know what she's up to."

"That doesn't surprise me. I don't trust Vania." Dad looked grimmer.

"That's why I went to Under-the-Hill with Herne. After Vania proved that she wanted me to mend the rift alone, I thought that Herne was the second most powerful being and we had to get him on our side. He wanted me to see where the dark fae live." Keelie hoped her words reassured Dad.

Instead, Dad grabbed her arm and pulled her into the corner. Keelie saw Elia's wide, curious eyes on them.

"Herne is a powerful being," he said, his voice low. "He's a nature god. If he wants you, then I'm powerless against him, even in his weakened state. You should not have gone with him. What promises have you made him?" His face was lined with worry.

"I haven't made any promises. Give me a break, Dad, I'm sixteen." Keelie thought of the intoxicating feelings she experienced whenever Herne was near. Darn him for doing this to her. Dad didn't know just how dangerously attractive the Green Man was, but she still had to find a way to smooth things over. "Anyway, when I was there with him, I found out some things about Grandma Jo. She was pure-blood fae."

"Pureblood?" Dad echoed, surprised.

"There's more," Keelie said quickly. "Queen Vania turned

her into a brownie, cursing her for a love affair she had with a mortal man. My grandfather."

A frown creased Dad's forehead. "Before your mother was born?"

Keelie nodded.

"That means that Katy was—that you are—"

"Dark fae. It's why I can go Under-the-Hill." Keelie didn't add how at home she felt there. "Herne told me that my dark fae side is strong enough, along with my elven blood, to make me not human. I'll have the lifespan of an elf or greater."

Dad didn't seem overjoyed. "Your mother never told me all this. If the elves discover it, they may consider you more dark fae than elf. It won't help matters."

Grandmother Keliatiel knew. Keelie didn't say the words aloud, but it looked like Grandmother had kept the secret well. Was this the reason why Mom had left Dad and the Dread Forest all those years ago? Had she feared her dark fae blood would be revealed? If so, she'd had nothing to fear.

Keelie jumped up. "I thought you'd be happy, Dad. I won't live just eighty years. We'll have more time together."

"I never doubted it." He said the words as if he really believed them.

Keelie was astonished. "You've never said that before."

"We'll talk about that later. One thing at a time, Keelie." Dad sighed heavily and sat down on the bed. "Norzan insisted you were the one to help. Mother convinced me you could handle yourself among the fae, after the superb way you managed the situation in the redwoods."

"Grandmother said that?" Keelie was pleased. A compliment from her rigid elven grandmother was high praise indeed, and rarely given.

"I wasn't going to let you come here, but she convinced me, along with Dariel." He scowled at his younger brother.

Dariel shrugged. "We all trust Norzan." Keelie caught the implication that Dad had agreed with Norzan, also.

"Elia wanted to visit her family, and with Sean and Knot along to protect you, I thought you would be safe. Dariel thought Elia would be safe with her clan."

"My clan did not welcome me. I felt unloved and dismissed." Elia blinked several times. "They didn't even celebrate the hope of the child."

Dad nodded. "We didn't expect the hostility and anger toward you both or we wouldn't have sent you into such an uncomfortable situation, much less such a dangerous one."

"Dad, I don't think anyone knew about the rift other than Vania. What I don't understand is how Peascod and the goblins have been able to collect the wild magic to make themselves stronger."

The dwarves' singing had stopped. Silence filtered through the motel walls, punctuated with an occasional "huzzah." Uncle Dariel and Elia walked over to the door, where he embraced her.

"Get some sleep. We have much to discuss in the morning. Sean's jousters and the dwarves will take turns keeping watch for goblins and Herne, so you'll be safe. Dariel and I must go speak with Terciel and King Gneiss about our next strategic move against the goblins."

Elia walked over to the bed, pulled back the covers, and slipped in.

Dad kissed Keelie's cheek and held her close for a moment. "I won't let anything happen to you Keelie. You are my life."

Tears pricked her eyes. "I love you too, Dad." She closed the door after him and turned to Coyote and Knot, who seemed to be asleep on the floor. "I know you guys are faking it. Get up. We need to talk."

"Will you shut up?" Elia said. "I'm trying to get some sleep."

Coyote's ears pricked up. "First talk to Herne. He's waiting for you outside."

Elia levered up on her elbows. "Not him again."

Keelie whirled and ran to the window. Sure enough, the forest god was outside. He waved.

"What nerve! After what he did to us. We're stuck in this fleabag motel and he's out there laughing." Keelie frowned at the horned Green Man.

"Gotta admit, it was pretty funny," Coyote's black lips curled up in amusement.

"Well, I'm not going out to talk to him. The guards will probably see him and kick him out anyway," Keelie said. As if the guards could even touch him.

"You're delusional." Coyote threw his head back and howled in glee.

Herne must have heard, because he grinned at her.

"Shut up. You'll bring the guards over here."

"So go talk to him. What can it hurt?" Coyote's tongue lolled.

"Zeke will kill her. That's what it's going to hurt," Elia said. "Don't take advice from an ugly dog."

"I'm not a dog." Coyote narrowed his eyes.

What could it hurt? Herne could whisk her off to Under-the-Hill again, that's what. "You're supposed to be protecting me," Keelie accused Coyote. "Whose side are you on?"

Knot opened one eye. "Yeow's the trickster."

"See, even the cat agrees with me," Elia said.

"Yeah, I'm getting that." Keelie glared at Coyote. She turned to look back out the window and stifled a shriek. Herne's face was pressed up to the glass. She turned around to tell Elia, but the elf girl was suddenly asleep.

Keelie yanked the door open. Her elven guard lay on the ground, snoring, his eyes wide open.

"That's just wrong. What did you do to him?" she asked.

"Sweet dreams," Herne said, with a wave of his hand.

"Get in here before anyone sees."

Herne shook his head. "You come out. These buildings are full of iron."

Keelie rolled her eyes and stepped outside. She turned to look back. "Stay in there and don't make any noise."

Coyote looked at her innocently. "Who, me? She's making enough noise for all three of us." He motioned with his paw at Elia.

Knot closed his eyes, but she knew he was the biggest faker. She stepped outside and closed the door gently behind her.

Herne offered her a plastic bottle full of soda.

"This isn't some fairy trick, is it?"

"No, it came from that machine over there. It's human food, though it doesn't seem to have any food in it."

"Why are you here?" Keelie pulled the top off the soda, heard the fizz, and took a sip.

"I came to show you something." Herne called a goblin to him, one of the little ones she'd seen all over Under-the-Hill. Keelie backed up, ready to jump back through the motel room door.

"Stop, it's safe. He's mine, look."

The goblin came up and squatted at Herne's feet, putting its spidery arms around the forest god's booted leg. His skin looked chitinous, a shiny black that glowed in the slanting arctic sun. His round, protruding eyes looked up at her.

"I thought Peascod controlled the goblins. Did you kill Peascod?"

"No. I'm not sure where the accursed fool went, but I discovered that when he's not around, his influence fades, and the goblins look to me. At least they still band together. It's easier to control them that way, when I can."

"Permanently? What happens if he comes back?"

Herne shrugged. "I don't understand the power Peascod has over the wild magic. But I don't think he's working alone."

"I still can't figure out how you lost control," Keelie said. "I mean, you're a god, right?"

Herne's expression turned stoney. "I was."

"What's the difference between a god and a fairy?"

"Power. Much of my power came from my worshipers, although most of it comes from nature itself. Few practice the old ways." He seemed reluctant to say the words.

"Don't look at me. I'm not a worshiping kind of girl."

Herne met her eyes. "I could make you."

Keelie shivered, sure that he could. She wondered how many other gods there were. Eager to look away from Herne, she glanced down at the little goblin. He was hideous, but seemed content to sit there. The little fellow looked up at Keelie and his eyes zoomed to her soda. He licked his lips.

Keelie offered it to him, careful to keep her hands away from his sharp talons. He snatched the bottle, ripped it in two and poured the liquid out, then calmly chomped down on it.

Keelie stared. "Do they all do that?"

"Table manners are not part of goblin life."

"No, I mean eat plastic."

Herne looked at the little creature. "I suppose. They eat all kinds of garbage."

She remembered how clean Big Nugget had been. No wonder. And of course, that's why cities were full of goblins. They ate garbage. Plastic. The idea excited her—a recycling solution. Although if the cities were full of goblins, you sure couldn't tell the difference.

"I have to go to bed," she said to Herne. "Thanks for coming by. I'm glad the goblins seem to be yours once more."

He bowed. "I'll see you soon. This alliance idea is so amusing."

"No more mention of consorts, okay?"

Herne's eyes flashed. "Oh, yes." Keelie felt that tingle again and stepped back.

"Don't fight it, Keelie. You are dark fae, and your blood sings to me."

She stood tall. "I'm also part elven and part human, and you have no sway over those."

Herne grinned again. "So you think." He bowed, and vanished.

Her elf guard moaned from the ground. She needed to go inside before he saw her out here or he would tell Dad. She put a hand on the doorknob, and the trees moved with a breeze that spoke to her in Herne's voice. *I do love a challenge.*

Two hours later, as Keelie tried to read the dragon magic book, her eyes closed. She swore she smelled the familiar scent of Ermentrude's charcoal cigarettes and the purring of Knot as he snuggled up against her.

She felt as if she were falling, and then she landed in a valley tucked between snow-capped mountains. The air was crystal clear and the grass was soft beneath her feet. Sunlight shone on her shoulders, warm on her skin. Knot played among the red and blue flowers. In the spring-green grass, Coyote rolled on his back with his legs up in the air.

It all seemed so real. It had to be. Keelie wished Sean were here with her. It would be a calm, serene place for her to pour her heart out to him, and he'd understand.

"It is beautiful, isn't it?"

At the sound of the voice, Keelie almost fell over. She

didn't turn around. She didn't want to look for fear the speaker wouldn't be there.

"We're here, Keliel," Grandmother Josephine said.

Keelie turned. Her grandmother's voice was the same as she remembered, but in this place she was so young and beautiful. Another woman stood slightly behind Grandma Jo, and as she stepped forward, Keelie cried out with every bit of grief and anguish in her heart and soul.

"Mom!" The word floated and echoed around the mountain.

The wind blew and rustled her mother's dark hair. Tears streamed down Keelie's cheek as she stared at her through blurry eyes.

"Hey, sweetie," Mom smiled lovingly at her, but there was sadness in her eyes. "You've grown so much."

Knot and Coyote ran to Keelie's side, then bounded in front of her, blocking her way as she was about to run to her mother.

"No, Keelie," Coyote yelled. "They're here to give you a message, but you cannot touch them. The fairy magic that flows within you, and within them, is what is allowing the contact between this realm and the spirit realm."

"The magic is leaking into the spirit world," Grandma Jo said. She placed her hands across Mom's shoulders as if to give her comfort.

"What?" Keelie wanted to run to Mom so badly, but Coyote stopped her by sinking his teeth into her shirt and tugging her back.

"There is a dark force who wants to release the dead to

do his bidding, if he is allowed to be free. He has slept for a long time. You have to mend the rift within the Earth to stop him," Mom said. "Mend the rift first, to stop the wild magic. Then you'll be able to use your tree magic to mend the crack in Gaia's Dome."

"Our time is almost up," Grandma Jo said sadly.

"What? You just arrived," Keelie protested.

"I know, my darling," said Mom.

Knot rubbed his head up against Keelie's leg. He purred. "Meow time."

"It can't be time."

Keelie looked at Mom, wanting to memorize everything about her so she'd never forget what she looked like. "Mom, I'm sorry I said I didn't love you the morning you left. I love you. I love you. I love you."

Tears formed in Mom's eyes. "I know, Keelie. I love you, too. Rest your heart. I know you didn't mean it."

Grandma Jo turned her head. "They're calling us. We have to go. Beware of the jester, Keelie. He is very dangerous, and he seeks your death to gain your power."

Fear pulsed through every fiber of Keelie's being.

"Will I ever see you, again?" she asked.

Coyote turned to Knot. "Let's go."

Keelie wanted to shout *no*. Mom and Grandma Jo were beginning to fade, growing smaller as if they were being pulled away.

Mom's voice wafted back, as pale as her image. "Keelie, tell your father that I love him."

Pain lanced through Keelie as she felt herself leaving the

mountainside. She whirled through a smoky vortex of fire, and she landed on the lumpy motel mattress with a loud squeal of bedsprings.

Knot and Coyote crashed to the motel floor in a bundle of fur.

"Yeow off meow."

"Get off of me, you fat cat."

A red ember of smoke from a lighted cigarette glowed in the dark room. "Told you it was a dragon magic book."

Keelie's head pounded like she had cannons going off inside her skull. "Was that real?"

Ermentrude clicked on a light, and though she was still in human form, she had claws instead of hands. She was knitting with them, rapidly working yarn. Knot and Coyote were still trying to disentangle their legs from one another.

"Yep, it was all real." Ermentrude took another puff of her cigarette. It smelled like a charcoal grill in the small, cramped room. Keelie wished desperately for some Febreze.

"The magic is leaking into …" She didn't quite know how to explain it to Ermentrude.

"The spirit world," Ermentrude answered.

"Yeah, the spirit world."

"Exciting stuff." Flames appeared in Ermentrude's nostrils, then snuffed out.

"I saw my mother and grandmother."

"You were given a rare gift."

"Yes, I was."

"You miss your mom, don't you?" Ermentrude asked.

Keelie nodded. If she said anything, she'd choke on the words.

"I wish my daughter would miss me. She's too busy avoiding me."

"Is your daughter a … ?"

"A dragon. Yes."

Ermentrude untangled her claws from her knitting, then put out her cigarette in an ashtray. She picked up her knitting again and threaded the loops onto her claws. "Yeah, but she's working, traveling around the United States from faire to faire. I'm hoping she'll get it out of her system, come back, and hatch some eggs. I'm ready for a batch of granddragons, but she has to meet the right guy first."

Keelie had a sneaking suspicion she knew Ermentrude's daughter. "What's your daughter's name?"

"Rose. Her father's idea, to name her after her grand-mother. You might know her. She goes by her father's name. In dragon society, it's the mother's name that is passed on."

"What is the name she goes by?"

"Finch."

Keelie sat down hard. Finch, the horrifying administrator from the Wildewood Faire who hated Keelie's guts. She was not one bit surprised that Finch was really a dragon.

"Do you know her? She's got great people skills." Ermentrude sounded as proud as any mother bragging about her kid. Keelie wasn't going to tell her otherwise. "She's working at a faire in Colorado this year," the dragon added.

"Really." Keelie shuddered. Whenever this drama in the Northwoods was over, she and Dad were going to the

High Mountain Renaissance Faire in Colorado. She briefly wondered who was minding their woodworking shop there while Dad was here.

Ermentrude stood up and packed her knitting bag. "I'll leave you to sleep. You haven't had much of that lately."

She left, and Keelie got ready for bed. She wanted to slip back into her dream world, to freeze Mom and Grandma Jo's images in her mind. Maybe she could go there alone if the magic walls were thin. It suddenly occurred to her that she hadn't asked how Grandmother Keliatiel had discovered about their dark fairy blood.

Something hard landed on her stomach.

"Ah." Keelie bolted upright. It was Coyote.

He stared at her. "Don't try and go there without me or Knot. If you get stuck, your soul can't return back to your body. And you can't go where your kin have gone unless you're dead."

She'd be stuck on that hillside forever, alone. "I've got it. I won't go back." Unless she really needed to.

twenty-two

"How did you two get there?" Keelie asked Coyote and Knot the next morning as they walked to Ermentrude's room for breakfast. She was still thinking about the dreamworld.

Coyote shrugged one furry shoulder. "I'm a spirit walker. I've told you before that I walk between worlds."

Knot swished his tail, and Keelie heard a distant sound of meowing.

"And that means you can walk to the world of the dead? Agh—" Keelie almost tripped over several tabbies and calicos sitting outside Ermentrude's door. The cats didn't flinch, just stared at her.

"What's with the cats?" Keelie looked at Knot for an answer. He lifted his nose in reply. Keelie knocked, then opened the door. Inside, Ermentrude sat at a tiny dinette table. Elia and Dariel stood next to her, their arms wrapped around each other.

"I have to leave," Dariel said. "We're still in Council meetings with all the big wigs. Herne is sending trolls."

"When will you be back? I'm starving," Elia said.

"Soon. Don't leave. I'll send food." Dariel kissed her and headed for the door.

Elia sat down gloomily. "I need to eat now, and if I don't get anything I'm going to be very grumpy."

"As an expectant mother should be," Ermentrude said soothingly. "I've decided to knit you a baby blanket."

Elia smiled tentatively. "Thank you." She moved to sit at the tiny table with Ermentrude.

"Don't worry, all of my yarn is fireproof." Ermentrude dug through her bag and pulled out a skein of fluffy white yarn spotted with ash.

Knot hopped on the arm of the chair and purred at Elia. She ignored him. Coyote sat at her feet like a loyal lap dog. Outside the motel, the cats' meowing escalated.

Keelie covered her ears. "Are you using some kind of elven cat charm?"

"I don't know," Elia snapped. She ran her hands through her golden curls.

The door suddenly crashed open. "Goblin attack!" the elven guard cried. "They've set the motel on fire."

Everyone leaped to their feet. "Ermentrude, can you put it out?" Keelie cried.

"I only start fires," the dragon snapped. "Get your coats and go outside."

Elia was already struggling into her cloak. "I have to pack my ceremonial robes, and my pink gown, too. Keelie, don't forget to get my hairbrush."

"No time." Keelie pushed her out the door. Obviously the Lore Master did not teach fire safety to elven kids.

Outside there was chaos. Armed men rushed back and forth in the motel's smoky parking lot and Keelie could hardly see for the choking, acrid gray billows.

She held her sleeve over her face and Elia bent over, coughing. Ermentrude didn't seem to have any trouble breathing smoke, and she helped Elia get away from the motel.

Three figures appeared out of the gray haze and followed them. Keelie turned to confront them, unsure what she could do to defend herself, when she saw that they were armed elves.

"We are to escort you to a place of safety," one said. His eyes were half-shut against the smoke. A wind arose, clearing the smoke but fanning the flames.

"Why don't we go into town to the Crystal Cup?" Ermentrude suggested. "It's enclosed and you could defend the doors, and maybe the goblins left some food inside."

"Maybe I can call on Herne to send a troll out there with us," Keelie added.

Sean jogged up to them, his chain-mail shirt jingling. "Dariel sent me to help guard you."

"Good," Elia said. "We're going to the Crystal Cup."

"Dariel didn't say anything about the Crystal Cup."

"He forgot my breakfast," Elia cried. "He doesn't love me. I'm going to starve, and my clothes will all be burned to ashes."

"Let's feed the pregnant elf—she's scarier than the goblins," Keelie said. Behind them, flames flickered from the long, low motel and black smoke billowed up and was pushed back down by the wind.

Ermentrude leaned on her walking stick. "It smells a bit like gasoline."

Keelie could only smell smoke. "If the goblins are trying to smoke us out, where would be the most logical place for us to go?" She spoke softly.

The guard elves leaned in. "Back to Grey Mantle," one suggested.

Another nodded. "Or to the City Hall building. It's sturdy, all brick."

Sean eyed Keelie, a smile growing on his face. "I get what you mean. The roads to those places might hold an ambush, but the way to the Cup won't."

"Right." Keelie nodded in Elia's direction. "Besides the hysterical mother-to-be, we have a dragon on our side. I think we'll be pretty safe, especially with you guys along."

"Let's hurry then," Sean said. "Walk behind the women," he told the elf warriors. "I'll take the front."

Ermentrude went to Elia and put an arm around her shoulders. "Come on, dear, let's get you something to eat. I'm afraid we'll have to walk."

"This is the worst trip of my life," Elia sobbed. "I want to go home."

"I understand, dear."

Keelie stomped after them. She felt the same way, but she wasn't about to whine about it to the world. Warmth for Sean flowed through her. She knew he was doing this as much for her as for Elia.

"Let me give you some relationship advice," Ermentrude said, glancing back at Keelie. "I dated an elf once, and they need time to think about things."

"You dated an elf?" Elia asked in a disbelieving tone.

The dragon chuckled to herself as if she was savoring a sweet memory. "He was very athletic."

Keelie didn't want to know.

When they finally reached the abandoned streets of Big Nugget, Keelie tried to ignore the fact that about fifteen cats and at least twenty crows were keeping pace with them. Knot and Coyote walked at either side of Elia, who seemed oblivious of the animals. "How far to the Crystal Cup?"

"Just a little bit more." Keelie, Ermentrude, and the elves kept a wary watch for goblins.

At the café, Keelie and Elia went inside. The building seemed frail compared to the No-Tell Motel. The cats and crows, dragon and guards stayed outside while Elia hunted frantically for food. There were some old bagels under a glass dome. Keelie would have loved to have some coffee, but the coffeepot had been destroyed. No other food remained.

Elia sat down with a bagel and sniffed it. "I guess this is it."

"This is it."

Outside, the skies darkened and a cloudy sense of doom enveloped Keelie. "Elia, we need to go. This was a bad idea."

Elia was reading the menu as she gnawed on the bagel. "I'm not leaving. I'm eating."

"We need to leave now." Keelie grabbed Elia's wrist.

"Not until…" Elia stopped and looked around as if she sensed something was wrong, too. "I think maybe you're right."

Keelie heard the discordant jangle and her stomach dropped down to her feet. She was going to have to face a pissed-off Peascod and protect Elia.

The floor cracked and splinters flew everywhere. Peascod and several goblins spun upward.

Elia ran to Keelie, and she wrapped her arms protectively around her.

"What are we going to do?"

"I don't know."

Keelie tried to telepathically contact the trees, but it still didn't work.

Peascod stood in front of Keelie, and he didn't look happy. He waggled his index finger. "No, no, no. Trees can't help you now." His jester's suit was stained and ripped. He sneered at her, and from underneath his creepy mask, his green bloodshot eyes glowed with hatred.

"Because of you, I have lost my position with Herne. Because of you, Keliel Heartwood, my plans for obtaining the magic have been ruined, but I'm going to enjoy killing you and your pregnant friend. That baby contains a lot of magic, and it will make a worthy gift to my master."

Elia hid behind Keelie, and she shielded her with her body.

Peascod chuckled. "It won't help to hide, elf. If you'd been smart, you would have stayed home in the Dread Forest where you and your child were safe."

Keelie sought out the Earth magic running through the ground beneath the café, and it was weird. It felt like soil that had been tainted with blood. She'd sensed this before, in the Redwood Forest, but this was a darker form of magic.

She stared at Peascod, who laughed. "Yes, blood sacrifice strengthens our magic."

"I knew you were evil, but this goes beyond what I'd imagined."

"Thank you. I've been working on my evil ways for many years."

At that moment, a loud pounding on the door erupted. "Kill him!" Peascod yelled to the goblins at his side.

Keelie knew Sean was outside, probably circling around the café ready to attack, and he was walking into a trap.

Cats, birds, and squirrels crashed through the window, shattering glass everywhere. They scrambled in and attacked Peascod. Crows pecked at his face, squirrels dangled from his clothes, and the cats scratched at his exposed skin with sharp claws. The nasty jester shrieked underneath the attacking mass of fur and feathers. Coyote rushed in and bit him on the butt, ripping his jester pants. Oh, gross! Peascod went commando.

Grabbing Elia by the hand, Keelie guided her toward the

back of the café. They could make their escape through the kitchen. Sean came charging in the back door, sword drawn.

"Keelie, Elia, this way."

"Where do you think you're going?" an armored goblin yelled. He looked like something from a video game.

Sean attacked, smashing his sword down on the goblin's head.

That had to hurt.

Keelie had to get Elia out of there while Sean kept the goblins busy. As they exited the back door, she looked all around, but she wasn't expecting what happened next—Peascod spinning up from underneath the ground in front of her. She shielded her face from the flying debris as the disgusting jester blocked their escape.

"Where do you think you're going?" Blood dribbled in rivulets from the scratches on his face and his arms.

A mop in a bucket of water stood at the back door. Keelie grabbed the mop and shoved it at Peascod's face. Mop water as a weapon worked for Dorothy in *The Wizard of Oz*; maybe it would work for Keelie.

Peascod laughed. "That's not going to work." He seemed to know where she was going with this.

From his red and black pants pocket, he removed a glass sphere and tossed it up in the air. "You're going to die, just like she did." He laughed maniacally. "Linsa was powerful, like you, and her blood was a very good vintage." His eyes glittered madly.

An image of a lifeless Linsa formed in the reflection of the glass. Peascod was standing over her body.

"This is not the image you showed Herne," Keelie said.

"No, Lord Herne has not seen what really happened to the Shining One he loved. Nor does he know that I killed her. Linsa had discovered that I was gathering my own goblin army, and she was on her way to tell Herne when—oops! Somebody died. It was easy to make it look as if Herne had done the deed, and Queen Vania believed it." Peascod laughed. "Linsa's death caused the rift, which widened. Now there's a rift among the creatures of the Northwoods, too. The symbolism is rich."

"I'm shocked you even know what symbolism means," Keelie said.

Peascod narrowed his eyes. "You're a mongrel. You're a mixture of everything, and you'll never truly belong."

He wasn't going to try this psychological angle on her.

"You know, I've heard the same thing over and over," Keelie retorted. "Living with elves toughens you up to the real world."

Peascod carefully moved forward. "It's always a rewarding experience to be sure of one's self."

Keelie heaved the mop at him. The smell of Pine-Sol filled the air and some water droplets landed on him.

Looking past the shrieking jester (who knew he could jump that high?), she saw Sean sneaking up behind Peascod. But he whirled around in time to stop the surprise attack.

"Oh, look, I'm caught in a love triangle. Shall we all kiss and make up?" Peascod began laughing. He threw the glass sphere up in the air, and as it rose, it arced over toward her.

"Keelie, watch out," Sean shouted as he barreled over to her.

Peascod spun around and disappeared into the soil. The sphere stopped midcourse and then turned, hovering as if it was on a seek-elf trajectory. It zoomed toward Sean.

"Sean!" Keelie screamed.

He lifted his arm up and shielded his face.

As Peascod spun back into the ground like a mad harlequin dancer dancing a frenzied dervish, Keelie picked up the bucket of mop water and threw it. It splashed everywhere, but missed its intended target. The ground was wet and muddy where Peascod had dug his hole.

Blood dripped down Sean's arm. He'd been protected by his armor, but some of the glass had penetrated the exposed skin. Small fragments were embedded in his face.

"Sean, are you okay?"

"Yeah! What about you? Elia?"

"Elia—she's not here." Panic filled Keelie as she remembered what Peascod had said about Elia's baby being a worthy gift for his master.

"We need to find her. Don't move. I need to see where the tracks lead us," Sean said, his armor clinking as he ran.

Keelie bit down on her lips. She needed to calm down. She closed her eyes and reached out for the trees. *I need your help.*

Peascod's dampening field of magic had been removed. She dreaded to think what else he had up his jester hat.

Milady, what can we do?

I need to reach Dad. Elia has been taken by goblins. He needs to bring the elves.

"Hurry, Keelie. I think I know where she is," Sean said.

She followed him down the street. Hundreds of muddy

paw prints marred the sidewalks. She had never been so relieved to see anyone in her life as she was to see Elia with Ermentrude.

She ran to Elia and hugged her. "I'm so glad you're safe."

Elia hugged back, pressing her teary face into Keelie's shoulder. "Me, too. I was so scared for my baby, especially after what he said."

Ermentrude handed Elia a handkerchief embroidered with dragons.

"I know," Keelie said.

Elia pulled away from her. "Knot and Coyote guided me out of there, and the cats and crows came around and attacked the goblins. We got away, but some found us, but when they saw Ermentrude they ran."

Knot and Coyote grinned at Keelie.

"Good job, guys." She nodded toward the dragon. "Thank you."

Ermentrude shrugged. "I'm a mother myself. I understand these things. Mess with a baby, you mess with me."

Keelie looked up at the black ribbons flying from the maypole, where the goblins had been dancing. The place was filled with negative magic.

She closed her eyes, concentrating on the current of energy beneath them, and found it—tainted with dark magic, oily with evil. She touched the wood of the maypole, and to her surprise discovered the same essence she'd detected in the Under-the-Hill grove. It had the same telepathic imprint.

"We need to leave," Ermentrude said in an urgent tone, looking around nervously. "I've sensed this darkness before."

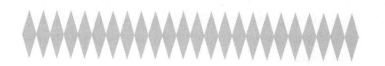

twenty-three

"Ow! That hurts," Sean yelled as Keelie pulled out the last small shard of glass with tweezers from the side of his face. They were back at the No-Tell Motel, which had a charred wing but was still habitable. Their new rooms were smoky, but it was actually an improvement.

Elia was asleep in a different room, guarded by Coyote and Knot. An army of cats patrolled the motel, along with additional Dread Forest jousters and Northwoods elves. Ermentrude had given them orders to let her know if they saw any goblins.

The dragon dug through her huge purse and pulled out

a tin of salve. "My very own creation. I make a batch every hundred years. I use crushed fire blooms, which grow at the base of an internal volcanic pool. It's highly prized among the dwarves."

It was hard to concentrate on Ermentrude or think about Elia. Sean was shirtless, and Keelie wanted to run her hands down his chest and over his chiseled abs. His skin was warm, and she wanted to press her body against his.

"Keelie? Keelie!" Ermentrude's voice rose.

"What?" She forced herself to look at the dragon, who gave her the pot of salve. "Thank you." She looked at the little pot's label. The letters were written in a scratchy calligraphy, but she knew what they said. *Fire Bloom Salve.*

"Can you read that?" she asked Sean.

"No. Can you?"

"Yes."

"I don't understand how you can read that. It looks like code to me. Runes, maybe?"

"You drank the tea Herne gave you. It enhanced your fairy abilities," Ermentrude said.

"Herne again." Sean snorted. He reached out and pulled Keelie closer to him, as if the very act would shield her from the nature god.

Keelie pushed him away, but he reached out for her hand and squeezed it. "Is it a permanent change?" he asked, staring at her. "Is it to make her more like him? More like a dark fae?"

Keelie didn't look away from Sean, but she'd had the same thought.

Ermentrude returned to the lumpy chair in the motel room. "Due to the fairy blood flowing through a matriarchal lineage, the answer is yes. But the tea wasn't bad for her. It just makes her magic work more efficiently."

"I still don't like it," Sean said.

Ermentrude sniffed. "Of course not, but you're going to have to accept the fairy magic within Keelie because it's part of who she is, and you certainly do like the rest of the package."

"It's always wise to listen to the words of a dragon." Sean quirked an eyebrow. "Practical advice."

"How do you know that? Ermentrude is the only dragon you know, and you just met her." Keelie tried to open the salve, but the lid seemed to be welded closed.

"Sean's grandfather is well-known among the dragons, Keelie," Ermentrude said. "He defeated a mighty tyrant and has our gratitude."

Sean shrugged. "It's family lore."

Keelie wondered what else Sean had never told her. It must be an elf-guy thing, because she'd uncovered a lot of her own history when she visited her father's house in the Dread Forest for the first time.

"I'm going to check on Elia. Make sure the cats and elves are keeping guard." Ermentrude shoved her bag onto her shoulder.

Keelie wrenched the tin of salve open and scooped up a glob of the medicinal-smelling stuff. "You said you wanted us to be honest, but you never bothered to tell me about dragons." She rubbed the salve on Sean's shoulder where a goblin had stabbed him.

Sean jumped. "Easy."

"Sorry." She'd applied it a little more roughly than she'd meant to do.

"That's okay. I think it's helping." He moved his shoulder. "My grandfather battled an evil dragon named Avenir and put him into an enchanted sleep, not far from here. Avenir had hurt hundreds of humans."

"How near here?" Keelie felt a tingle in her neck, which didn't stop until it hit her tailbone. "Wait a minute. Your grandfather didn't kill the dragon? Could Avenir be awakened from his enchanted sleep?"

"Not that I know of." Sean shook his head. "It was hundreds of years ago. And I don't know exactly where it happened. Under a mountain, according to our family lore."

She absentmindedly rubbed some more salve, gently, on Sean's wound. Amazingly, the wound began to heal before her very eyes.

"Wow. Ermentrude was right, this stuff works. No wonder the dwarves want it." Keelie ran her hand over Sean's shoulder and down his chest. He lifted her face until she was level with his gaze. His green eyes burned, intense.

"I've thought about what you said, about Herne saying you would live as long as me." Sean lips were close to hers. "I know this has been one of the things that has kept you from wanting to take our relationship further."

He wrapped his hand around her neck and brought her face closer to his.

"Yes," she said.

"Good." Sean kissed her, and frissons of delight traveled through Keelie's body. She realized she'd been afraid to enjoy her relationship with Sean, but not anymore. She leaned against him and deepened the kiss.

When their lips gently parted, he pushed her back against the wall and pressed his body against hers. Resting his forehead against hers, he said, "I think your father will probably hear about us being in a motel room alone."

Keelie laughed. "And you're half-dressed, Lord Sean o' the Wood."

"You've seen me like this before, in the smithy." Sean's hand rested on her backside.

"Yeah, well, we weren't alone there."

The door opened and Knot and Coyote marched into the room. Knot's cat jaw dropped, and Coyote snickered.

"I think our moment is over," Sean said.

Knot glared at Sean, and a low growl rumbled from his throat.

"You're right," Keelie said. She leaned close to him. "But we can meet later."

"We will." Sean kissed her lightly on the lips. Knot fell over onto his side and placed his paws over his eyes.

Sean shrugged into his shirt. "I'll go and help Bromliel. The goblins could still be in the area, and we're trying to pick up their trail."

Keelie nodded. "I think I'm going to work on some notes. I want to write it all down while it's fresh in my mind. Dad wants to know more about the Under-the-Hill forest."

Sitting down at the motel-room desk, Keelie drew a sketch of the forest and made notes on the page about the differences in the trees in the grove. She sketched the mountain, too. Ermentrude had said that somewhere underneath the mountain was a volcanic pool that was bubbling through the rift. Perhaps the way the Under-the-Hill trees gathered energy to live was widening the rift.

Or not.

Earth magic, quicksilver, and fairy magic … all were used in the areas where goblins had been seen. Keelie couldn't see how the dots connected, but it was there. She leaned her head into her hand.

Peascod had killed Linsa when she'd discovered he was forming a goblin army. Vania needed to know the truth about her sister's death. If the truth was revealed, then maybe Herne and Vania would work together to help seal the rift. Not that Vania would believe them. They needed to capture Peascod and force him to tell Vania what he had done. Keelie sighed, frustrated.

Knot rubbed against her legs, warm and furry. She reached down to rub his head, but he swatted at her. She pushed him away with her foot and he purred, an old game of theirs.

Keelie looked at her drawing again. She didn't have all the pieces to the puzzle, but maybe others had some answers. It was time for everyone to put their cards on the table.

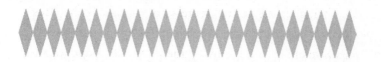

twenty-four

That evening, Elia and Ermentrude brought their suppers to Keelie's room—cold sandwiches and warm cola. Miszrial, on guard duty, joined them, oblivious to the "go away" vibes the others were sending her.

Keelie ate the unappetizing meal with them, thinking that it still was better than the twigs-and-mushroom steak the Grey Mantle elves had served.

"I still find it strange that humans could use magic," Elia said. "At the Ren Faires, humans think that every trick is magic. Are you sure they were actually accessing the rift?"

"You saw what was going on in Big Nugget before the

goblins came." Keelie took another eye-watering sip of cola. "Kids floating through the air, people with wings. We didn't get to stick around to see it all, but it was the real thing."

"Dariel said the spirit world's gate might come down, too." Elia shuddered.

Ermentrude nodded. "I'm afraid it's true. When the rift first opened, I had the ghost of a dwarf take up residence in one of my treasure chests. Claimed the gold was his. He's still there. Sings all the time. Drives me crazy."

"So you knew there was going to be a problem with the dead, and you didn't tell me." Keelie stared wide-eyed at Ermentrude. "Everyone's keeping information to themselves around here."

"I didn't know if it was the one ghost or if we were going to have a problem with a crop of them." The dragon woman smiled. "I really could use a smoke, but I'm not going to light up around Preggers. If you ladies will excuse me, I'll be right back."

Once Ermentrude left, Miszrial turned to Keelie. "I can talk to the other elves and try and convince them to listen to you, but Terciel has convinced the others that you're behind the problems, especially after Herne's proclamation that you are his consort."

"Herne is still part of the solution. I need for you to convince them of that, and to meet with the fairies and the dwarves. I've been looking at everything I've learned so far"—she gestured toward her notes—"and there are a lot of holes in the story."

"You ask for a lot, Keliel Heartwood." Miszrial glared.

"We're all united by one common purpose: to seal the rift," Keelie said.

"Except Herne has goblins in his realm," Miszrial said. "How can I guarantee my people you're not bringing them to attack us? Terciel is not the only one to question your alliance with the Green Man, and the fact that you're part fairy yourself."

Keelie felt insulted. "I was asked here for that very reason. And if I was allied with goblins, then we wouldn't be sitting here."

"Yes," Elia said. "The Grey Mantle elves were the ones who sent for us, so I suggest you tell the Council that the fairies, the dwarves, and whatever else needs to show up is coming, and they should get over their snitty attitudes and work for the common good."

Pregnancy had turned Elia into a warrior elf.

Miszrial's eyebrows rose. "I will go and talk to my people, and I will contact you as to their decision."

A weak answer, but it was a start. Keelie nodded and watched Elia walk the elf woman the short distance to the door, then close it behind her.

Two cats had jumped inside while the door was open and now twined around Elia's legs, rubbing their heads against her.

"Why are you attracting all these animals?" Keelie asked.

"Yeow child calls them," Knot said.

Elia looked horrified and shrank against the mildewed wall, warrior elf no more. "I'm going to find Dariel. Maybe he can make sense of this."

Keelie looked up from the drawing on the table. "Don't go alone."

"The guards are right outside. One of them will walk with me." Elia slipped out quickly, as if she couldn't wait to get away from Knot's explanation.

Moments later, the door banged open and Fala and Salaca entered. The cats hissed and scooted out the door.

"Hello, Keliel." Fala picked up the dragon magic book and thumbed through it. Salaca skipped the greeting and was scanning the map on the table.

"Nice manners," Keelie said, outraged as well as shocked to see them. She stormed over. "How dare you go through my stuff?"

"Dragon magic?" Fala held up the book. "Expanding your repertoire."

"Where were the court fae when we were fighting the goblins?" Keelie demanded. "The dwarves and elves joined together with Herne's forces—but we could have used you." She struggled to keep a calm voice. She wanted to scream at them.

"This is very interesting. Look, Fala." Salaca tossed Keelie's drawing of the Under-the-Hill grove to him.

Catching the sketch with one hand, Fala laughed. "Our Keliel has been a busy girl indeed. Hanging out with dragons. Visiting Under-the-Hill. Who is collecting this information?"

"I'm trying to solve the problem of the rift," Keelie said.

Fala whistled. "Trees that use the magic of crystals. This

is very new indeed, even for Fairy. Makes you wonder what Herne is really up to."

Keelie reached for her sketch, but Fala turned away, keeping it out of her grasp "No. no. Queen Vania wants to see this." He rolled her sketch up like it was a parchment.

"Are you ready?"

"For what?"

"We're off to see the queen," Salaca said as he reached for Keelie's upper arm. Before she had a chance to shrug away, Fala snapped his fingers.

Keelie suddenly found herself back at the Quicksilver Faire, with Fala and Salaca at her side.

"Why did we have to tramp up the hill and through the door the first time, if this is so much faster?" she asked.

Fala shrugged. "It's fae magic. Elves who travel here must use the long way."

Gone were the crowds and music. The empty streets were silent, lined with shuttered shops that were eerie and bereft of life.

Keelie wondered if Maemtri was still here. She was an ally who straddled the different realms of Fairy. Or Keelie hoped she was an ally—you could never tell with fairies. It was one of the rules she'd forgotten.

Knot popped in beside her.

"You can teleport, too? This is so unfair."

"Meow secret."

She wasn't going to argue with him. She was glad he was here.

In the center of the faire, the vortex light pulsed and

rotated. One thing Keelie had learned lately was that she hated traveling through vortexes or whooshing places. The elven and human parts of her wanted to keep her feet on the ground, and to stay in a place where time progressed forward one minute at a time.

"Knot, go to the Timekeeper and get us a reprieve. I need half an hour. I sure don't want to go back and find out a week has passed and the world has ended."

Knot blinked at her. "Meow can do that."

Fala put a hand in the small of her back and urged her forward toward the vortex. Keelie didn't struggle; she was eager to speak to Queen Vania. Without the crowds to impede them, they were soon facing the vortex.

"Before we go, can you tell me what you know about Linsa?"

A look of sadness passed between the two fairies. "She was the queen's younger sister, and she made unfortunate decisions," Fala replied.

"She loved Herne," Keelie said.

"Yes, a mistake we have learned you're repeating," Salaca said disapprovingly. "The queen is angry you went to Under-the-Hill."

"Enough time for talk. It's time to jump." Fala motioned toward the vortex.

Keelie closed her eyes and leaped.

She landed facedown on the cold marble floor of the castle's Great Hall.

"Bring her to my chamber." The queen's voice echoed

around the room. Keelie levered herself up, but she didn't see Vania sitting on her throne chair.

Fala and Salaca escorted Keelie to the queen's tower chamber. This was the same room in which Keelie had observed the rifts in the atmosphere and in the crust of the Earth.

Fala handed the sketch to the queen, and she unrolled it.

"How did you like your tour of Under-the-Hill?" The queen's eyes were on the drawing.

"It was very interesting," Keelie answered. She hoped Herne wouldn't get mad at Queen Vania seeing her sketches and notes, although since he hung around up here in disguise she shouldn't be too worried. She had a feeling that the queen had never been to Under-the-Hill. Not her kind of place.

Keelie wasn't as frightened as she had been earlier, but the discussion she was about to have with the queen was going to be extremely uncomfortable, and possibly dangerous. She also remembered that this was the fairy who had turned her grandmother into a brownie because she'd fallen in love with a human.

Salaca handed the queen the book on dragon magic.

She turned the pages, not really looking at them. "Accepting courting gifts from Herne. He can be quite charming. My sister found him so, and it was the death of her. Did you know he tried to convince her to come after my throne?"

"I heard that they were in love."

"Love. That is an emotion for humans and maybe some elves, but since fae runs through your veins, I give you the same warning I gave to her, and may you make better use of it. Herne is evil, and he will use you to meet whatever goal he has in mind. He wanted my throne for himself, uniting Under-the-Hill and the High Court."

"He loved Linsa," Keelie said. "And I think he is quite content with his realm."

Vania turned away, and then whirled around. "She said the same thing, but he killed her. Who do you think is behind the rift? It is his goblins draining the magic."

"Who told you this?" Keelie asked.

"His jester told me. That Peascod."

"It wasn't Herne who killed Linsa. It was Peascod."

"Do you have proof?"

"He told me when he tried to kill me. He said he sacrificed Linsa so that her blood would open the rift for his master. But his master is not Herne."

"He lied to you because he was my spy in Herne's court." Vania paled as she spoke.

Keelie stared disbelievingly at the queen. "He was your spy?"

"Yes, and he is loyal to me." Vania bridged the distance between them until she was almost nose-to-nose with Keelie. "You believed Peascod when he told you he killed Linsa."

"You believed Peascod when he told you Linsa was plotting with Herne to take over your throne. He's poisoned your mind. Turned you against your own sister." Keelie could see a flash of doubt pass through the queen's eyes.

"How do you know he's telling you the truth?" Vania demanded.

"Because I'm not important to Peascod. I'm in his way. He doesn't need to lie to me, so as he kills me, telling me he killed Linsa gives him immense pleasure. Finally, he can tell someone, show how clever he is. Whereas with you, if he can manipulate your feelings with lies, he will."

"Why would Peascod kill my sister?"

"Linsa had discovered Peascod was involved with the goblins, and that they were serving another master. He was betraying Herne. Peascod has been playing both you and Herne. It's kept you divided, so he could go about collecting the magic for whomever he's serving."

"It can't be."

"It's true, and now you have to join forces with Herne, the elves, and the dwarves to stop the rift. We both saw the crack in Gaia's dome."

Vania pulled up the image of the Earth. "I don't know if I can do that." She paced.

"Linsa would tell you to do so. From what everyone has told me about her, she was a kind fairy."

"I miss her." Silver tears streamed down the queen's face. She turned away from Keelie and circled around her in a counterclockwise motion.

"I understand the pain is still raw, and it feels as if your heart will never heal," Keelie said. "I lost my mother almost a year ago."

Vania turned and walked in the other direction, as if her mind was driven to keep her body moving in rhythm to frantic thoughts.

"There's another reason we have to work together," Keelie added. "It isn't just the veil between Fairy and Earth and Under-the-Hill that is being torn apart. The veil between us and the spirit world is opening, too."

"How do you know?" Vania asked. "You don't have the magical ability to talk to the dead."

"Because my mother and Grandmother Josephine came to see me."

Vania paled and wrung her hands nervously. She really needed to take up a hobby. Maybe Ermentrude would have a suggestion.

"I know what you did to my grandmother—Willow, you called her. You turned her into a brownie, and it was Linsa who offered her a life as a human."

Vania lifted her head and stared at Keelie. "Yet you're here. Do you wish to have your revenge for what I did to Willow?"

Keelie knew honesty was the best policy. "I would be lying if I said no."

The queen's eyes widened.

"But, I can put that aside and work with you to seal the rift. And I think the women in my family wouldn't want me to take that path. They would want me to help heal." Keelie held her head up with pride and looked Vania squarely in the eye. "We need to act now to close the rift."

"I see. I will let you know about my decision and working with Herne. I will give it some thought. Still, I don't know if what you're telling me is true."

"You'll have to trust me, and we're running out of time."

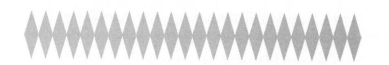

twenty-five

Quivering on the inside, Keelie couldn't believe she'd just talked to the queen the way she had...all the time she'd spent around Grandmother Keliatiel had paid off. You had to project authority and not let them smell the fear. Still, Keelie hoped her conversation would result in Vania cooperating. She thought about Elia and the baby. Vania had to join her magic along with the others to stop the rift.

When Keelie returned to the Great Hall, Knot was waiting for her. His tail twitched agitatedly. "Yeow okay?"

"Meow okay. I'm ready to go. Did you get what I asked for?"

He turned his head and she saw a small pocket watch hanging from his neck by a slender blue ribbon.

Fala gestured toward the vortex. "Are you ready?"

Keelie nodded. "Knot."

He sauntered over to her.

Before they reached the vortex, Fala stopped. "Keelie, I wish you success in closing the rift."

Stunned, Keelie didn't know what to say.

"If you can find a token Linsa gave Herne, and if he can show it to the queen, it will prove to her that Linsa didn't plot a betrayal."

"Do you know what this token is?" Keelie asked.

"Herne will know," Fala advised. "And you're going to need this." He returned her book of dragon magic. "I snitched it when she wasn't looking."

"Thanks." Keelie took the book warily. "Why are you helping me?"

"I want to save the High Court and serve my queen, but common sense tells me that there is truth in what you say." He bowed.

Keelie and Knot jumped into the vortex. Disorienting lights pulsed around her and she held her breath, as if that was going to help. She thought about the No-Tell Motel. The image of Sean popped into her mind, along with the memory of how his skin had felt under her hands that morning ... and then she landed with a painful thud outside the motel office.

She spat out a mouthful of dirt. "Gross!"

Knot appeared in midair. An oak tree reached out its

branches and caught the cat, who then landed on top of Keelie's head.

"Ow! Do you have to keep landing on me like I'm your personal air cushion?"

Knot jumped down, meowing underneath his breath. Keelie got up, wincing. She mentally contacted the tree. *Thank you.*

You're welcome, Tree Shepherdess.

She smiled, and reveled in the contact with the oak. It was so different to be in contact with the greenness and the living essence of Earth, which was what was missing in the Under-the-Hill trees. Their alien consciousness had haunted her ever since she'd been in contact with them. Grandmother and Mom had to get to the root of the problem. Maybe she needed to return to Under-the-Hill and study the roots of the grove trees again.

"Keelie." Sean was standing at the edge of the building. He walked over to her. "Where have you been?"

"The High Court, to talk to Queen Vania."

"You went alone."

"I was summoned. Actually, kind of kidnapped. Fala and Salaca came and got me, and all my notes and map, too."

"Are you okay?"

"I stood up to Vania, and Knot talked to the Timekeeper so that we got back right away." She told Sean what the fairy queen had said. He listened, and then kissed her forehead.

"I can't say I'm happy you went, but she needs to be involved in the alliance and I'm proud of you for standing up to her. Let's go tell your father and King Gneiss."

"Sean, I have to return to Under-the-Hill to speak to Herne." She saw Sean's muscles tense.

"Can't he come here? He's shown up here often enough."

"I need to examine the trees in Under-the-Hill again. There's something about them that's important to the rift, but I don't understand what it is. I wish Sir Davey could come with me." Sir Davey's knowledge of Earth magic might identify the strange way the trees shared a consciousness, like a hive.

Sean sighed. "I'm going to be honest. I don't want you to go, but I know you have to. Just don't make any rash decisions about..."

"I've already made up my mind, and you should know that." She sighed. Elves. You would think, as long-lived as they were, they'd pick up some wisdom about the way girls think.

"Keelie."

She reached up and kissed him.

He pulled her close and Keelie felt something fat and furry attach itself to her leg with sharp claws. She glanced down at Knot just as a familiar whoosh sensation made her knees buckle. Sean's arms tightened around her. Before she opened her eyes, she knew where they were.

"What was that? Where are we?" Sean pushed her behind him, ready to defend her against an invisible enemy. He looked up, amazed, at Under-the-Hill's seemingly endless sky, its eternally reddish dusk illuminating the tall black spikes of the haunted forest.

"We're in Under-the-Hill by the grove, the trees I want to study." Keelie's voice came out in a whisper.

"How … ?" Sean didn't have a chance to finish the question. Knot popped in beside Keelie, his fur sticking out in different directions. His tail had a kink in it.

"Serves you right for bringing us here without a warning," she told the cat. She knew better than to touch him. He looked grumpy and might bite her to make himself feel better.

"Knot brought us here?" Sean asked. "I thought this was Herne's doing."

She didn't tell him that if Herne had been responsible, Sean would still be standing outside the No-Tell Motel. "I need for you to keep a cool head. I need your help in persuading him to join the alliance. We all need to put aside our differences to make it work."

Sean tucked a stray curl behind her ear. "I will. For you."

Goose bumps dotted her skin and her knees felt loose. They were definitely about to enter a new stage in their relationship, or maybe it was the influence of Under-the-Hill. She stepped away from Sean so that she could think.

"This is the grove that Linsa and Herne planted together. It symbolized their relationship. They brought the trees from Earth and used quicksilver and different combinations of magic to keep them alive."

"Maybe the trees will give you some insight as to why we're here?"

Keelie opened her tree sense. Nothing but a rumbling from the roots, which quickly grew into a loud roar. She stumbled at the onslaught of magic and energy that crashed into her.

Sean rushed to her. "Keelie, what was that?"

"The trees. Magic," she gasped.

A familiar discordant jangle ripped through the air as Peascod stepped from behind one of the trees. "Not what you expected?"

Sean moved forward, but Peascod threw a glass sphere filled with a swirling green glow, which expanded and flowed across Sean, then sealed into a perfect bubble again, enclosed around him. It was as if he was stuck inside an upside-down fish bowl. Keelie saw him shouting and pounding on the glass.

"Let him go."

"I'm afraid I can't have him going around being all heroic." Peascod laughed. "It was a good thing I didn't kill you. I have a new plan for you."

"I don't care why you've had a change of heart." She wouldn't let him see how frightening he was to her.

"I don't have a human heart, so don't become all sentimental. Let's just say you'll be useful to the end. Your end. Now, I need for you to focus your attention on the trees."

Keelie flicked her eyes over at Sean, who was now pacing back and forth. If she cooperated with Peascod, it would give Sean more time to find a way out.

"What's wrong with the trees?"

"Can't you tell by touching them? And you call yourself a tree shepherdess."

"You call yourself a jester, but I haven't laughed yet."

He scowled.

"One question, though. This is Herne's garden. I thought he banished you."

"He did, but with the magic leaking, I'm becoming stronger. So much stronger that I can travel between the realms." He tilted his head. "And Herne is ever so weak, as you've discovered. Seems he needs you, too."

The ground rumbled beneath Keelie.

"No more chitchat. Let's get to work."

"What do you want with me?"

"We need you here to release one of our own."

"A goblin? I thought you had plenty of those."

"We have a surplus, no thanks to you and your killing kin, but buried beneath the roots of the trees, one of our comrades has awakened. He wants to be set free, but for that we need a tree shepherdess' special magic."

"What are you talking about?" Keelie felt the ground rumble and wondered if there was a volcano below them. Hadn't Ermentrude mentioned that fire blossoms grew at the edge of the volcanic pool? They might be standing in the middle of a time bomb. The rift was probably making it unstable.

She saw that Sean had gone still, his ear was pressed to the bottom of the glass orb. Fear had widened his eyes. He met her gaze and mouthed a word that chilled her.

Dragon.

Fear washed over Keelie as she realized what was making the rumbling underneath the ground. "You're releasing a dragon."

"Clever girl. I didn't think you would figure it out. But not any dragon. This is Avenir."

"And the trees are dead." Keelie realized that the consciousness she'd been feeling before, when Herne had brought her here, had been the consciousness of just one being. She hadn't been talking to trees. The dragon had answered her queries.

"Funny thing about Avenir. Your history is tied to his— he was once the mate of a dragon friend of yours. And your Sean is descended from his captor. He will be so pleased to see Sean o' the Wood." Peascod laughed. "You should see the look on your face. I can read you so easily. No, there was no love lost between Ermentrude and Avenir."

"I'm not going to help you." Keelie shuffled her feet to maintain her balance as the ground roiled, something below desperately trying to surface. Unearthly screams came from the walled merchant town, and the air was full of confused dark fae.

"He's getting impatient. Let's help him, shall we?" Peascod grabbed her hand. Keelie pulled against him, but the jester was strong and dragged her away from the trees, then pulled her hand open and slashed a knife blade across her palm.

Keelie screamed as pain seared through her hand. Blood dripped in a steady stream onto the soil. The dirt opened like a mouth to suck the blood in.

Something pushed her to the ground and she kicked away from the slurping mouth in the dirt. A black stag stood over her, facing Peascod with lowered antlers.

Peascod laughed again. "My impotent lord. Come to see my triumph? Your little mongrel will be Avenir's first meal, and her power will seal your doom."

One of the dark trees fell, its branches cracking the glass

orb that held Sean. He pounded his shoulder against the crack and broke free, racing toward them with drawn sword.

"Keelie," he shouted, "run."

She couldn't. The earth buckled and shook, and huge rocks fell around them. A huge silver claw scratched through the ground and was soon joined by another. Avenir was twice as big as Ermentrude, and she'd only seen two of his toes.

Herne dissolved to his humanlike form and turned to Keelie. "Grab Knot and touch a tree, then think of the maypole in Big Nugget. The cat will get you there."

Sean rushed toward Peascod. The jester laughed, then reached within his pockets and pulled out another glass sphere. He tossed it up into the air, and when it landed in his hand, he disappeared. The tree trunks were beginning to crack, and the ground all around them burbled. It reminded Keelie of the time when Alora had emerged as a huge tree.

She wished she knew more about dragons. Remembering her dragon magic book, she reached into her jeans pocket. She opened the teeny-tiny book just as another claw erupted from the ground. The rumbling was becoming stronger. Sean stumbled over to her. He ripped a strip of material from his shirt. "I need to wrap your hand."

Keelie could read the dragon script, but it was super small. She finally saw that it seemed to be a spell to turn a dragon into its human form.

Herne snatched the book from her hand. "Clever girl, but you must leave this battle to me." He turned to Sean. "Go with her, elf, and make sure that she's safe."

The dragon's head emerged among the broken tree

roots, dirt and boulders showering from its massive jaws. He roared, and a spray of flame illuminated Under-the-Hill, making it look even more hellish.

"Leave the battle? Really?" Sean was already drawing his sword.

Keelie agreed with the sentiment, but before she could look for a weapon, Knot snagged her leg and ripped his way up her body.

"Yeow leave!" His claws dug deeper and Keelie staggered toward one of the strange trees and grabbed its trunk.

The dragon lifted hellish dinosaur jaws and roared again, flaming the cavern roof. Flame arched back down and licked at Sean's hair.

"Come with us, Sean!" Keelie reached an arm toward him, but he only glanced at her, nodded to Knot, then turned back to face the dragon, sword lifted, arms in the air, blade dangling behind his back as he readied it for a mighty swing.

A strange look came over Sean's face. Next to him, Herne had the book open and was shouting the words on the page as streamers of magic poured from the fingers of his upthrust hand. The magic swirled around him, and as the body of the dragon rose from the pit, it transformed into a man. A tall, broad-shouldered man with long silver hair, in full armor. From the smoke rolling from his ears, he was ready to murder. He howled and ran toward them.

Sean stalked toward him, sword still raised, as Keelie felt the whoosh and Under-the-Hill disappeared.

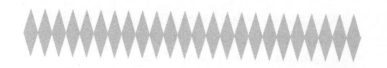

twenty-six

Light exploded around her. For a half second, Keelie thought the dragon had flamed her, but then she realized it was the sun. She was on the street in Big Nugget, by the remains of the Crystal Cup. Her relief was short-lived, however. A goblin jumped onto an overturned car, followed by another. Three more came around the ruined building, and all had their eyes fixed on her. Knot hissed at them and grew taller, his claws out and a sword appearing at his side. He drew it.

"Knot, what's behind us? I'm afraid to look." The back of her neck itched.

Knot leaned forward, slashing his sword at the goblins. Keelie threw a quick glance behind them. Nothing. The goblins rushed.

"Run," Knot yowled.

Keelie backed away quickly, just as a rumble vibrated through the street. Exactly what she needed—an earthquake. She assessed the area for earthquake safety, ingrained in her from her California childhood. Except for the attacking goblins, the treeless spot where she stood was the safest. Too bad.

She turned and ran, then fell hard to her knees as the ground came up to slap her. Knot tripped over her and landed on her back. She wheezed and watched, amazed, as the street before her buckled and flattened like a tablecloth being shaken. The light poles that lined one side of the street fell over, glass exploding as it hit the hard ground.

"What's going on? Earthquakes don't last this long," Keelie yelled. The ground still shook. She lay flat, looking back toward the goblins who were also hugging the ground, eyes wide. One of them leered at her, then got to his feet and staggered toward her.

"Meow mask shop, hurry." Knot tugged her up, and something pulled at her hair—a *bhata*. Others flew ahead, and the air was suddenly bright with pinpoints of pixie light. The lights flew behind them, back toward the goblins.

Across the street, the mask shop door hung open, held there by a mound of sticks. The *bhata* had come to help them. The doorway would be a safe spot until the earthquake was over, and then they could barricade themselves inside until help came.

If help came. Keelie's feet bounced on the ground as she moved forward; it was like dancing on a trampoline with a mind of its own. The middle of the street ruptured, chunks of payment flying upwards then landing around.

The crack in the ground widened, and as Keelie grabbed the door frame, she wondered how Sean was. Everything was happening so fast. Knot pushed her inside and blocked the door, sword raised, but the goblins hung back, maybe still freaked out by the earthquake. The little *bhata* crowded inside with them.

A horn sounded from the hilltop and echoed from the buildings that still stood. Knot froze and lifted his face to sniff the air. He grinned, showing his fangs.

"Who is it? The good guys?"

He nodded, holding onto the door frame as another tremor shook the building. A panicked group of goblins sped by the door, barely glancing at them. At their heels, axes and pikes swinging before them, came the dwarves, armored and scary looking.

They pounded past, then down the street. Excited, the *bhata* followed them.

Keelie pushed Knot aside and went out. "That was weird. Come on, let's see how far the hole goes down. There must be a fault here."

Knot growled, but let her walk toward the edge of the crevasse that split the street down the middle for two blocks. A sound like the metal-on-metal of bad brakes filled the air.

Keelie covered her ears and looked over the edge. Two goblins were holding on to rocks on the side of a deep pit, their claws scrabbling for purchase. Suddenly, one let go, and his scream faded as he vanished into the darkness below. The other one tried to pull himself up onto a boulder, then slipped. He, too, fell into the abyss.

A surge of magic hit Keelie from below. She fell back, her hand on her rose quartz to shield herself from the Earth magic that now filled the air. A sharp-nailed hand closed over her arm and hauled her to her feet.

"Avenir has torn open the rift and brought it with him to this world." Vania stood next to her, tall and queenly, her eyes flashing like jewels in the reflected aurora borealis light.

From behind a row of buildings, hunting horns sounded and the battle cry of the dwarves floated like banners over them. The goblins were on the run, but there were so many of them that Keelie was sure they hadn't seen the last of them.

A sulfurous stench rose from the abyss. Horrified, Keelie saw a giant, silver-taloned dragon paw clutch the edge of the remains of the town road. A wing tip taller than the surrounding buildings rose behind the paw, and then Avenir was among them.

He had grown huge on the rift's magic. "Ermentrude," he bellowed. Fire charred the remains of the maypole. Keelie tried to back away, but Vania held her fast.

"He will not harm us," the fairy queen said. "His battle is with Herne."

"Why Herne?" Shocked, Keelie struggled to free herself. "We have to help him."

Vania laughed. "He's a forest god. He can help himself. Do you think the magic can be drunk only by the dragon? Do you not feel it, Daughter of the Forest?"

Keelie looked down at her arms, which were covered in waves of colored light that seemed to be coming from inside of her. She glowed with power. But it was wild magic that she didn't know how to use.

A movement behind the dragon's massive leg drew her attention. It was Sean, dragging himself to his feet. Bloody, but still armed, he stabbed at the back of Avenir's knee, searching for a vulnerable spot.

Avenir roared and swatted at Sean, knocking him into one of the shop walls. He got back up, but Avenir's attention had turned to the huge stag that now faced him. Herne's deerlike body was huge, muscles rippling under the smooth reddish hide, and his antlers were broad and thick, ready for battle. His hooves trailed magic, and wherever he stepped, green life sprang up.

The dragon magic book flew out of the crevasses and slid to a stop at Keelie's feet. Vania shrieked, but Keelie reached down and snatched it up before she could take it from her. She tossed it to Knot, who sprang away with it in his furry arms.

Avenir roared again, spread his wings, and turned his long head to examine Herne. Big as he was, the forest god looked puny next to the Godzilla-sized dragon. The battle definitely looked uneven.

Elven war cries sounded, and Keelie hoped Dad knew she was alive. A flight of silver-tipped arrows hit the dragon, and some stuck, like sewing pins, in his hide. He screamed with fury and flamed the street in the direction of the pharmacy.

Keelie smelled burning wood and paper. If the humans ever returned, they would have to rebuild.

"Let's get someplace safe to watch the fun." Vania tried to drag Keelie away.

Sean had gotten to his feet and was bracing himself with one arm against the wall. He looked up at Avenir, then at Herne. He sheathed his sword, then took a deep breath and launched himself at the dragon's leg, crawling up swiftly, from scale to scale, until he reached his back.

Avenir was so huge, and his focus was so entirely on Herne, that he didn't seem to notice the elven knight between his shoulders. Keelie held her breath as Sean drew his sword and slashed downward, causing Avenir to scream and try to reach him, to no avail. Sean held tight to the sword and rode it, tearing, to the edge of the dragon's wing before being once more dashed to the ground.

Keelie fell back against Vania as Avenir's wings buffeted the air. His injured wing dragged, but finally the dragon was able to fly. Flapping painfully, he made his way toward the mountains.

Elven victory cries sounded from the other side of town.

Herne turned his majestic, antlered head and walked toward them, morphing with every step, becoming more human looking, until finally he stood before them, the forest god once more. He was breathtaking, and Keelie could see why her human ancestors had paid him homage.

"Unhand Keliel Heartwood, Queen Vania. She is not your enemy." Herne's voice was deep and resonant. A god's voice.

"You cannot command me. I am not the besotted fool my sister was." Vania lifted her head.

"How can I convince you of my innocence in her death?" Herne did not look at Keelie.

"You cannot. I have searched for the one thing that would prove the guilt of my sister's killer. On the day of Linsa's birth, our father forged a quicksilver heart in the fires of the Earth's core. Her birth gift, as mine was my scrying room. That heart could not have been taken from her in life, and when she died, it should have returned to me, yet it has never appeared.

"I know of the heart. Linsa showed it to me," Herne said. "It did not return to you because it was no longer hers to give. When we bound our true hearts together, she gave me a token of her unending love. I have Linsa's heart."

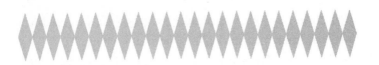

twenty-seven

Keelie gasped when she saw the silver heart hanging from a chain around Herne's neck. He removed it and gently held the heart in the palm of his hand. Ribbons of light and magic flowed through the quicksilver. A slight fluttering from the center of the heart made it appear as if was alive and beating.

Vania reached out with trembling fingers. "Give it to me."

Another rumble from the ground, and the fairy queen almost lost her balance but steadied herself. Sean reached out for Keelie and stabilized her as she swayed to the left.

Herne protectively clasped Linsa's heart. "She gave it to me as a token of her undying love."

Vania scowled angrily. "That heart belongs to me."

He draped the chain back around his neck and hid it beneath his shirt. "It was freely given to me by the one I love."

Vania blasted Herne, pinning him to the ground with a mighty wave of magic. Keelie sprang back and watched, amazed and terrified. Pulling strands of wild magic from the air, Vania wove an invisible net that held Herne.

The clash of metal on metal signaled that another battle was taking place nearby. Keelie heard her father's voice call to her. "Dad!" she screamed. She saw the elven army turn the corner, her father at its head.

Above them, Avenir dove into view, a sinewy silver streak mirrored with the colors of the aurora borealis. He was beautiful, and his questing gaze fell on the Lord of the Forest. His wings swept back and he prepared to dive.

"Dad, look out—Avenir at eleven o'clock!" Keelie's voice echoed in the rubble-strewn streets.

Dad looked up, and the elven archers around him nocked their arrows.

Vania whipped around and gestured toward Keelie. Strands of magic wrapped around her, burning, taking her oxygen. Her vision faded, and then all was black.

Keelie was hot, and the air had a heated mineral smell that reminded her of the hot springs she'd visited with her old friend Laurie when they were in eighth grade. She opened her eyes, but she wasn't in California. The dark cavern's soaring ceiling reminded her of Under-the-Hill, but the red light that flickered against the walls was from only one source, and the searing steam cooking her right side came from a vent in the rock that burbled with a hidden, molten river.

Vania was standing near the vent, as if the heat did not bother her. Fala stood before her in fanciful armor that seemed more decorative than useful. Knowing the fae, it was probably enchanted.

"Take your army and wipe out the elves. I will handle Herne."

Fala's expression did not change. "He is injured, your majesty. Surely we can pick him off easily?"

"He is a god once more," Vania said, sounding grumpy. "The wild magic has restored him. Peascod has failed. Must I do everything myself?"

"What about the girl?" Fala's eyes flicked toward Keelie, but then quickly back to the queen.

Fala knew she was awake, but he hadn't betrayed her. Yet. Would he really fight against the elves? Keelie wondered if Dad was still alive or if the dragon had killed him. In any other forest, she would have felt him; he would have spoken to her mind-to-mind. The trees would have talked of nothing else. But here . . .

Vania walked toward the vent in the rock and looked in, seeming to enjoy the blast of heat. "Leave her. I'll need her later."

Fala bowed to the queen and left just as Peascod and his large band of goblins spun up from beneath the earth, dirt spewing everywhere. A glow of magic shone over their avocado skin and their eyes were bright with madness. Keelie could feel that they were much stronger than they had been. They pulsed with energy from the wild magic.

She very carefully reached for the rose quartz clasped at her belt loop. She was going to need all the magical backup she could get, because another battle was about to take place. As she stretched her mind to the trees, pain ripped through her head—she felt strong magic blocking her telepathic connection. It was like the dampening field she'd experienced earlier. She cried out from the sudden headache.

Peascod grinned at her. A cold foreboding slipped through Keelie—it looked like she was going to be on her own. It wasn't a comforting thought, even as the pain eased. The goblins surrounded her, and Keelie saw no way to escape. She had to come up with a plan.

Vania tried to motion toward her with her hand, but it seemed she couldn't move it. Panic flashed across her face.

"I wouldn't do that, Your Majesty," Peascod chuckled. He was holding a bright green cut-glass container. Its quicksilver lid pulsed with magic. One of the goblins reached over and grasped the queen's wrists. It smiled, exposing horrible rows of sharpened teeth.

"You dare touch me." Vania kept her steely gaze level with the goblin's. "You'll die," she whispered.

The goblin licked his mud-brown lips with his serpentine tongue as if he was anticipating the first taste of death. "You'll die first!"

As the goblins crowded around Vania, relishing her fear,

Keelie glimpsed a shadow creeping up on her. Fed up with being dragged around, she jumped up in a karate kid pose, then dropped her arms as she realized that it was Ermentrude, finger to her lips, beckoning for her to follow. The dragon woman looked into her eyes for a second, then nodded, satisfied at what she had seen.

Goblin screams filled the cavern, sounding like bad brakes, and Peascod cursed. "Hold them!" he ordered.

As the goblins charged toward them, Keelie and Ermentrude sprinted into a corridor. Their footsteps echoed oddly in the space, as if they were five hundred people instead of two. As they reached an intersecting tunnel, a wave of elven soldiers and dwarf warriors poured out and ran past them.

"Dad! Where are you?" Keelie cried. She let go of Ermentrude and ran after the soldiers. Intent on the battle ahead, they didn't listen when she asked if Zekeliel Heartwood was still alive.

Behind her, Ermentrude huffed and puffed. "Maybe I should cut back on the smoking."

The running army clashed with the armored goblins in the huge cavern. The echoing sounds were deafening. Ermentrude pulled Keelie to safety on a jagged boulder near the vent. Keelie scanned the scene below for her father and Sean, but it was impossible to tell one fighter from another. Drums sounded as more goblins poured into the cavern.

"This is the caldera," Ermentrude yelled in Keelie's ear, pointing at the vent. "The rift starts here."

Keelie looked down at the opening in the rock. This was the rift, the source of the wild magic. She could see the golden river that sloshed and bubbled beneath it. No wonder it was so warm in Big Nugget now, and there were earthquakes—they were in a volcano!

Panic rushed through her as she saw Avenir charge into the fray. His human form was mighty, almost as scary as his dragon shape. His gaze fell on Ermentrude. Cutting a swath through the warriors, he fought his way toward her.

Ermentrude shoved Keelie behind her. "This might get ugly, kid."

Might get ugly? A war was raging around them, and it wasn't pretty. It smelled even worse. Keelie wanted to cry or run away. At the same time, she wanted to grab a sword and hack into some goblins.

Then she saw Peascod, flitting behind Avenir and looking around anxiously. He stopped and straightened his mask. Keelie followed his gaze and saw that the fae army had arrived. They were doomed.

Fala raised his sword and called to Queen Vania. She smiled and extended her hand to him from across the carnage of the cavern floor, just as if they were in the High Court's ballroom. Fala saluted her with his blade, then stepped aside to reveal Herne, in his man-form, fully restored.

"Traitor!" Vania screamed. "You betrayed my army to the enemy?"

Avenir stopped his surge toward Ermentrude and turned to face Herne. "You," he bellowed. "I thought I had killed you for good."

Herne laughed. "I was here long before you, lizard. I will be here long after."

Avenir roared and instantly began to change into his dragon form. His mighty, clawed feet extended and the goblins ran to safety. The elves and dwarves turned their attack toward him. At Fala's signal, Salaca led half of the fae army to flank the dragon.

"Don't kill Herne," Vania screeched. "The fool has Linsa's heart and has not declared to whom it should go. Give me the heart, Herne. It belongs to me."

Peascod stepped away from the dragon as fire blazed out of the caldera. The gash in the rock was widening. Fire encircled Avenir's body, which had grown huge within seconds. Instead of burning him, however, the magical flames seemed to empower him as he finished his transformation. The elves and dwarves froze, unsure of how to attack. Peascod smiled with pleasure.

Avenir has to be stopped, Keelie thought desperately. If he killed Herne, then the fae, elves, and dwarves would all perish. She didn't want to speculate about what would happen if Avenir and the goblins were free to roam the world, killing and destroying.

"Little human child, come to me," Peascod said, striding toward Keelie. Her skin crawled as if the cockroaches from Maemtri's shop were walking on her body.

"Keep away from her," Ermentrude warned.

"I need another blood donation," Peascod continued, ignoring Ermentrude. "I need your human heart, beating with your life force and magic, and this is the perfect place to work the ritual."

Flames danced along Avenir's wings as he hovered above

Peascod. The downdraft blew smoke and ash around the cavern, fanning the flames so that they grew ever larger.

Peascod bowed his head slightly. "The rift will make you invincible."

He had been speaking to Avenir, but Keelie felt the power that filled the room. She suddenly knew that she could work this sort of power, just as Vania had.

"Don't do it, kid," Ermentrude exclaimed, as if reading her thoughts. "You'll end up like her."

Keelie slid back, her heart racing. She had to figure out a way to use her Earth magic, not the tempting but dangerous wild magic that was filling the cavern.

Lava erupted from the caldera, spattering the wall. A goblin, splashed by the lava, burst into flames and ran shrieking through the now-silent crowd. Vibrant light surrounded them like a malevolent rainbow. Keelie took the opportunity to slide down the other side of the boulder, closer to the caldera and hidden from Peascod and Vania.

She crouched down and duck-walked across the rock floor to the left, toward the caldera. The heat was unbearable, but she wanted to see what was going on. Suddenly her left foot rolled and she heard a crunch. Keelie fell to the ground. As she scrambled to get up, chills spread over her skin. She was sitting next to a pile of bones that resembled a rib cage. For a split second her mind blanked; then she realized it was a human skeleton. No, not human ... fae.

The bones shimmered. The bony hands were outstretched as if the person had pleaded for his or her life before the end came. Bits of red hair clung to the skull.

"Oh. My. God." Keelie jumped to the side and gulped down air, which wasn't a good idea. It burned her trachea.

Peascod sprang up next to her. "Thought you'd hide from me?" He peered down at the skeleton, then bent lower to examine it. "It's amazing how skin decomposes. You would think that as a fae, Linsa would've stayed preserved a little longer."

The blood drained from Keelie's face. "This is Linsa." Of course. Who else would it be?

Herne appeared on the rock. He looked down and cried out in anguish.

Peascod's eyes glinted through his mask. It glowed, and ripples of color crossed its shining surface. "Yes, Herne, her sacrifice gave us a lot of power. So much so that we were able to open the rift fully and release the wild magic. Her blood allowed us to control it." He kissed his gloved hand and blew it toward the remains of Linsa. "So sweet were her screams as the life force drained out of her."

Fear coursed through Keelie. Her fate might be the same as Linsa's.

Avenir swooped over the widening rim of the volcano, unaffected by the lava. He flamed the ceiling again.

Keelie laughed, thinking she was close to hysteria. It seemed ridiculous—the mere idea of stopping a dragon was preposterous, especially when he was the size of a three-story house. Peascod frowned; it wasn't the reaction he'd been anticipating from her. She knew she had to find a way to stall him.

Vania appeared, motioning with her hands, and moved

toward the pitiful remains on the ground. Keelie stood up and backed away respectfully. The queen needed a moment with her sister.

To her surprise, Vania just kicked Linsa's bones out of the way. "She was a fool." She looked up at Herne, who towered over her on the rock, his eyes still on the red-haired skull. "If only she hadn't given you the heart, it would have come to me at her death. How was I to know?"

Were Avenir and the fairy queen working together? The idea made Keelie queasy. If Avenir and Vania controlled the wild magic, the world would suffer.

Avenir flapped his wings and rose again from the caldera. Hot wind blew Keelie's hair back and her eyes watered. She blinked several times and swore she was seeing a heat mirage, but she wasn't—Ermentrude was rising behind Avenir, molten gold in the brilliant light of the overflowing caldera.

Avenir turned, startled to see his former mate ready to attack. "Good to see you in fighting form, my love," he chuckled evilly. "You must still love me if you've come back for more."

"No more, Avenir! I thought your evil hide had been buried for good."

Ermentrude flamed Avenir, and the two dragons crashed into the ceiling and walls as they battled. The cavern was immense, but dueling dragons require space. Below them the armies scattered, seeking safety.

Sean broke free from the elven army and rushed toward

Keelie, but Peascod stepped in his way. "I'm afraid we can't let you rescue your Keliel."

Vania grabbed Keelie by the arm. "Her fae blood makes her mine. I command her."

"No one commands me," Keelie shouted. "I am the Tree Shepherd's daughter." She closed her hand once more around the rose quartz. This time, she felt Earth magic respond to her call. Around the cavern, the dwarves screamed out their battle cry as they felt the pull of the Earth magic, and above them the dragons echoed their cries of fury.

Vania whipped around to face Keelie, shock on her face. Then it turned to delight. "You are so much more powerful than I thought."

Herne pointed to the fairy queen. "You are outnumbered, Vania."

Vania smiled. "You're a fool, just like my sister. So optimistic. Both of you so in love." She rolled her eyes. "Love is for humans. And optimism will destroy you. Give me the heart, Herne."

Vania looked more beautiful than ever. Keelie felt the bump of the queen's magic and realized that it was her glamour. She was using magic to enhance her appearance.

Herne lifted a hand and pixies swirled around Vania, pulling at her hair and pinching her. Vania cursed and swatted at them. A swirl of magic left her mouth, a purple stream of fog that quickly filled the cavern.

Keelie clutched the rose quartz tighter and pulled up an edge of Earth magic, its clean power surging through her. The fog bounced off of her, but all around her, the elves, fae, and dwarves froze in place. Dismayed, Keelie saw that Herne, too, had gone still in mid-motion.

Ermentrude, flying above the fog, screamed as Avenir slammed her into the wall. He caught her in his massive claws and dropped her into the caldera.

Keelie couldn't breathe. They had lost the battle. Numb, she watched as Avenir landed in front of Vania.

"Kill the fae girl so that the magic comes to me," he said, glaring down at her.

"You monster," Keelie yelled. If she could gather enough Earth magic, it would shield her from Avenir's flame. She felt a strong thread, stronger even than when she'd tugged on Earth magic in the Wildewood. She felt a tickle in her mind and closed her eyes—and the image of the old woman came to her.

Mother Tree leaned on her twisted staff. *What are you waiting for? I see the roots.*

Keelie scanned the area, but she didn't see any tree roots. Only poor Linsa's bones.

Then Keelie felt a tug of magic and turned to see the glowing heart, fluttering beneath Herne's shirt. Avenir's neck rippled with muscles as he turned to look at Keelie. His talons clicked against the stones.

Mother Tree's presence had vanished the minute Keelie saw the heart, and so had the Earth magic she'd gathered. If she didn't replace it now, she would die. Dad was probably dead, and Ermentrude certainly was. But Keelie couldn't give up. She would not let Peascod, Avenir, and Vania win, even if it meant her own death.

"If you're not going to sacrifice the girl, then I'll eat her. Bones and all," Avenir said in his deep, dark voice.

Keelie drew deep on the Earth magic. The rose quartz, cool in her hand, was a balm against the caldera's scorching heat.

Vania turned away from examining Herne's still form. "Bones mixed with magic contaminate the ritual. How many times do I have to explain this to you?"

The now-glowing rose quartz was a pink ball of light in Keelie's hand. She fixed her gaze on Herne and realized that if the heart was still with him, he must be alive. She saw him nod imperceptibly. He was only pretending to be enchanted, and he'd understood her unspoken request.

She pulled on the wild magic through the rose quartz, and its pulsing light brightened from pink to blinding white. Avenir closed his eyes and staggered back to the edge of the rift. Keelie stared at Herne's chest as she tightened her hand around the rose quartz.

Herne suddenly pulled the chain from around his neck. Vania gasped. Linsa's heart dangled from his outstretched fingers. The wild magic surged toward it.

The heart healed all. Would it mend the rift?

Keelie looked down at Linsa's skeleton. She reached for a femur, shuddering as her fingers closed around the rough bone. She held it and the rose quartz together. Herne nodded.

"For you, Linsa," Keelie said. "And for all who have died this day."

"No!" Vania screamed, running toward Herne, magic blasting from her outstretched hands.

Herne hurled Linsa's quicksilver heart toward the caldera. Vania's magic caught it and it rose, floating above the rift as if it weighed nothing. Vania made a pulling motion and the heart drifted toward her, but before she could reach out and grab it, Ermentrude rose from the caldera, spewing lava as she rocketed toward the ceiling. Her wings hit her former mate, and as Avenir tried to catch his balance, Ermentrude dropped down on him and pushed him toward the caldera. Keelie picked up a discarded sword and hacked at Avenir's armored side, and Herne grabbed at the quicksilver heart.

Vania's push of magic had left her drained. She fell back, and as she hit the floor, the bespelled warriors were released from the enchantment. Sean ran to Keelie, took the sword from her hand, and plunged it between two of Avenir's toes. The dragon screamed, releasing his grip on the edge of the caldera. He toppled backwards into the lava-filled chasm.

Peascod had run toward Avenir, but he skidded to a stop as the dragon vanished beneath the lava. He looked back at Keelie. Hate flowed from his eyes, but he turned and started to run, his goblins stumbling after him. The fae and elven armies, still recovering from their frozen state, didn't give chase.

Keelie had time to think about Peascod. She had to seal the rift, and seal it now, while Avenir was still in it.

She stretched out her arms and envisioned roots from far beneath the earth. Roots of the first trees, when the planet had been shiny and new. In her mind, she saw the roots pushing up through the wild magic and the aurora borealis pulsing with magic.

Keelie, wait for me.

Astonished, Keelie turned. It was Dad's voice in her head, and now here he was, in battered armor and splashed with goblin blood, striding toward her through the gathered armies. She ran to him and threw herself into his arms. He grasped her tightly to him.

"My girl, my girl. I thought I'd lost you."

Weeping, Keelie could only nod. She sniffed. "Dad, we have to finish this."

"Agreed." Zekeliel Heartwood, Lord of the Dread Forest, straightened.

Fala came forward, with a small, backward glance at his fallen queen. He was joined by King Gneiss and finally Norzan, who, limping, was helped into the chamber.

Herne waited for them by the caldera, along with Ermentrude—who was once more in human form, looking magnificent and really in need of a shower.

They moved together, in ceremonial silence. The thought hit Keelie that if she could talk to Dad, she could talk to the trees. Mentally, she reached for all of the trees growing in and around Big Nugget, Grey Mantle, and throughout Canada, and then farther away in the Dread Forest. She felt waves of the green energy flowing toward her.

Dad squeezed her hand. He knew what she was doing.

In Keelie's mind, she saw the Mother Tree laughing. One of her roots reached out into the world. Light, and silver magic, and a thread of green magic all pulsed around the Mother Tree as her root stretched ever farther.

Keelie felt a different kind of green magic bolster hers, darker and older. It was Herne.

He gazed at the gathered representatives of their different races, and at the hundreds of witnesses behind them. Then he stretched his hand over the caldera and opened it, watching as the quicksilver chain glimmered out of sight, soaring down into the lava that formed the magical core of the world.

The Mother Tree's roots now wove in and out around the chasm, aided by Keelie and Dad and Norzan. Herne's power drove the magic forward and stitched the rift closed, like a doctor sewing a wound together. In Keelie's mind, Mother Tree reached her branches toward the sky. As the leaves swiped Gaia's Dome, the broken crack repaired itself and the ceiling became solid.

Exhausted, Keelie opened her eyes.

To her surprise, she found herself back on Big Nugget's main street, crowded now with the armies that had been below. She watched as the magic wove stitches in the ground, like the kind Grandma Jo had created when she embroidered. The ground was merging closed, leaving only broken pavement where the abyss had been. The green magic seeped away into the earth.

Keelie tilted her head back and sighed with relief. In the skies above, stars twinkled and a crescent moon glowed in the dusky evening. No aurora borealis glimmered against the sky.

She looked at Herne. He winked. Keelie winked back, and the nature god seemed surprised. He turned to help Ermentrude, who was limping badly, and the two magical beings exchanged whispers. Ermentrude's red hair was spilling down her back in a messy tumble, and her right eye was swollen.

Keelie felt a green tickle in her mind and heard the laughing of an old woman. It was the Mother Tree. When she looked back, several treelings had sprouted through the former abyss.

When the citizens of Big Nugget returned, they would be surprised to see trees growing in their street.

Keelie suddenly felt nervous. She scanned the area. "Where's Peascod? And Queen Vania?"

"The fae have Vania," Herne assured her. "They will take care of their own." His eyebrows narrowed. "Peascod has probably returned to the hole he crawled out of. I must go and meet with the goblins he's left behind, to see if they will serve me."

"Are you just going to let Fala give Vania an aspirin and let her get back to her evil business?"

"He is King Fala now. And the fae deal harshly with traitors to the High Court. Vania murdered her sister. They will show her the same mercy."

Keelie shuddered. "And the goblins? How can you trust them?"

Herne grinned. "I'm a god, remember? They worship me."

"You are so full of yourself."

His eyes darkened. "Heed me well, Keliel Heartwood. Our business together is not finished."

Dad was standing nearby, so Herne only nodded and walked away. Darn it.

Keelie didn't think she'd seen the last of Peascod, either. When she encountered his evil again, she would be prepared for the deadly fool.

twenty-eight

The following evening, there was a celebration in the Council building at Grey Mantle to recognize all the brave elven warriors. Dad would be giving a speech. Keelie had slept all night and all day, awakening right before the party to find Sean being treated like a hero by the Grey Mantle elves and all the elf girls swooning over him.

Neither the fae nor the dwarves had been invited to the celebration. Keelie had hoped for unity, but despite how the races had come together to seal the rift, everyone was still blaming each other for the rift in the first place, and for allowing Queen Vania to gather power unchecked.

When the party was in full swing, Keelie decided she needed some air. She left the building and strolled through the empty streets of Grey Mantle, Knot and Coyote at her side. Something moved in the woods and her animal companions rushed to check it out, leaving her alone.

Yesterday, she thought she'd die. Now she was bored and lonely. Maybe it was her human side that was so fickle, but she missed everyone. Herne had disappeared, along with the goblins who had pledged allegiance to him. Ermentrude had returned to her home underground to rest and heal from her injuries. The dwarves had gone with her, still singing war songs.

Uncle Dariel and Elia were already on their way back to the Dread Forest—Elia had wanted to return home as soon as possible. The Grey Mantle clan might be her relatives, but Elia knew where she belonged.

Keelie didn't even have that. Although she'd been one of the ones to mend the rift, all the Northwoods elves were ignoring her, even Miszrial. It was as if they were under orders not to associate with her.

That didn't stop them from singing a new song titled "Seven at the Rift." Keelie had only been awake four hours and she'd already heard it three times. She hoped they choked every time they had to say "brave Keliel" as they named the seven: Norzan, Keliel, Zekeliel, King Gneiss, Ermentrude, Herne, and Fala.

"Really, you would think some appreciation would come your way," a stag said, stepping out of the woods. "A parade. Maybe some solemn chanting. A boring dinner followed by boring speeches. But you only receive veiled threats." Down by the stag's hooves, a small spidery goblin chomped on a plastic soda bottle.

Keelie smiled. "They're cute when they're little."

Herne's brown soulful eyes sought out hers. "Wood sister, forest friend. I owe you much."

He swiftly transformed into his human form. Long dark hair curled on his shoulders, mingling with the moss that trimmed his cloak. Antlers still grew from his forehead.

She liked the nature god/rock star look.

Herne leaned down and kissed her softly on the cheek, as if she were his little sister. "I'll be watching your back." Magic glowed around him as he changed back into a stag, and the goblin climbed onto his back. With a last look at her, he galloped away into the forest.

Keelie smiled. Knot reappeared from the bushes and glowered up at her, as if he knew what she was thinking and disapproved.

Salaca stepped out from behind a tree. "I'm glad we court fae weren't the only ones not invited to the party."

Keelie jumped. "The fae don't need help having parties."

Salaca bowed. "Our new ruler wishes to speak with you."

Keelie's blood chilled. She remembered Herne's words, that the fae dealt harshly with their own. Had he come for her? "Do you seek revenge?" she asked.

Salaca's lips twitched. "No, Tree Shepherdess." He turned

and bowed to someone behind him. Fala stepped forward, dressed in silky blue robes.

"So it's true. You're the new King of the Shining Ones."

"Yes." Fala smiled at her. "I want to thank you for restoring the balance among us. Even though the rift has been sealed, some wild magic remains. The humans here will be ever strange, but the fae, dark and light, will be as brothers once more. Herne is once more welcome in the High Court, and we will help him to rebuild the underworld."

His eyes flickered to a spot behind her and she felt Sean's warm hand at her waist.

"Of course," Fala added, "I'll need a queen." His eyes twinkled. "Know any powerful fairy girls?"

"No, she doesn't." Sean pulled her back against him.

King Fala bowed, and he and Salaca vanished.

"What did you do that for?" Keelie asked, turning to him. "Fala wasn't threatening us. You totally overreacted."

Sean's eyebrows slammed together. "I did not. You know how dangerous they are. We can't trust them. We had a temporary alliance, but now things are as they were."

He must have forgotten the fae blood that flowed through her veins.

Taking her hands in his, Sean said, "Keelie, you need to decide what you want. I know sixteen years seems like a small number next to my age, but now that you know you will not live a mortal life, don't play with my heart."

She looked into his green eyes—elven eyes, just like hers. Their expression was earnest, but with a bitter flatness of hurt lurking just behind, as if he was preparing himself for the worst.

Sean had been her hero from the start. He'd never called her names or looked down on her for being part human. She touched her rounded ear. *Was* she playing with his heart?

Herne and Fala were not for her. She didn't belong in this alien forest, nor in the High Court, nor Under-the-Hill. She belonged in the Dread Forest, with her family. Maybe with Sean, too. She stroked his cheek and kissed him. He closed his eyes, breathing in her scent, then drew her close to him. Keelie didn't fight free of his embrace, although she knew Dad might be aware of it now that he could speak to her telepathically once more.

"Keelie..." Sean started.

"Shh," she said, putting two fingers against his lips. "It's the wild magic talking. Let's discuss this when we're back home."

His face brightened with relief.

"Keelie!" someone called. Sean snarled.

"Keelie, where are you?" It was Dad.

"Out here."

"Don't you want to hear my speech?"

"Coming, Dad." She and Sean walked back toward the Council building, holding hands.

Tomorrow morning, she and Dad would be leaving for the High Mountain Renaissance Faire in Colorado, where all her adventures had begun. She couldn't wait to see her old friends—Raven, and her mother Janice the herb lady, and Tarl the Mud Man and his filthy crew of jokesters.

Cameron, the birds of prey lady, would surely be there. And of course, Sean and his jousters would be coming too.

She glanced up at the tall trees that she'd never befriended, and the mountains that had been filled with dragons, goblins, and fae. What a place.

Dad was waiting on the broad path that led to the building. Keelie blew a kiss to the stag watching them from the forest's edge.

"That's Herne, isn't it?" Sean glared at the deer.

"Yup." She smiled at Sean. "Goodbye fairy drama, hello Ren Faire fun."

Sean glanced toward her father, then kissed her. "I personally guarantee your good time."

"Really?" She grinned. Oh yeah, she couldn't wait to get to Colorado.

epilogue

The next day, as they took their seats on the sleek twelve-seat Healer helicopter that would take them to the airport in Yellowknife, Dad warned her for the umpteenth time not to radiate her feelings while in the air.

"You don't want to broadcast your emotions to the forests below," he cautioned.

"Yes, sir. I'll probably sleep the whole way, and I've still got the Compendium to study." Lord Elianard would have a conniption when he found out that the book had stayed in her room the whole time, unread. Of course, now she could probably add a chapter or two to it.

Keelie jammed her backpack under the seat in front of her. Her spare T-shirt rolled out of the top of the bag and she stuffed it back in, then did a double-take. The pack's plastic buckles were gone.

"Weird. Looks like my pack's been mutilated."

"Knot probably did something to it." Stowing his bag in a compartment next to their seats, Sean didn't seem concerned.

A splash of cool water hit her ankle and Keelie looked down, startled. A little black goblin grinned sheepishly at her, the bottom of her water bottle still dangling from its shiny lip. She saw a chewed-up paper tag dangling from the goblin's wrist, and reached down gingerly and pulled it up. The goblin let her stretch up its spidery little arm, its oversized hand tipped with impressive talons.

Take care of him and he will take care of you, the mutilated tag read. It was signed with an *H*.

"Missing buckles explained. He must have eaten them." Sean was staring down at the goblin, eyes wide. "How are you going to explain him to your dad?"

Keelie sighed. "Maybe he'll just be pleased that our woodshop will suddenly be tidy." She reached for a candy bar wrapper someone had tucked into the seat pocket in front of her and handed it to the goblin, who brightened and munched it down.

The summer ahead had just gotten way more interesting.

About Gillian Summers

A forest dweller, Gillian was raised by gypsies at a Renaissance Faire. She likes knitting, hot soup, and costumes, and adores oatmeal—especially in the form of cookies. She loathes concrete, but tolerates it if it means attending a science fiction convention. She's an obsessive collector of beads, recipes, knitting needles, and tarot cards, and admits to reading *InStyle* Magazine. You can find her in her north Georgia cabin, where she lives with her large, friendly dogs and obnoxious cats, and at www.gilliansummers.com.

Watch for Book III
of the Scions of Shadow Trilogy.